ALI'S PRETTY LITTLE LIES

alloy**entertainment**
Produced by Alloy Entertainment
151 West 26th Street
New York, NY 10001
www.alloyentertainment.com

Library of Congress catalog card number: 2012950661
ISBN 978-0-06-223336-3

Typography by Liz Dresner

12 13 14 15 16   CG/RRDH   10 9 8 7 6 5 4 3 2 1
❖
First Edition

Ali's Pretty Little Lies

A PRETTY LITTLE LIARS PREQUEL NOVEL

SARA SHEPARD

HARPER TEEN
An Imprint of HarperCollinsPublishers

To K

If you're going to be two-faced,
at least make one of them pretty.

—MARILYN MONROE

SWITCHEROO

Once upon a time, there were two identical twin sisters, Alison and Courtney. They were alike in every way: Both had long, blond hair; huge, clear, round blue eyes; heart-shaped faces; and winning smiles that melted hearts. When they were six, they rode matching purple bikes up and down their family's driveway in Stamford, Connecticut, singing "Frère Jacques" in a round. When they were seven, they climbed up the big-kid sliding board together and held hands the whole way. Even though their parents gave each of them her own bedroom with her own canopied princess bed, they were often found sleeping on the same twin mattress, their bodies entwined. Everyone said they shared that indescribable twin connection. They made promises to be best friends forever.

But promises are broken every day.

In second grade, things started to change. They were little things at first—a dirty look, a slight shove, an indignant sigh. Then Courtney showed up in Ali's Saturday art class insisting she was Ali. Courtney sat at Ali's desk in school on a day her sister was sick. Courtney introduced herself as Ali to the UPS man, the new neighbors with the puppy, and the old lady at the pharmacy counter. Maybe she pretended she was her sister because Ali had a little extra sparkle, a certain something that got her noticed. Maybe Courtney was jealous. Or maybe Courtney was forced. *Ali made me do it,* Courtney told her parents when she was caught. *She said if I didn't pretend to be her for the day, something awful would happen to me and you and all of us.* But when their mom and dad asked Ali if this was true, her eyes grew wide. *I would never say something like that,* she answered innocently. *I love my sister, and I love you guys.*

Suddenly, Courtney and Ali were getting into screaming matches on the playground. Then Courtney shut Ali into a bathroom stall at lunchtime and didn't let her out. Teachers called the girls' parents, their voices full of concern. Neighbors pulled their children close when they passed Courtney, worried she might hurt them, too. The final straw came that flawless spring day when the girls' parents found Courtney sitting on top of her sister, her hands around Ali's throat. Doctors were called. Psychiatric evaluations were performed on both girls. Ali handled it with poise, but Courtney panicked. *She started it,* she insisted. *She threatens me. She wants me gone.*

Paranoid schizophrenia, the doctors said in grave tones. That sort of thing could be treatable, but only with a lot of care. It was up to Ali to make the final decision, though—and, tearfully, she decided that her sister should go. And so a facility was found. Off Courtney went, away from her family, away from everything she knew. Her parents reassured her that they would bring her home as soon as she was better, but weeks passed, and then months. Suddenly, Courtney was sort of . . . *forgotten.*

Sometimes, a family is like an ear of summer corn: It might look perfect on the outside, but when you peel the husk away, every kernel is rotten. With the DiLaurentises, the girl who seemed like the victim might just have been the tormentor. Sending Courtney away might just have been Ali's master plan. And maybe, just maybe, all Courtney wanted was what she deserved—a happy life.

This is Rosewood, after all—and these are Rosewood's most mysterious twins. And as you know, in Rosewood, nothing is ever as it seems.

The first thing Courtney DiLaurentis heard when she woke up the morning her life changed was the ticking of the clock on the wall. It was telling her, in a not-so-subtle way, that time was running out.

She looked around the unfamiliar bedroom. Her parents had moved from Stamford, Connecticut, a few years ago to avoid the shame of putting a daughter in a mental institution. They'd relocated to Rosewood, Pennsylvania, a filthy-rich suburb about twenty miles from Philadelphia where even the dogs wore Chanel collars. Because they knew no one when they moved, they didn't have to tell anyone about their crazy daughter in the hospital. They'd even changed their last name from Day-DiLaurentis to simply DiLaurentis in hopes that it would keep nosy neighbors from Connecticut away.

The guest room Courtney was staying in smelled like mothballs and had a twin bed with an old plaid comforter, a wicker dresser too shabby for even a mental ward's day room, and a small, chipped bookshelf containing dated cooking magazines and a bunch of boxes marked TAXES and STATEMENTS. The closet was filled with Christmas decorations, pilled afghans her grandmother had crocheted, and ugly sweaters she couldn't imagine anyone wearing. In other words, the room was a repository for everything her family wanted to forget about—Courtney included.

Courtney pushed the covers back and walked into the hall. The house, a huge Victorian, was designed in such a way that the upstairs overlooked a great room, giving Courtney a bird's-eye view into the kitchen. Her older brother, Jason, was hunched over the table with a bowl of Frosted Flakes. Her twin sister, Ali, flitted around the counter. Her hair was a perfect blond wave spilling down her back, and her pink T-shirt gave her clear skin a healthy glow. She lifted a pile of newspapers and looked under it. Then she opened a silverware drawer and slammed it shut.

"Alison, what's the matter?" asked Mrs. DiLaurentis, who wore a gray Diane von Furstenberg wrap dress and heels. It looked like she was going to a job interview instead of taking her daughter to a new mental hospital.

"I can't find my ring," Ali snapped, opening the trash bin and peering inside.

"What ring?"

"My initial ring, *duh*." Ali opened another cabinet and slammed it hard. "It's the one I wear, like, every *day*." She whipped around and faced her brother. "Did *you* take it?"

"Why would I take it?" Jason answered between bites.

"Well, I can't find it," Ali snapped. "Just like I can't find my piece of the flag," she said, giving Jason a pointed look.

Jason wiped his mouth with a napkin. "Even if I did know about your stupid piece of the flag, anyone is legally allowed to take it—even the people who helped hide it. The stealing clause, remember?"

"Maybe you took it to give it to someone else." Her gaze drifted to the second floor.

Courtney stepped away from the railing. Back in the bedroom, she opened the flowered suitcase she'd had since third grade and studied its contents. Inside was a T-shirt almost the same shade of pink as the one Ali was wearing. She found dark indigo jeans that matched Ali's, too. She slipped them on.

Time Capsule was a long-standing tradition at Rosewood Day, the private school Ali and Jason attended, and finding a piece of the torn-up flag was a rarity for a sixth grader. All weekend, Ali had been boasting about the Time Capsule scrap she'd found—although, technically, Jason had told Ali where the piece was, which didn't seem fair. Ali had decorated her piece at the kitchen table after dinner two nights ago, giving Courtney, who was watching TV in the den, superior looks. *Look how important I am*, those looks said. *You're not even allowed to leave the house.*

But Ali hadn't had that look on her face when her flag went missing yesterday. In the privacy of her pathetic little guest room, Courtney had run her fingers over the silken fabric and Ali's puffy silver drawings—a Chanel logo, a Louis Vuitton design, a cluster of stars and comets. Courtney had drawn a little wishing well in the corner, just wanting to make her mark on something her sister coveted so much. *Then I'll give it back*, she'd promised herself. But Jason had gotten to it first. He'd seen Courtney looking at it in her room and rushed in, saying, "Do you really want things *worse* between you guys?" Then he'd snatched it back before she could say a word.

Courtney was about to shut the suitcase when her gaze drifted to the pamphlet tucked into the suitcase's pocket. *The Preserve at Addison-Stevens*, the front said. There was a photo of a bouquet of irises beneath the title. They were the same sorts of flowers her parents had gotten for her grandmother's funeral.

She opened the booklet and stared at the first page. *We assist children and adolescents in developing effective coping skills and building self-esteem to be able to return home and back to school,* it read.

Tears sprang to Courtney's eyes. She'd been in hospital care since she was *nine*—three whole years. And even though she'd gotten used to the Radley the same way a mouse might get used to living in a cage, she'd seen horrible things she never wanted to witness again. Ever since the hospital announced it was closing its doors and converting into a luxury hotel, Courtney had assumed her family would bring her back to Rosewood to live with them. When her father had driven her here on Friday, he'd said as much—this would be a trial visit that would perhaps turn into something more permanent.

But for some reason, circumstances had changed in the last twenty-four hours. Mrs. DiLaurentis had knocked on Courtney's door last night and told her to pack her things at once, slipping the pamphlet for the Preserve into her hands. "We think this will be the best thing for you," she cooed, stroking her daughter's hair.

Courtney leafed through the pamphlet's pages, staring at the photos of the patients. They had to be models—they looked too happy. She'd heard terrible things about the Preserve from other kids who had gone there. People called it "death row" because so many kids committed suicide while inside. Others called it "Rapunzel's tower" because parents left their kids in there for years. No Internet, television, or phone calls were allowed. The nurses were like extras from *One Flew Over the Cuckoo's Nest,* and the doctors on staff had no qualms about tying kids to their beds to keep them calm. Parents loved it, though, because the place looked beautiful from the outside. And it was super expensive—it *had* to be good, right?

But she *wasn't* going. She'd been formulating a plan all night to figure out how. Now all the pieces were fitting into place . . . except the opportunity she needed. She hoped one would arise—and *soon*. Her parents were taking her away in forty-five minutes.

She buried the pamphlet under her packed clothes and wheeled the suitcase to the top of the stairs. Then she walked down the stairs. Something caught her eye out the back window. Four girls were standing behind the bushes, whispering. They looked about Courtney's age, and she could hear their voices through the screen.

One girl, a blonde in a field hockey skirt and a white T-shirt, placed her hands on her hips. "I was here first. That flag's mine."

"*I* was here before you," a second girl spouted. She was a little on the chubby side and had frizzy brown hair. "I saw you come out of your house only a few minutes ago."

A third girl stomped a purple suede boot. "You just got here, too. I was here before *both* of you."

Courtney ran her tongue over her teeth. Were they here for Ali's flag? And they'd made a reference to one girl coming from next door—that had to be Spencer Hastings. Mrs. DiLaurentis had mentioned her name at dinner on Friday, and Mr. DiLaurentis had made a sour face. He'd said Spencer's parents were such show-offs, building a third addition to their house, converting that perfectly good barn into a luxury apartment for their oldest daughter. *As if a bedroom isn't good enough?* he'd railed.

"Do you see them out there?" Courtney asked Ali, who was now standing at a counter, angrily whipping through a magazine, headphones in her ears. Jason was gone, and by the sounds of it, their parents were still upstairs, getting dressed.

Ali's head snapped up. She tore the headphones out. "Huh?"

"There are some girls outside. One of them is the girl who lives next door."

"She's in the yard?" Ali looked annoyed and walked to the window. But when she peered out, she frowned. "I don't see Spencer. Thank *God.*"

"You're not friends with her?"

Ali snorted. "*No.* She's a bitch."

And you're not? Courtney thought.

Ali turned to face her as if Courtney had said it out loud. A nasty smile settled across her lips. "Cute shirt. But it's giving me déjà vu."

Courtney grabbed a banana from the basket. "I liked the color."

"Yeah, right." Ali sauntered to the counter and grabbed a donut from the open box.

"Careful," Courtney said, strolling toward her. "Donuts will make you fat."

Jelly dripped down Ali's chin. "So will mental hospital food, *schizo*."

Courtney winced. She wasn't a schizo, and Ali knew it. "Don't."

"*Don't*," Ali imitated, her features turning ugly.

Courtney sucked in her stomach. Ali always used a nasal, dumbed-down voice to mimic her. "Stop it," she snapped.

"*Stop it*," Ali imitated.

Courtney felt the old fire rise up inside, the one that had gotten her in trouble before. Although she tried her hardest to suppress it, something broke loose. "Guess what," she spat. "I *do* have your Time Capsule flag."

Ali's eyes widened. "I *knew* it. Give it back."

"It's gone," Courtney said. "I gave it to Jason. And he doesn't want to give it back to you." It wasn't exactly the truth, but this version sounded better.

Ali glowered at Jason, who had just reappeared in the doorway. "Is this true? You knew she had my flag?"

Jason looked back and forth between the girls, his gaze lingering on their matching outfits. "Well, yeah, Ali, but—"

Ali's gaze darted to something in Jason's pocket. The shiny blue fabric peeked out. She snatched it out halfway, her eyes widening at the wishing well that was now wedged between the manga frog and the bubble-letter *awesome*. Her eyes narrowed on Courtney. "Did *you* draw this?"

Jason grabbed it back from her and stuffed it back in his pocket. "Ali, just let it go."

Ali squared her shoulders. "You're *always* on her side!"

"I'm not on anyone's side," Jason said.

"Yes, you are!" Ali glowered at Courtney. "It's a good thing I told Mom that you threatened me last night. That's why you're going to the Preserve, you know."

Courtney's eyes widened. "I didn't do anything to you!"

Ali tipped her chin down. "Maybe you did. Maybe you didn't. Either way, you're not welcome here, bitch."

"Ali, enough!" Jason shouted.

"*Enough!*" Ali imitated with a sneer. When she brushed past him for the stairs, she shoved him. Jason staggered backward and crashed into a wrought-iron bookshelf. The whole thing wobbled, and a platter with the New York City skyline on the top shelf shook precariously. Jason lunged forward, but it was too late. The plate shattered on the wood floor.

The silence after the crash was deafening. Jason glared at Courtney, who had frozen in the corner. "Why did you have to start things with her?" he hissed.

"I couldn't help it," Courtney said weakly.

"Yes, you could," Jason said. And then, letting out a frustrated groan, he pushed out the back door.

Courtney's insides turned over. "Jason, wait!" she yelled, running to the window. Jason was her only ally—she couldn't have him angry at her. But when she gazed out the glass, Jason was gone. The four girls were still cowering in the bushes, though.

She glanced over her shoulder into the kitchen. Pieces of the New York City plate lay all over the floor. Soon enough, her mother would appear from wherever she was and discover the mess. She would call to her two daughters to ask what had happened. One would appear from upstairs. What if the other daughter was outside, talking to a few girls from school? It wouldn't be Courtney out there, after all—she didn't know anyone. She wasn't even *allowed* outside.

This was it. Her opportunity. If she went out there, their parents would think she was *Ali*, not Courtney. It would be the first time she'd ever impersonated her sister without Ali making her. *The first thing you need to do*, she told herself, *is channel her. No one will believe you're her if you don't.* So she shut her eyes and channeled her sister. A beautiful bitch. A manipulative queen bee. The girl who'd ruined her life.

Her skin prickled. It wasn't even that difficult: Courtney had been the queen bee of a group of popular girls at the Radley, scoring the best table in the day room, controlling what shows they watched on TV, putting on the best performance for the ward's talent show. And even before she'd gone to the Radley, kids had loved her—more than her sister, in fact. People felt at ease with Courtney; they picked her first for kickball, they teamed up with her for art projects, she got more valentines than anyone else in the class. Ali, however, sometimes put people off. She was too pushy, too intense. She yelled at people when no adults were watching, pouted when she didn't get the best gift in the Secret Santa exchange, and once even kicked a girl's brand-new kitten that she'd brought to show-and-tell. Yes, Ali was beautiful—a teensy bit more beautiful than Courtney, in fact—but she wasn't the most-loved. It was why she'd worked so hard to get Courtney out of the picture. She wanted to be the one and only star.

Courtney noticed Ali's blue wedges sitting by the door and slipped them on. To ensure her mother would see exactly where she was—and where her sister *wasn't*—she casually knocked another plate off the shelf. As it fell with a loud, hard-to-ignore crash, Courtney pushed the screen door open and watched as the girls, who were now arguing loudly, fell silent and looked up. By the intimidated, reverent expressions on their faces, she knew she already had them fooled. Of course they thought she was Ali.

"You can come out," she yelled in the most confident voice she could muster.

The girls didn't move.

"Seriously, I *know* someone's there," she said. "But if you've come for my flag, it's gone. Someone already stole it."

Spencer emerged from the bushes first. The others followed. And then it just . . . *happened*. They assumed she was Ali, and they asked her questions. Answers spilled from Courtney's mouth so naturally, like this was a role that was perfect for her. And when Mrs. DiLaurentis appeared on the porch, her gaze flickered cautiously at the girls in the yard—these definitely *weren't* Ali's friends. But when she looked at her daughter, she didn't suspect a thing. She just assumed Courtney was Ali. And when she closed the door again, the family was in the car within minutes. They drove away. Just like that.

Courtney was so excited and nervous and scared that she could barely keep up her apathetic act with the girls in the yard. She felt like she was about to burst. She felt like giving every tree in the yard a huge hug.

By the time Courtney returned to the house, she felt like she'd just run the distance to the Radley and back. Her head felt light. Her limbs felt heavy. She looked around the kitchen. Pieces of the plates were still on the floor. A flower vase had been knocked over, too. The quiet house seemed to reverberate with the phantom sounds and voices of what had just transpired. Violent, desperate screams echoing in the air. A scuffle to get into the car. A protest that they had the wrong twin.

She walked through the silent rooms, her sister's wedges clomping on the floor. Her plan had worked. But suddenly, panic struck her. Now she had to *keep it up*. This wasn't something that might only last a few days or weeks before people caught on that the wrong girl was at the Preserve. She had to figure out a way to stay home forever.

She ran upstairs to her sister's bedroom, taking the stairs two at a time. Her gaze scanned Ali's black-and-white bedspread, the cutout magazine ads and pictures of her friends on the walls, the bulging closet full of clothes. She darted to Ali's bed and slid her hand under the mattress. Ali's diary was buried precisely in the middle, just as it had been yesterday. She sat down, opened to where she'd left off, and read.

But when she got to the end, the fizzy feeling in her stomach had intensified. The diary was all about Naomi Zeigler and Riley Wolfe, and it made a lot of shadowy references to secrets and inside jokes that Courtney would have no way of knowing. There was no way she could remain friends with Naomi and Riley—she'd have to ditch them and form a new clique. Only, who?

The four girls in the yard popped into her head. Spencer, Aria, Emily, and that last girl, the chubby one. She ran to Ali's fifth-grade yearbook and scoured the pages. *Hanna*—that was her name. They hadn't signed her yearbook—none of them knew Ali well. *Perfect.*

Slam.

Her head whipped up, and she shoved the diary back under the mattress. Only an hour had passed. Had they returned already? Had they figured it out?

She peeked out the front window. There was a black car chugging at the curb; she couldn't see the driver. Footsteps sounded across the kitchen floor, then creaked on the stairs. She remained stock-still as whoever it was padded down the hall. A figure appeared in her doorway, and she almost screamed.

Jason looked at her with narrowed eyes. "Did they already take her?"

Courtney nodded, still not daring to breathe.

Jason's mouth became small and tight. "Well, I guess *you're* happy now, huh, Ali?"

He shook his head and continued toward his room. The door slammed loudly, rattling the walls. A few seconds later, the opening bars of an Elliott Smith song blared.

Courtney ran her hands down the length of her face. He'd called her *Ali*.

She walked to the mirror. The girl in the glass wore a deep-pink shirt and wedge heels. She had glossy hair, a heart-shaped face, and an impish smile. After a moment, she threw back her head and tossed her hair over her shoulder, just the way Ali did, and then gasped. She'd nailed it.

Euphoria washed over her like a tidal wave. She was going to rule the school. Become fabulous. Turn into the best Alison DiLaurentis possible. She *deserved* it, damn it. And her sister? She thought of Ali's face as her parents shoved her into the car, the life she would lead in the Preserve. But what was done was done. And it was only fair.

She stood up straighter, admiring the girl in the mirror. Suddenly, she remembered something, ran back into the guest room, opened the top drawer of the ugly bureau, and pulled out the silver ring she'd stolen last night when Ali had taken it off to wash the dishes. She pulled it out and held it to the lamp. A small *A* was engraved into the face. Smiling to herself, she slid the ring onto her right pointer finger, the same finger Ali wore it on.

Then she stared at the girl in the mirror again. "I'm Ali," she said to her reflection. "And I'm fabulous."

1

THE PRINCESS OF ROSEWOOD DAY

Alison DiLaurentis strode down the hallway at Rosewood Day Middle School, her kitten heels clacking, her blond hair bouncing, and her plaid uniform skirt riding high on her thighs. The earth science teacher poked his head out his classroom door and raised his eyebrows. The overhead lights, which made everyone else look washed-out and pale, brought out the honey tones in Ali's skin and the green flecks in her eyes. Her footsteps seemed to march in time with the school's "between classes" classical music. And as she rounded the corner toward the cafeteria, the crowds parted for her as they might a regal queen.

Which she sort of *was*.

It was springtime, almost at the end of her seventh-grade year, and Ali and her friends ate at the best table outside, a large, square four-top that had an excellent view of the baseball diamond. Emily Fields, Spencer Hastings, Aria Montgomery, and Hanna Marin were already seated and taking out their lunches: sushi rolls from the Fresh Fields counter and soft pretzels from the cafeteria.

Ali waved at them from the doorway. Spencer brightened. Hanna pulled an extra container of sushi rolls out of her bag and set it in Ali's place. Emily gazed at Ali with a small, excited smile, perfunctorily brushing a few stray leaves off Ali's favorite seat. Aria laid down her knitting and gave Ali a huge smile.

As Ali walked across the courtyard, everyone's eyes were on her yet again. She could hear the admiring whispers and the appreciative whistles. Devon Arliss, who was in Ali's history class, ran up to her as she passed and slipped her that afternoon's homework, which she didn't even have to ask Devon to do for her anymore. And Heather Rausch, whose sister worked at the Sephora in the mall, handed her a gift bag full of samples from the newest makeup line. "You're the only person besides the employees who gets to try these out," Heather said proudly.

"Thanks," Ali said to Devon and Heather, shooting them aloof smiles. It felt like she was a VIP celebrity: She was so precious and desirable, you had to be on a waiting list just to get near her.

Ruling a school was, in a word, *awesome.* She had trends to launch (she'd single-handedly gotten everyone at Rosewood Day to wear lime-green nail polish this spring); people to cut down (planting that fake love note from Kirsten Cullen to Lucas Beattie was perfect revenge for when Kirsten had criticized her field hockey skills); parties to plan (the spring-summer season was the busiest); and girls to upstage. Including her very best friends.

She walked up to them at the table. "Hey, bitches!"

Her friends smiled brightly. "Hey, bitch!" they all said in unison, though Emily looked embarrassed. Even the teachers barely flinched when they heard *bitch* in the halls, but Emily had practically been brought up Amish, and she was still cagey about swearing.

Ali pulled out the old Polaroid camera her father had given her and snapped a photo of them, the girls grinning happily. Even though Aria was the group's official photographer/videographer, the Polaroid was Ali's thing—she never went anywhere without it. At first, she'd carried it around so she wouldn't forget certain details about her new life in case she got caught and sent to the Preserve. She wanted proof of the cute boys she was friends with and the sunniest spot on the patio where she and her friends sat for lunch every day. Now, taking regular pictures had become a habit.

"So what's up?" Ali asked as she lifted the lid of the sushi. Hanna had picked Ali's favorite—spicy tuna roll with extra wasabi.

"I saw Lara Fiori after gym," Aria said. "She was wearing the same Marc Jacobs sandals you had on last week. A total copycat."

Ali snorted. "*Not it*," she said, referring to the game

she'd repurposed from her brother, Jason. It was the catch-phrase she and her friends said about anyone unpopular or uncool.

"Agreed." Spencer fished something out of her bag and handed it to Ali. "Kirsten Cullen gave me an invite to a party at her country club this weekend. Should I say yes for us?"

Ali studied the invite, which was on creamy card stock. "It looks perfect, Spence. Definitely."

Spencer looked pleased. "We'll have to shop for dresses, huh?"

"Ooh, Bloomie's got a new shipment of DVFs in," Hanna said excitedly. "I called them obsessively all morning and had the salesgirl put some on hold for us."

"Nice," Ali said, holding her Vitaminwater bottle up to Hanna's in a toast.

Emily leaned forward. "Have you heard from Matt today?"

Ali picked at her nails. "Only a million times." Matt Reynolds had been Ali's boyfriend, but he moved to Virginia last week. He wanted to do the long-distance thing, but she wasn't feeling it. Although he was the cutest boy in seventh grade, she'd never really been that into him. But as the cutest *girl* in seventh grade, it was only right that they dated.

"I'm over him," Ali went on. "I'd rather hang out with you guys any day."

Her best friends of a year and a half blushed just as

gratefully as they had the time Ali had recruited them to be her new clique. And Ali had a lot to thank them for, too. If they hadn't been in her family's backyard that day, right at that critical moment, things would be very different. Everyone at Rosewood had accepted Ali's new group quickly, and the other girls' popularity had skyrocketed. It was a win-win for everyone.

They'd had a lot of fun times. Like at her family's mountain house in the Poconos. Or at the many parties they'd been invited to, holding court while all the other girls tried to impress them. Or that time last year when they'd skinny-dipped in Pecks Pond, the many sleepovers they'd had, the hundreds of hours of phone conversations and shopping trips and spa days. Ali had made these girls over. They'd gone from nothings to somethings, all because she was Alison DiLaurentis.

Of course, what they didn't know was that she *wasn't* Alison DiLaurentis. But Ali didn't like to think about her past anymore. It was something she'd learned in group therapy a zillion years ago: If you think only positive thoughts, it will lead to a positive life. Her old existence as Courtney was gone.

She looked at Aria, who'd just picked up her knitting needles and a skein of pink mohair. "Are you making another bra?"

Aria nodded, then held up half of a C cup. "You like?"

Ali fingered the soft fabric. "You could seriously sell these at Saks." Then she looked at Spencer, who was penciling something into her day planner's calendar. "God, Spence, you have the *best* handwriting."

Spencer brightened. "Thanks!"

Ali told Hanna the new sunglasses she'd bought from H&M were amazingly chic, and she tugged on Emily's ponytail and said the boatneck T-shirt she was wearing really showed off her muscular shoulders. Paying the girls compliments felt good—not only because they complimented her back, but also because it drew them closer together. There was nothing in the world more powerful than a clique of girls who were honestly best friends—not just frenemies. It was something Ali had wished for all her life.

All the same, Ali couldn't resist asserting that she was just *slightly* better than the rest of them. She pulled out her cell phone, looked at the screen, and mustered a laugh. "Cassie sent me the funniest text earlier," she said, referring to Cassie Buckley, a girl on the JV field hockey team with Ali. "She's so hilarious."

"You're still hanging out with her?" Emily sounded wounded. "Field hockey's been over for months."

"We got pretty tight," Ali said breezily. "In fact, I'm hanging with Cassie and a few other girls from the team this afternoon."

There was a pregnant pause. Ali peeked at her friends, satisfied by their worried, intimidated expressions. She knew they wanted her to invite them along, but excluding them was the whole point. It wasn't to be mean, exactly.

It reminded her of what Spencer's labradoodles, Rufus and Beatrice, did in the Hastingses' backyard: They would play for a while, and then Rufus would climb on top of Beatrice and pin her down to remind her who was the alpha.

"Hey," Spencer said after a moment. "We need to figure out what we're doing for the end-of-seventh-grade sleepover. If you don't already have plans that night, Ali." Her tone was light, but she gave Ali a cautious look.

"Please say you don't have plans!" Emily said anxiously.

"I wouldn't miss our sleepover." Ali looked at Spencer. "What if we had it in your barn?" The Hastings family had an old barn in their backyard that they'd converted into a gorgeous apartment for Spencer's older sister, Melissa. With its lofty ceilings, enormous closet, and marble bathroom complete with a soaking tub, it was the ultimate bachelorette pad.

Spencer twisted her mouth. "Not unless we want Melissa playing truth or dare with us."

Ali rolled her eyes. "Kick her out for the night! It would be perfect, don't you think? We could set up sleeping bags in that big main room, watch movies on the flat-screen, maybe even invite some boys . . ." Her eyes sparkled.

"Like Sean Ackard?" Hanna asked excitedly.

"Noel Kahn?" Aria braved a smile.

Spencer picked at her nails. "What if we had it in your backyard instead, Ali?"

Ali made a face. "Have you forgotten about the gazebo

we're building? My backyard is a disaster area." Then she laid her head on Spencer's shoulder. "Please ask Melissa? I'll be your best friend."

Spencer sighed, but Ali knew she was considering it. That was the power she had over all of them. They would do *anything* for her, even things they didn't want to.

Just like she had done for her sister, all those years ago.

The bell rang, and everyone stood. "Call us later?" Hanna asked Ali, and Ali nodded. Usually the girls did a five-way phone call at the end of the day to catch up on gossip.

Ali held her head high as she rounded the corner toward the gym, her next class period, the jealous gazes of her classmates like warm summer sun on her skin. But suddenly, something in the hall stopped her short. There was a new display in one of the cases, called ROSEWOOD DAY DRAMA CLUB: A LOOK BACK. In the center of a poster board was a picture of this year's drama club after the performance of their play, *Fiddler on the Roof*—there was Spencer, who'd played a supporting role, right in the front. Fanning out in a sunburst pattern around that central photo were pictures of plays from even earlier. Ali spied a younger Spencer playing a tree in *A Midsummer Night's Dream*. There was a picture of Mona Vanderwaal, her hair arranged in pigtails and her mouth full of braces, playing a cowgirl in *Annie Get Your Gun*. There was a younger Jenna Cavanaugh, singing a solo, her lips naturally pink, her hazel eyes wide, seeing everything.

And right next to that, delivering a line to eye-patch-wearing Noel Kahn, was her own face. Except this was a play before sixth grade. Before Courtney had become Ali, and Ali had become Courtney. If you really concentrated, the differences between the two girls were obvious. Her sister's eyes were wider and a little bluer. She stood straighter, and her ears didn't stick out as much. But not a single person had ever noticed those differences—people rarely paid attention to details.

Ali thought about the Preserve at Addison-Stevens. She'd visited a few times, and it was even worse than the rumors. The patient ward had peeling blue walls, dark corridors, and bars on the windows. Kids shuffled through the halls despondently, some of them muttering, others screaming, most twitching. Her sister was one of them now. She'd been insisting she was Alison DiLaurentis for over a year, working herself into a lather. It was a beautiful catch-22: The more the real Ali insisted she'd been unjustly imprisoned at the Preserve, the more ammunition that gave the staff to keep her there. They had her on so many meds she was drooling most of the time.

Ali glanced over her shoulder, suddenly getting the queasy sensation that someone was watching her. That feeling struck her now and then, though mostly she just chalked it up to being stressed about graduating.

She turned back to the photo. It felt dangerous, somehow. Ali could never, *ever* let anyone find out her secret; she wasn't going to the Preserve as long as she lived. She twisted open the latch of the display case, stuck her hand inside, grabbed the picture of pretty, fifth-grade Alison, and slipped it into her bag. She would burn it when she got home tonight.

Out of sight, out of mind. Just like she used to be.

2

SMOKE GETS IN YOUR EYES

Later that afternoon, Ali sat in Cassie Buckley's Jeep, in Cassie's driveway. Cassie had just gotten her driver's license, and she loved giving the girls rides home. They faced Cassie's rickety Victorian house, where they and a few other girls on the field hockey team had been hanging out after school. The place had a wraparound porch, stained-glass windows, and a chicken-shaped weathervane on the roof. To the right was Cassie's long and narrow side yard, which contained a garden that needed weeding, a stone wall that separated it from the neighbors, and an old claw-foot bathtub that wasn't out of place here in funky Old Hollis. Ali actually preferred Hollis's shabby-chic vibe to Rosewood's uberfussy perfection, but, as it didn't seem like an opinion Alison DiLaurentis would have, she never let on.

After she finished checking her mirrors, Cassie turned the key in the ignition. "I hope we pass some hot seniors on the road."

"Which ones?" Zoe Schwartz asked from the backseat.

"I don't know," Cassie said. "Someone hot."

"I'll find you someone." Zoe flipped through the pages of the latest *Mule*, Rosewood's yearbook, which had just come out that day. No one knew why it was called *The Mule*—it was an apocryphal, private-school inside joke that the yearbook staff felt superstitious about messing with.

"Ian Thomas is pretty cute," Zoe decided, pausing on Ian's senior picture. His smile was wide, his eyes were ultra-blue, and he actually looked cute in the graduation cap.

"Not as cute as Ali's brother." Cassie grabbed the communal Marlboro Light that was being passed around and took a long drag.

"Ew!" Ali said.

"What? He's gorgeous." Cassie nudged her. "Can you get me a date with him?"

"You wouldn't *want* a date with him," Ali said. "He's so moody." Then she straightened up in the front passenger seat, plucked the cigarette from Zoe's hand, and puffed, doing her best not to wince when the smoke hit her lungs. The other girls were sophomores or juniors; she was the first seventh grader to ever make the team, even beating out I've-played-field-hockey-since-birth Spencer. But when Ali sat in Cassie's Jeep with them, smoking and talking about boys, it was like they were all the same age.

"Ian's actually really nice," Ali said. "I hang around him all the time."

"Really?" The girls looked at her. "When?"

Ali loved that she had their attention. "He dates Spencer Hastings's sister. He's over there a lot."

Cassie wrinkled her button nose. "Melissa Hastings? What a waste."

"She's so prissy," Zoe agreed. "What does he see in her?"

Ali picked at her manicure. Ironically, her brother had had a crush on Melissa Hastings, too. She didn't know what to think of Melissa, though. Of all the people in Rosewood, Melissa was one of the few who didn't bow down to her. Sometimes, when she was in her yard, Melissa stood at the window of the barn apartment at the edge of the Hastings's property and just stared at her.

Cassie blew a smoke ring. "What are our summer plans, people? School's ending in a month."

Brianna Huston, who had glossy black hair and thick goalie's legs, lowered her sunglasses. "Lose ten pounds. And get a boyfriend, of course."

"A summer romance would be awesome," Zoe sighed.

"I want a boyfriend, too," Ali declared.

Cassie gave her a questioning look as she braked at the stop sign. "Don't you already have one?"

Ali pictured Matt's tearful face when he'd climbed into his family's minivan for Virginia. She'd only responded to his earnest, love-struck texts twice. "I'm not into the long-distance thing."

They passed Hollis College. Students were sitting on benches with cups of iced coffee or talking on the stone steps. When Ali noticed three shirtless guys playing

Frisbee on the lawn, she reached over and pressed on the horn. The guys looked up and grinned. Ali blew them a kiss as Cassie drove away.

"Like them, maybe," Ali joked.

Cassie's jaw dropped open as she looked at Ali. "You should be my new bestie," Cassie said. "I'll kick aside these bitches and make you my co-queen bee."

"Hey!" Zoe said good-naturedly.

"I'm *kidding*," Cassie said, then gave Ali a wink.

They drove out of Hollis and wound through the streets of Rosewood, where the houses got bigger and more spread out. Cassie cranked up Jay-Z, and all the girls sang along. They passed the white monolithic King James Mall, a sign for the brand-new Rive Gauche French bistro on the marquee at the entrance. Then they looped down one of the back roads past the Marwyn trail, whose parking lot was filled with cars and bikes. Next, they crossed the old covered bridge, which everyone loved to tag with graffiti, and then drove past the neighborhood of enormous, secluded mansions where Sean Ackard, Hanna's crush, lived.

Cassie entered a neighborhood full of McMansions to drop off Zoe, then pulled up to Brianna's gated horse farm. When it was just Ali and Cassie in the car, Cassie lit another cigarette, took a drag, and passed it to Ali. "So guess what? My mom is actually going to be home long enough to come to the sports awards ceremony next week. I guess she, like, felt guilty or something."

"That's awesome." Ali squeezed Cassie's hand. "Now we just have to get *my* mom to come to my graduation."

Cassie looked at her sympathetically. "Is she still out all the time?"

"Yep," Ali said tightly. "Miss Socialite Jessica DiLaurentis." She rolled her eyes. "My dad doesn't even go to events with her anymore."

When Ali had told her friends that she and the field hockey girls talked about deep stuff, she wasn't entirely lying. They talked about their parents a lot. Cassie's were jet-setters, never making time for her. To the other girls, she made it sound like it was a good thing—her empty house was perfect for parties, she could wear whatever she wanted to school, and her parents didn't even notice the ding she'd made in the front fender of the Jeep. But to Ali, she told the truth because Ali's parents were also on their own planets—her mom had attended three benefits this month for her cause célèbre, children with mental illness, but rarely spent time with Ali or Jason.

They turned onto Ali's street. The familiar houses Ali had looked at every day for a year and a half now gleamed in the late-afternoon sun. Mona Vanderwaal made loops around her family's five-car garage on her Razor scooter. Her friends Phi Templeton and Chassey Bledsoe sat under a willow tree in her front yard, playing with a yo-yo. All three of them looked up, slack-jawed, as they saw Ali and Cassie pass. *Dorks.*

The Cavanaugh house, a rambling Colonial with a big

backyard, was next. Ali gazed at the large oak tree that still bore the remnants of the wooden ladder that had led to Toby Cavanaugh's tree house. Suddenly, she noticed a face in the front window. Jenna Cavanaugh stared out, big wraparound sunglasses over her eyes. Ali felt a pull in her chest. She held up two fingers to the car window, her and Jenna's old secret sign. Not that Jenna saw.

Cassie pulled into Ali's driveway, coming to a stop behind a construction truck filled with ladders and shovels. Next to it was a battered black sports car, its interior full of Burger King cups, empty wrappers, and schoolbooks. "What's going on in your backyard?" Cassie asked.

Ali sighed dramatically. "My parents are building gazebo-zilla. It's going to seat a zillion people for all their parties. Those disgusting workers showed up yesterday to consult with my parents about what needed to get done."

Cassie raised her butt off the seat and gazed at something in the backyard. "They don't look so disgusting to me."

Ali followed her gaze. A trio of guys in sweat-stained shirts and ripped jeans traipsed through her yard, passing the tree house in which she and Emily had spent many hours talking. One of the workers had tattoos up and down his arms and carried a shovel over his shoulder. Another had dirt all over his face and was talking on his cell phone. But the third guy, who was younger, was staring right at Ali, his green eyes piercing, an impish smile on his face.

"Oh my God, I'm in love," Cassie whispered.

"With Darren Wilden?" Ali made a face.

Cassie gaped at her. "You know him? I've only seen him in the halls."

"He's Jason's friend." Ali made a noise at the back of her throat. "His idea of fun is tagging the wall outside the tennis courts."

"Bad boys are hot." Cassie pulled out a tube of sheer lip gloss and slowly spread it across her lips.

"He's all yours," Ali murmured.

They fell silent as Darren approached, still staring at Ali. Finally, he cleared his throat. "You shouldn't be smoking, Ali," he said sternly.

Ali looked down. The Marlboro Light Cassie had lit was still in her hand, white ash curling into the air. Anger flared inside her. Darren was a fixture at her house, as moody as Jason and just as irritating. Who did he think he was, her dad? As if he had any power over what she did!

Ali took another long drag of the cigarette, then flicked it out the window. She stepped out of the car slowly, her eyes on his. She sauntered up to him, not saying a word, until she was right next to him. Then she pulled up her skirt and gave him a little peek of leg. Darren's eyes went right there and widened not with horror or disgust, but with what was definitely inappropriate lust. Smirking, Ali waved good-bye to Cassie, then turned and strutted into the house, knowing he and Cassie were still staring.

There. She was the one in control, after all.

3

PARTY ON THE DOWN LOW

"One Swiss fondue with four skewers." A waitress laid a bubbling cauldron of melted cheese in the center of the table. "Enjoy!"

Ali's mother, a tall, elegant woman with long blond hair, a heart-shaped face, and a perma-Botoxed forehead, placed her napkin in her lap and daintily picked up a skewer. Her father made an *mm* sound and smacked his lips, which Ali had always thought were a tad thick and rubbery. A long string of cheese stretched uncouthly from the skewer to his mouth. *That* was probably the reason her mom never brought him to her charity dinners.

Ali wrinkled her nose in disgust. "What is this? It looks like Velveeta."

"It's fondue." Mrs. DiLaurentis pushed a skewer toward her. "You'll love it."

"I'd probably love full-fat ice cream, too, but you don't see me eating *that*."

Her mother sipped from her glass of white wine. "It's French, honey. Therefore it has no calories." She twisted her mouth like it was a funny joke.

Ali folded her hands across her empty plate and gazed around the restaurant. It was Thursday night, and she was with her family at Rive Gauche, the new French bistro that had opened up in the luxe section of the King James Mall. The place was decorated with distressed mirrors, retro alcohoɪ ɔds, and Paris street signs. Groups of well-dressed Main Line women shared mussels and French fries at almost every table. A group of college kids who looked like they'd stepped out of the pages of J. Crew tucked into tureens of French onion soup in the corner.

Ali considered taking a Polaroid of the cool new restaurant, but then decided against it—this place was awesome, but she'd rather take a photo of it with her friends. She couldn't even believe her family was out to dinner; they hadn't done this in ages. Even so, her parents sat as far apart as possible in the booth, as though they were two awkward junior high kids at a dance. Mrs. DiLaurentis was glued to her cell phone as if she were messaging with the President, and Mr. DiLaurentis kept peeking at a sheaf of legal briefs he had in his bag.

"Jason, you'll try some, won't you?" Mrs. DiLaurentis placed her phone by her plate and nudged a skewer in Ali's brother's direction.

Jason's floppy blond hair fell into his eyes as he shook his head. "I'm not hungry."

"Don't you feel well?" Mrs. DiLaurentis reached out to feel Jason's skin.

Jason pulled away. "I'm fine."

Ali snorted. "Looks like someone's in one of his Elliott Smith moods," she said, referencing the moody, miserable music he always listened to when he was depressed.

Jason glanced at Ali for a split second, then sniffed and turned away. Ali wondered if he was pissed because he'd heard that she'd been smoking with Cassie, or maybe that she'd flirted with Darren. But why would he care about either of those things? Most of the time, Jason pretended like Ali didn't even exist.

Which really hurt. Ali was grateful her parents hadn't guessed who she was—they were too wrapped up in their own lives to pay attention. As long as she acted *enough* like Ali, they didn't question anything. But she'd thought Jason would have noticed something. Wasn't he supposed to know her the best of anyone? He'd visited her practically every weekend at the Radley, after all, playing spit with her in the day room, telling her about the girls he'd liked—one of whom had been Melissa Hastings, with whom he'd struck up a friendship. "This is how you get her to like you back," Ali had coached him, giving him pointers that she'd picked up from *Cosmo*.

But when she'd taken over her sister's life, she'd discovered that Melissa was dating Ian Thomas, and Jason was single. She'd wanted to ask Jason if he was okay, but it seemed out of character—Alison thought Jason was annoying and insufferable. If she wanted to play this part properly, she had to pretend she thought that, too. If she told even one person the truth, her secret would be one step closer to being revealed.

The waitress set down everyone's drinks. Across the table, Mr. and Mrs. DiLaurentis whispered.

"Now?" Ali's mother looked alarmed. "We should wait."

"It *can't* wait," Mr. DiLaurentis said firmly.

"Yes, it can."

"What can?" Ali asked, grabbing a piece of cheese-saturated bread and popping it in her mouth. The cheese melted warmly on her tongue. It was so good she almost swooned.

Her mother fumbled with her utensils. "Um, nothing, honey. We're just a little stressed right now. Sending Jason to Yale is quite an expense, and we're trying to figure out how to manage our finances."

Ali burst out laughing. "If you guys are so worried about money, then why are you building that huge gazebo in the backyard?"

There was a long pause. Mr. DiLaurentis jumped up to use the bathroom, shaking the table so hard he almost knocked over the fondue pot. Ali's mom's phone rang, and she answered in a false, bright voice.

Ali grabbed her mother's wineglass when she wasn't looking and took a long sip. *Whatever.* A year ago, she would've taken their bizarre behavior personally—maybe her parents sensed who she really was and refused to share things with her. But they kept lots of secrets, things they didn't tell Jason, either.

Mr. DiLaurentis returned from the bathroom and immediately reached for his wineglass. When Mrs. DiLaurentis got off the phone, she looked at Ali. "So. We're going to the hospital this weekend."

Ali's stomach flipped. "*Again?* We were just there."

"*You* were there two months ago. It'll be good for you to visit your sister."

"I have plans," Ali said quickly.

Mr. DiLaurentis's brow furrowed. "Your mother didn't even tell you which day we were going."

"I have plans *every* day." Ali smiled weakly. "*Please* don't make me go. It's so *hard* on me emotionally. I spend hours crying in bed whenever I come back from there."

Mrs. DiLaurentis looked tormented. Ali felt a dart of triumph. Playing the emotional card always worked.

The rest of the dinner was stilted and silent, no one really talking. Mrs. DiLaurentis jumped up halfway through her entrée because she saw a few women she knew from the Junior League. As they pulled into their neighborhood, there were tons of cars parked on the curb. More cars were jammed in Spencer's driveway, most of them Jeeps, SUVs, banged-up BMWs, and Hondas. Loud bass thundered from the backyard.

"Looks like someone's having a party," Mrs. DiLaurentis murmured.

Mr. DiLaurentis made a face. "On a Thursday night?"

Ali got out of the car to get a better view. Kids stood on the Hastingses' patio and near the backyard barn where Melissa lived. Melissa sat with her legs crossed at one of the patio tables—with her chin-length blond hair and pearls, she looked like a clone of Mrs. Hastings. Spencer's father, who was tall and broad with a long, slender nose; strong jaw; and thick head of curly dark hair, stood on the deck, swirling a snifter of cognac.

Mr. DiLaurentis rolled his eyes as he slammed the driver's door. "Do they have to be so damn showy? That third tier to the deck looks ridiculous."

"And she's always dropping hints that they only serve Dom Pérignon at parties," Mrs. DiLaurentis added. "How tacky!" But even as she got out of the car and walked inside, her gaze remained on the crowd. She looked almost wistful.

Jason went inside without commenting. After a moment, Ali was the only one left on the driveway. She peered through the hedges. Most of the kids she recognized: There was Justin Poole, a hot soccer player named Garrett Flagg, and Reed Cohen, whose band almost got signed at a Philly music festival last year. Ian Thomas, with his straw-colored hair and confident, golden-boy good looks, stood by the barn's front door, holding a red plastic cup that was almost certainly full of some sort of alcohol. But when Ali saw the girl *next* to Ian, flirting up a storm, her mouth dropped open.

It was Spencer.

Instantly, Ali started across the lawn, not caring if her brand-new white Maloles flip-flops got grass stains. She wriggled through the opening in the hedges and marched past the crowd of kids until she was right next to Spencer and Ian. When Spencer turned, she paled. "Oh!" she chirped nervously.

Ian glanced at the two of them, then wandered away to talk to another senior. Ali faced Spencer and smiled sweetly. "You didn't tell me there was a party tonight."

Spencer's eyes darted back and forth. "Melissa put it together at the last minute—she got into Penn on a full scholarship."

"Yay for her," Ali said. "But you could have texted me."

"I'm sorry." Spencer looked nervous. "I didn't think you were home. I saw your car pull out earlier."

Ali placed her hands on her hips. "So?"

Spencer set her mouth in a line. "Ali, it wasn't—" Then her eyes clapped on someone behind them. Ian was sauntering back over, now with a plate of food in his hand.

"Who grilled these burgers?" He took a juicy bite. "They're amazing."

Spencer brightened. "I did, actually."

"Seriously?" Ian looked impressed. "Can you do steaks?"

Spencer sank into one hip and gave him a long, sultry stare. "I can do anything."

Ian's smile broadened. Suddenly, Ali wondered if *he*

was why Spencer hadn't told her about the party. Maybe she wanted him all to herself.

She inserted herself into Ian's field of view. "Heeey, *Eee*," she said, calling him by the nickname her sister had used in her diary.

Ian turned his attention to Ali. His smile widened, and he looked her up and down. "What's up, Ali?"

She batted her eyelashes. He was way too old for her, but it was so much fun to flirt with him—*and* she couldn't resist those sexy dimples when he smiled. "Is that Dom Pérignon you're drinking?" She pointed at the cup.

Ian shrugged. "It's champagne, but I have no idea what kind."

Ali looked at Spencer. "Apparently your mom bragged that she *only* serves Dom Pérignon champagne at parties. It seems kind of tacky, though, don't you think?" She loved needling Spencer with the snarky things her parents said about the Hastings family.

"Who cares if it's tacky if it tastes good?" Ian said. He proffered the cup to Ali. "Want a sip?"

"Ian?" Melissa interrupted from the patio just before Ali accepted his cup. She stood at the railing, glaring at them. Ali gave her a sweet smile, but Melissa's expression didn't change.

"Coming," Ian said, snatching the cup back from Ali. He shot the girls a parting smile and said he'd see them later. When he slung his arm around Melissa's shoulders, Spencer made a tiny, tortured whimper.

"Is someone out to get her sister's boyfriend?" Ali teased.

Spencer's face reddened. "Of course not!"

Ali rolled her eyes. "Oh, please. It's written all over your face. '*I can do anything*,'" she added in a breathy voice. "'*Come to me, big boy. Give me a big, wet kiss.*'"

"Shut up!" Spencer screeched. "You flirted with him, too!"

Ali shrugged. Of course she'd flirted with him. There was something in her DNA that made her want to flirt with *every* boy Spencer liked. She needed to prove that she was better. In fact, Ali and Spencer had a running contest this year to see who could kiss the most older boys. Spencer kept insisting she was winning, but Ali was convinced she'd cheated. "I wasn't *serious*," she said. "Admit you have a crush on him and I won't be pissed that you didn't tell me about this party tonight because you wanted Ian all to yourself."

"But I didn't *know*—" Spencer started.

"For the record?" Ali interrupted. "I think he's gorgeous. You should totally go for him."

"You think?" Spencer's eyes lit up. "Even though he's with Melissa?"

"Why not?" Ali asked. "All's fair in love and war."

In truth, she thought it was kind of sketchy to go for a senior, but she hoped softening Spencer up a bit would get her to confess even more.

Spencer sighed. "Okay. I *do* have a crush on him. But you can't tell anyone, okay?"

"Your secret is safe with me." Ali linked her arm with Spencer's and pulled her toward a table of food and drinks set up near the grill. And, lo and behold, there *were* a few bottles of Dom Pérignon on the table. But as she grabbed a bottle and glugged some of the uberexpensive liquid into a cup, it hit her: By admitting she had a crush on Ian, Spencer had also kind of admitted she *had* kept the party a secret from Ali after all.

Bitch.

4

NEVER TRUST SOMEONE
FROM CALIFORNIA

"Why didn't you go to the Hastingses' last night?" Ali asked as she climbed into Jason's BMW the following morning for school.

Jason, who had purple circles under his eyes as though he'd gotten no sleep, turned up the college channel on SiriusXM. "I didn't feel like it."

"Half your class was there," Ali argued. "It was a lot of fun." After she and Spencer had made up, they'd danced with cute upperclassmen for the rest of the night. Several guys had asked for her number, not that she'd given it to them. She still felt like there was something sketchy about dating someone that much older.

"I wasn't in the mood." Jason shot her a look. "And I don't like that *you* went."

Ali scoffed. "Melissa didn't care that Spencer was hanging out."

Jason flinched. "It's not like I'd jump off a bridge if Melissa did it first."

Ali crossed and uncrossed her legs. *You would have a year ago*, she wanted to blurt. But she doubted Jason had confessed his crush on Melissa to the *real* Alison.

She looked at Jason. "Do you think Mom and Dad are really stressed about sending you to college?" She gasped. "What if they're broke?"

Jason snorted. "They're not broke. I don't think that's what they're worried about, either."

"But they said . . ." Ali trailed off, thinking of her parents' weird behavior at dinner. "Do you think they lied?"

Jason hit the brakes hard behind a Mercedes coupe, not answering.

Ali ran her fingers up and down the seat belt strap. "What if they're talking about getting a divorce?"

Jason twisted his mouth. "I don't think–"

"It makes sense. They're never together anymore. And all that talk at dinner about telling us something–it's probably that, don't you think?" She pushed her string bracelet around her wrist. "I'm not surprised, really. Having a daughter like Courtney must really take a toll on a marriage."

The name *Courtney* hung in the air like a bad smell. Ali rarely said her real name out loud, and definitely never to Jason. He breathed out steadily and evenly, his expression giving away nothing. "Maybe," he finally said.

They pulled down the long, tree-lined drive to Rosewood Day. The stone-and-brick school rose up before them, giving Ali the same tingles she'd felt the very first time she'd come here in sixth grade. *This is what I was missing*, she'd thought as she'd smoothed her hands over her blazer. *I am so going to rock this place.*

And she had, of course. Everyone already knew her and bowed down to her. Oh, there had been challenges on the first day: getting lost on her way to gym, confusing Devon Arliss and Dara Artz—luckily they were just thrilled she was speaking to them at all—and flirting with Andrew Campbell, only to realize he was one of the nerdiest kids in school. A few people had given her strange looks when she'd sat down *inside* the cafetcria—apparently all the cool kids sat outside—but she'd played most things off with panache and ease. The very next day, though, she carried around her sister's old diary, which she'd begun writing in herself, as a cheat sheet to Ali's life.

Jason swung past the lower and middle schools and headed for the parking lot at the back, where all the upper-classmen parked. People spilled out of cars and talked boisterously. Ali bolted out the door as soon as Jason rolled into a space, and looked around for Cassie and her other hockey teammates. But then she spied someone else. Hanna stood at the far end of the parking lot with a tall, thin, dark-haired girl she didn't recognize.

"Ali!" Hanna waved her hands above her head. "Over here!"

Ali strutted over, squinting at the girl. She was pretty—
really pretty—and looked like she was at least a freshman.
She was carrying an emerald-green fringe bag with a Marc
Jacobs logo on the clasp. Ali wanted to think it was a
knockoff, but it looked way too nice.

"Ali, this is Josie." There were two bright pink spots on
Hanna's cheeks. "And Josie, this is Alison DiLaurentis."

"Nice to meet you." Josie stuck out her hand to shake.
Her nails were painted a dove gray Ali had never seen
before. She didn't even know gray was a popular color,
but it looked utterly chic. "I've heard a lot about you."

"Everyone has," Ali said primly. "But I've heard nothing about you."

"Josie's family just moved here from Los Angeles,"
Hanna butted in.

"It's so lame that they decided to move in May." Josie
rolled her eyes. "Couldn't they have waited until summer?
I wasn't even able to go to my ninth-grade dance, and the
hottest guy had asked me. *And* I had a friend who had
tickets to the Teen Choice Awards, so I couldn't go to
that, either."

"Oh my God, I would *love* to go to the Teen Choice
Awards!" Hanna breathed.

Ali's head was spinning. *Los Angeles? Ninth-grade dance?
Teen Choice Awards?* She leaned on the back bumper of
someone's VW Beetle. "And you know Hanna *how*?"

Hanna brightened. "I met her yesterday at Otter."

"What's that?" Ali asked. "A pet store?"

Small, almost pitying smiles appeared on both Hanna's and Josie's faces. "Otter is the new boutique at the mall," Josie said. "My dad owns it. I'm working there after school a few days a week."

"It's the best store, Ali," Hanna gushed. "People from the *Sentinel*'s style section were even there when I went in. They said they might do a write-up!"

"We're having an opening-week sale—you should stop by," Josie said, stepping out of the way as a battered Volvo gunned its way up the lot. Then she nudged Hanna. "Remember that fight those girls got into over that pair of Citizens jeans?"

Hanna looked at Ali. "You would have loved it. These two girls spotted a pair of skinnies they both wanted at the same time and got into a fight in the dressing area."

"*That's* how amazing the jeans were," Josie added.

Ali cleared her throat. "And *how* did you find out about this store, Hanna?"

"I read about it online." Hanna suddenly looked panicked. "I thought you knew about it, Ali. I would have said something."

"Since when do you go to the King James alone?" Ali said in a voice that might sound to anyone else like teasing but she knew would put Hanna on edge. "I thought we always texted each other if we were going." She didn't bother to bring up that *she* had been at the King James yesterday, too. But that didn't count—she'd been with her parents.

"She wasn't there for very long," Josie said cautiously, giving Ali a strange look.

"It's a personal, best-friends thing," Ali said tightly. Then she looked at Hanna again. This whole situation was wrong. Since when was Hanna receiving invites to boutique openings and not telling her about them? And since when was a pretty, older girl from Los Angeles choosing Hanna as her newest bestie? Okay, so Hanna was wearing a pretty silk blouse Ali had never seen before, and she always knew what to do with jewelry—today she had a bunch of silver bangles on her left arm. But she also had pink and purple rubber bands in her braces. There was a pimple on her forehead and another one forming on her chin. Her Rosewood Day blazer, which had fit at the beginning of this year, pulled at the chest and didn't quite button at the waist. She'd still be a dork if Ali hadn't scooped her up and given her a popular-girl home. More than that, she was *Ali's* dork, and Ali didn't want to share her.

Ali sniffed the air. "Um, Hanna?" She glanced down at Hanna's banana-yellow Marc Jacobs wedges. "I think you have dog poop on your shoe."

Hanna paled. "Oh my God." She scuttled over to the curb and furiously scraped her heel against the concrete.

Ali gave Josie an apologetic look. "We just can't take Hanna anywhere. One time, when we were in Philly together, she literally fell off the curb into a mud puddle!"

Josie's lips twitched, but she didn't laugh. She pulled

her bag up her shoulder. "Actually, I should probably go. I still don't really know my way around this place yet."

"You're leaving?" Hanna asked, returning from the curb.

"We'll talk soon, okay?" Josie practically fled from them, her ponytail bouncing as she ran down the hill. When she got to the door, a few pretty girls said hello to her, and she smiled back.

Hanna slumped miserably. Ali threaded her arm through her elbow. "I'm sorry, Han. People can get pretty grossed out by dog poop, though."

Hanna pulled her bottom lip into her mouth. "There actually *wasn't* any dog poop on my shoe. I checked."

"Really?" Ali asked innocently. She grabbed her hand and squeezed it hard. "I *swore* I smelled something, Han! My bad!"

Hanna's brow furrowed, perhaps sensing what Ali was up to. Hanna was smarter than Ali sometimes gave her credit for—she picked up on manipulative behavior much faster than the others did. If Ali ever stepped aside—not that *that* would ever happen—and if Hanna made herself over, she'd probably make a decent queen bee herself.

But Hanna said nothing. Ali clutched her arm once more. "Besides, I've heard that everyone from California is a major flake. You don't want to be friends with her, anyway."

She had Ali, after all, and Ali was all that mattered.

5

THOSE SUMMER ROMANCES ARE ALWAYS THE BEST...

"Bring it in, ladies!" Ali's field hockey coach, Mrs. Schultz, called as the two scrimmaging teams jogged in front of the field. Even though the season was long over, Mrs. Schultz liked to get the girls together to practice every once in a while to stay in shape for next year. Ali tramped toward the bleachers. The scent of fresh-cut grass tickled her nostrils, and as she got closer, she saw that Mrs. Schultz was setting out a big jug of fruit punch–flavored Gatorade, her favorite.

"You girls play great defense," Mrs. Schultz said when Ali and Cassie reached the stands. "You're going to be a force to be reckoned with next fall."

Cassie nudged Ali. "You're going to be an MVP even before you're a freshman."

"That's because I'm awesome!" Ali chirped, forming her arms into a V. But deep down, she couldn't even believe she'd *made* the team. She'd barely walked the grounds at the Radley, much less ran field hockey drills, but as soon as she heard that the high school team was opening up JV tryouts to two outstanding junior high players—Ali and Spencer—she'd made it her goal to make the cut. When her family later visited the hospital and "Courtney" found out that Ali had made the high school team, "Courtney's" face had paled. *Who's the better Alison now?* Ali had wanted to yell at her.

Ali grabbed a plastic cup from the stack and poured herself some Gatorade. Then she changed her shirt, threw her gear into her bag, said good-bye to Cassie and the others, and started toward the auxiliary parking lot, where Jason was supposed to be waiting to pick her up. Only a Honda Civic, a random school bus, and the rent-a-cop's Ford were parked there, the driver's seats empty.

She sat on the edge of the fountain to wait. Two cheerleaders whose names Ali didn't remember flounced out of the upper school and headed to their cars. An eighth grader who was always on the morning video announcements stood near the flagpole, talking on her cell phone. And standing by the doors to the gym were Naomi Zeigler and Riley Wolfe. They looked up and stared at her at the same time, then quickly turned away.

Ali's stomach flipped. It had been a year and a half since she'd ditched Naomi and Riley without an explanation, but she still felt uneasy in their presence. At first, the two girls had begged Ali's forgiveness for whatever they'd done—they just wanted to be friends again. They offered to do Ali's homework for the year. Whatever clothes in their closets she liked, she could have. They mentioned a place called the Purple Room and something called Skippies, which was exactly why Ali had dropped them— she didn't know what they were talking about. They would have sniffed her out as the Fake Ali so fast she would have been locked up at the Preserve in no time.

Her phone chimed, and she jumped. It was a text from Aria: *Want to come over tomorrow night? My parents are going on a date. Liquor cabinet, here we come!*

Yes and yes! Ali typed back.

She pushed her phone back into her pocket. Suddenly, she felt eyes on her back again, and goose bumps rose on her skin. Was it Naomi and Riley? But when she turned, it was a boy about her age, standing where the trees met the parking lot. She had no idea where he'd come from, and he was staring at her so intensely that Ali worried he could see into her thoughts.

"It's Alison, isn't it?" he called out as he moved closer.

Ali squinted. The boy was tall and lanky, built like the guys who swam butterfly on Emily's year-round competitive swim team. He wore a fitted black T-shirt, slim-cut seersucker shorts, and laceless canvas sneakers. His brown hair stood up in spiky peaks, and his eyes were an even more arresting shade of blue than hers. They *had* to be colored contacts.

"Alison?" he repeated when he was closer. His voice was gravelly and deep.

"Uh, yeah," she said slowly, pushing her hair behind her ear. "And you are . . . ?"

He looked astonished. "You don't remember me?"

Ali blinked. It has been a long time since she couldn't answer a question as her sister, and it made her feel dizzy, unmoored, and transparent. "Refresh my memory," she said, hating her words.

"It's Nick Maxwell." He sat on the edge of the fountain and placed his hands on his knees, which were tanned and had just the tiniest bit of dark hair on them. "From Camp Ravenswood."

That explained why Ali had no idea who he was. Her sister had gone to that camp the summer after fifth grade, a few months before the switch. "Of course!" she said brightly, hoping she sounded convincing, that dizzy feeling not going away. "How *are* you?"

Nick chuckled. "You *have* forgotten me. I guess you write stuff about guys on cabin walls all the time?"

"I . . ." It felt like Ali had been plopped into a foreign country without any knowledge of the language. She'd memorized her sister's journals word for word, and there'd been no mention of anyone named Nick in her diary. Maybe she'd worried her parents would read it and kept him a secret.

Nick ducked his head. "I'm sorry—you probably didn't know that I saw what you wrote." He drummed his fingers on the concrete. "The counselors made me wash it off. I think they thought I *made* you write it or something."

His gaze returned to her, and he smiled appreciatively. "Maybe I should have paid more attention to you back then, though. You've really grown up."

"You *should* have paid more attention," Ali repeated, the pieces slowly coming together. Had Ali written something desperate on a wall about a boy who she'd had an unrequited crush on? Had this guy actually said *no*?

She stood up and hiked her field hockey skirt higher on her thighs. All of a sudden, she really, *really* wanted Nick to like her. Imagine telling *that* to her sister in the hospital. She'd have a brain aneurysm.

"So what did you think about what I wrote?" she cooed flirtatiously.

Nick's eyes sparkled. "Well, it was really flattering, obviously. It's not every day a guy reads a message about how good of a kisser he is—especially when a girl he'd never kissed wrote it. I was wondering how you could tell."

"Oh, I've always had a good sense of how people will kiss just by looking at them," Ali said, eyeing his lips. They were pink and bow-shaped.

"Really?" Nick grinned.

"Yep."

They remained that way for a moment, grinning at each other. Then Ali reached for her camera. "Can I take a photo of you?"

"Only if I can get your phone number in return," Nick said.

Ali snapped a photo, then wrote down her cell number

on a piece of paper ripped from her math notebook. Then Nick took off, saying only "See you around, cutie." As he tilted away from her, Ali felt unsettled. Why hadn't he asked her to do something? He didn't want her yet in the way that he *should*. She thought of how she'd learned to hypnotize people recently, a game Matt's older sister had taught her one afternoon. *Count down from one hundred, touch someone on the forehead, and then say they're in your power.* Ali wished she could try it out right now and make Nick ask her on a date.

Then she saw a familiar figure cut across the hockey field. It was Ian Thomas, dressed in khaki pants and a kelly-green polo. He looked like a cross between a frat boy and a golfer, but a hot guy was a hot guy. Maybe there was another way to get Nick in her power.

She put herself in his path. And, like any good pawn, Ian grinned when he spotted her. "Hey, Ali!" he called, waving.

Ali blew him a kiss, and he teasingly blew one back. She didn't even need to turn around to know that Nick had stopped and was staring.

Maybe she was a better hypnotist than she'd thought.

6

SOMETHING'S ROTTEN
IN THE ANTIQUE BARN

Saturday afternoon, Ali parked her bike on the grass between the large, crooked wooden sign that read ANTIQUE WAREHOUSE and Aria's parents' battered, blue, bumper-sticker-plastered Subaru wagon. Aria had called her about a half hour ago—her family was coming here to shop for a table, and did Ali want to meet her? Ali had nothing to do, so she'd agreed. Besides, it was tense inside her house—doors kept slamming, her parents passed each other without speaking, and at one point her mother answered the ringing phone, said nothing but sighed, and then slammed it down. Ali needed to get out.

Ali pushed open the barn door and blinked in the darkness. The antique store smelled like a strange mix of mildew and freshly squeezed lemonade. An oldies station was playing on the radio, and everywhere she turned were piles of junk. Old toys, ugly rugs and blankets, and chairs that would definitely collapse if someone sat on them.

More clocks than Ali could count sat on every available inch of counter space. Aria's brother, Mike, who was in sixth grade, banged on the top of an old pinball machine to get it to work. Then he turned to Ali and gave her a long, amorous stare, just like he always did. Aria's brother was *so* into her—he'd once even tried to kiss her at one of Aria's sleepovers.

"There you are," Aria said, touching Ali's shoulder. Ali spun around and took in her friend. It seemed as though the pink streaks in Aria's hair had multiplied, and she wore long feather earrings that grazed her shoulders. Tucked under her other arm was her stuffed pig puppet, Pigtunia, which her father had brought her from Germany.

"Only babies carry stuffed animals," Ali chided.

Aria spun around and shrugged, holding up the puppet and making her oink. "Pigtunia wanted to go for a ride. How could I say no?"

Because she's a puppet? Sometimes Aria was such a freak.

"Hey." Aria touched a Tiffany-style lamp on the table with Pigtunia's snout. "What do you think? Aren't these things worth a lot of money? And look—it's only twenty-five dollars!"

Ali snorted. "I'm sure it's a knockoff." This was the Main Line, after all. Even junk shop owners knew what a real Tiffany lamp was worth.

Up ahead, Mr. Montgomery, who Aria called Byron, turned to a smaller, round table with a tile top. "How about this one?"

Mrs. Montgomery—Ella—sniffed. "That won't fit all four of us. Or is that the point?"

"What's that supposed to mean?" Mr. Montgomery demanded, crossing his arms over his chest. His tweed blazer had a hole in the elbow.

Mrs. Montgomery pushed a lock of her brown hair behind her ear. "Forget it."

"I don't *want* to forget it." Aria's dad guided his wife around a corner. They spoke in whispers. Mike looked up from the pinball machine, his brow furrowed.

Ali turned to Aria. "What's up with your parents?"

Aria shrugged. "They always get like this when they shop for antiques."

By the way Aria's throat bobbed when she swallowed, Ali knew she'd hit a nerve. But you had to be blind not to notice that Aria's parents' relationship had changed. In sixth grade, Mr. and Mrs. Montgomery spoke French at the dinner table when they wanted to say romantic things in front of their kids. These days, they barely ate dinner at the same time. And once, not that long ago, when Ali had slept over at Aria's, she'd gotten up in the middle of the night to use the bathroom and noticed that Aria's mom was sleeping in the guest room. Aria said it was because her dad snored, but the house had been awfully quiet that night.

Ali wanted Aria to confide in her if she was worried—maybe if Aria did, Ali could open up about her own family worries. But Aria didn't work that way. While the other girls had their own reasons for ingratiating themselves to Ali, spilling their secrets if she so much as asked how their day was, it was hard to get Aria to open up. In fact, Ali wasn't exactly sure sometimes what Aria got out of the friendship. Sure, she liked being part of a clique, but she often held Ali at arm's length, keeping her feelings close to the vest. Sometimes, it made Ali fight for her affection and attention even more. Other times, it just annoyed her.

Suddenly, Ali spied something on one of the tables. An old, silver pocket mirror with delicate engravings on the handle and the back was propped up next to a stack of books. Her doctors had used a very similar mirror during group sessions at the Radley.

She shut her eyes, a memory flooding back. Miss Anna, the psychologist, would pass the mirror around to each girl, telling her to look into it and share with the group what she most wanted to be. Most girls would give touchy-feely answers: *I want to be strong; I want to be better; I want to be happy.* But Ali had gazed at her reflection, her features matching her sister's. She hadn't said she wanted to be her sister, though, as most people at the hospital would have thought. She'd said, *I want to be free.*

She slipped the mirror into her bag and walked away.

"This place smells like my grandma's basement," she said, grabbing Aria's arm and steering her out the door. "Let's go outside."

They wove through the piles of wicker baskets and

around a large wooden butter churn and emerged into the late afternoon sun. The air was scented with lilacs. A horse neighed from a nearby pasture. Despite the idyllic setting, Ali suddenly felt that familiar prickle in her spine. A car passed, and when she looked through the windshield, Melissa Hastings's scowling face stared back. Ali flinched. They weren't far from their neighborhood, but this was a back road, not one that Melissa would have much reason to travel on.

Then Ali spied two guys emerging from the enormous Colonial-style house down the path from the barn. "Is that Noel Kahn?" she asked.

Aria whipped around. They both watched as Noel and a guy they didn't recognize grabbed a basketball from the grass and shot hoops in the huge, circular driveway.

"C'mon," Ali said, starting across the parking lot. "Let's go talk to them."

"Wait!" Aria shrieked, grabbing her arm. "How do I look?"

Ali inspected Aria, from her Technicolor hair to her sparkly blue eye shadow to the swirly patterned hippie top that showed off her skinny arms and big-for-seventh-grade boobs. "You look great," she said. "But ditch the pig, okay?"

Aria stuck Pigtunia on the roof of her parents' car, and then she and Ali started over. The boys looked up when they saw them coming. Noel's brown hair was tousled, and there was a smudge of dirt on his face. He and the other guy, who had curly blond hair, freckles, and pinchable cherub cheeks, wore sleeveless T-shirts, long mesh shorts, and white sneakers that looked enormous on their feet.

"Hey, Ali. Hey, Aria," Noel said.

Aria grabbed Ali's hand. *He knows my name!* the squeeze said. *Of* course *he does*, Ali wanted to tell her. She'd only introduced them six million times.

"Hey, Noel," Ali said. Then she looked at Cherub Cheeks. "Who's your friend?"

The guy stepped forward. "Mason Byers. I just moved here from Atlanta."

"He's going to be on the lacrosse team next year," Noel said. "Coach asked me to show him around." He gestured across the street. "Were you girls antiquing?"

"My parents are," Aria said, rolling her eyes. "They're obsessed with old stuff."

"That's cool." Noel turned his green eyes to Aria. "My parents are, too. My dad collects scale models of ships. They're taking over his office."

"My dad's into books," Aria admitted, fiddling with her fake nose ring. "Sometimes he goes to flea markets and brings back a whole crate of them, looking for one that's valuable. My mom wants to kill him most of the time—we don't have room for all of them."

"Flea markets can be pretty cool," Noel said. "I once found a killer neon beer sign at the one in Bryn Mawr."

Ali snorted. "Noel, when have *you* ever gone to a flea market?" Noel's family was one of the richest in Rosewood.

Noel gave Ali a playful poke. "I've been to plenty. And if you're not interested, when Aria and I go to a flea market, *you* don't have to come."

Ali rolled her eyes. "As if I'd *want* to."

A loud *beep* sounded from across the road. Aria's parents were trying to fit a round table with ornately carved legs into the back of their Subaru. The table fell to the ground with a *clonk*, and Mr. and Mrs. Montgomery started arguing.

Clouds rolled across Aria's face. "We should probably head back over."

"Good luck with that table," Noel said.

"Nice meeting you," Ali said to Mason as they walked away.

Once the boys went back to playing basketball and they were out of earshot, Aria grabbed Ali's arm excitedly. "Oh my God, he wants to go to a flea market with me!"

Ali snorted. "He didn't exactly say *that*."

"Still, it went well, don't you think?"

Ali glanced at her friend. Aria's eyes were shining, almost spinning, she was so excited. For whatever reason, it annoyed her. It wasn't like Noel would ever *really* go for Aria when he had someone like Ali as an option. He was just being nice, probably because Aria was Ali's best friend.

Suddenly, her cell phone buzzed. *Hey, cutie*, said a text from a local 610 number.

She frowned. *Who is this?* she wrote back.

You've forgotten me again? came the reply. *It's Nick from camp.*

Ali's heart flipped over. Finally! She'd been waiting for Nick to text. *My memory is coming back to me,* she wrote.

Just wanted to say hi, Nick responded. *Gotta run.*

Ali slipped her phone back into her pocket, feeling triumphant. She *knew* making him jealous would work like a charm.

She looked at Aria, suddenly feeling more magnanimous. "I think it went *really* well," she said.

By the time the girls were back across the street, the Montgomery parents had managed to get the table in the car. There were angry looks on their faces, but they straightened up once they saw the girls.

Mrs. Montgomery opened the front door and threw her purse into the footwell. "C'mon, Aria. We'd better get going." She glanced at Ali, then at Ali's bike, then at Mike, who'd already climbed into the back, his body contorted to accommodate the large table. "I'd offer you a lift home, Ali, but I don't think there's room."

"It's cool—I don't mind riding," Ali answered. Then she looked at Aria, who'd rescued Pigtunia from the roof and was cradling her in her arms. "Are we still on for tonight?"

Aria glanced at her parents, who were now sitting in the front seats of the car, staring straight ahead. Her throat bobbed as she swallowed. "Um, I actually don't think my parents are going out after all."

"Oh." Ali shrugged. "That's okay. We don't have to . . ." She mouthed the word *drink*.

"Actually . . ." Aria spun her blue string bracelet around her wrist, then glanced warily at her parents. "It's not a good night to come over."

Ali stepped back. "Why?" Aria stared at her feet, not answering. "Is something going on with your parents?" Ali demanded.

Aria looked wounded, almost like Ali had slapped her. *I'm just trying to be nice!* Ali almost protested, but Aria got into the car before she could. "I'll call you later, okay? Sorry."

Aria shut the door, leaving Ali standing next to the car, her arms dumbly at her sides. Ali stared at the bumper stickers on the car's back fender as it pulled away. PLANNED PARENTHOOD. VISUALIZE WHIRLED PEAS. A Darwin fish. Aria didn't even look out the window to wave good-bye.

Ali walked away as the car pulled out of the lot. As she reached into her bag, her fingers closed on something familiar. The silver mirror. She pulled it out and stared into the glass. For a moment, she didn't recognize the girl looking back—she looked sad, bereft, confused. Nothing like herself at all.

7

SO MUCH FOR BEING A MATCHMAKER

A few hours later, Ali and Emily lay on the long leather sectionals in Ali's den. Ali was flipping through prom issues of *Teen Vogue*, *CosmoGirl*, and *Seventeen*, and Emily was leafing through a dog-eared copy of *Horoscope Birthday Book*, which she seemed to never tire of. MTV's *My Super Sweet 16* blared in the background, and the house smelled like the baked chicken and corn on the cob Mrs. DiLaurentis had fixed for dinner. Jason stomped around upstairs, slamming his bureau drawers and opening and closing his closet door. Miserable rock music hummed through the ceiling.

"All these girls look hideous in mint green," Ali declared as she turned a page of a prom-dress fashion spread. "Any dress that's the same shade of a scoop of ice cream is *not* sexy."

Emily placed the birthday book on the ottoman. The spine was so worn that the pages splayed open without any encouragement. Emily had been reading the entry for June 6, Ali's birthday, for probably the billionth time. "I think *you'd* look pretty good in mint green," she decided after studying the picture of the dress.

"That's because I look good in any color," Ali said, only half joking.

"You do," Emily said earnestly, and Ali wanted to hug her. Emily was always good for a pick-me-up. After Aria had mysteriously canceled, Ali had called up Emily asking if she wanted to come over here instead. Naturally, Emily had given her an emphatic *yes*.

Emily doodled a picture of a girl in a prom dress on the cover of one of her notebooks. Instead of keeping a diary, Emily displayed her thoughts, likes, and dislikes in doodles on her notebooks: On this particular one, she'd penned her favorite swimmer's name, Michael Phelps, in bubble letters; a picture of the Rosewood Day shark mascot in blue Sharpie; and Ali's, Spencer's, Aria's, and Hanna's names in calligraphy, followed by the letters *BFF*.

The air conditioner kicked on again, fluttering the curtains on the bay window. Ali stood up and pushed the curtains back, revealing the view of the Cavanaughs' house across the street. It had been through this very window that Toby Cavanaugh had spied on them last year on the night everything happened.

Emily must have been thinking the same thing, because she cleared her throat. "I think I saw Jenna today. Maybe she's home from school."

"I saw her, too," Ali said.

Emily twirled her pen between her fingers. "Do you ever . . . *think* about her?"

"Not really," Ali lied.

"Do you ever think it's weird that Toby confessed to something he didn't do?"

Ali yanked the curtains shut. "He *did* do it, Em. End of story."

"But—"

"End. Of. Story." Ali pointed to the string bracelet on both of their wrists. There were a lot of things she'd considered telling Emily since that night. What she'd seen just before the firework went off. The discussion she'd had with Jenna even *before* that night. But she'd been lying for so long that she couldn't start over now. And anyway, the truth wouldn't change what had happened.

She tugged at Emily's ponytail. "I'm so glad you could come over tonight, Em."

"Totally." Emily ducked her head bashfully. "We haven't had a night alone since February."

Ali smirked. "Of course you'd keep track of something like that." Emily was like the friendship secretary, keeping minutes of exactly how much time they spent together. Sometimes, she'd announce that they'd been friends for two hundred and thirteen days, or that they'd spent four hundred minutes on the phone the past week, or that they'd exchanged sixty-seven emails or written a hundred and nine texts, or that they'd shared fourteen secrets.

Emily looked worried. "Is it weird?"

"Nah." Ali hugged a pillow. "Well, maybe weird in a cute way." If the others were around, Ali might have dogged Emily a little more for it, but when it was just the two of them, she could tell her what she really thought. When Ali was with Emily and only Emily, being so polished and perfect didn't matter as much.

Footsteps sounded in the hall, and the girls looked up. Mrs. DiLaurentis emerged in the kitchen in a sundress, a thin leather bankbook in her hands. She stopped short when she saw Ali and Emily in the den. "I thought you girls were going to the mall," she blurted, hiding the book behind her back.

Ali cocked her head. "We never said that."

"Oh." Mrs. DiLaurentis looked flustered. "Well. Don't stay up too late, okay?"

The garage door slammed. Ali waited for her mother's Mercedes engine to start, but it didn't. She was half-tempted to go out into the garage and see if she was just sitting in her car, talking on her phone—she did that some-times. *Freak.*

Bzz. Ali's phone vibrated in her back pocket. She had a new text from Nick. *Hey, cutie*, it said. *Write anything about anyone on a cabin wall lately?*

Ali's stomach swooped, and she let out a happy squeal. *Sorry, haven't met any good kissers*, she replied.

"Who are you writing to?" Emily peeked at Ali's phone from the couch.

Ali turned the phone over. "Someone from hockey." She didn't want to share Nick quite yet. It was nice keeping it quiet until she was sure something was actually happening between them. Besides, Emily would probably criticize her for moving on too quickly from Matt, breaking his heart. Emily was a softie like that.

She looked up at Emily, taking in her long strawberry-blond hair, light eyes, and cute, freckly face. "We need to find you a boyfriend, Em."

Emily looked startled. "We do?"

"*Duh!* You haven't even had a first kiss!" She clapped her hands. "I think I might've found someone perfect for you. He just moved to Rosewood—his name is Mason Byers. He's playing on the lacrosse team, so he's sporty, too. And he seems really sweet, Em—he's from somewhere in the South. I bet you'd really like him."

She jumped to her feet, getting even more and more excited. "I could call Noel right now and ask for his number. He's supercute, Em—he has freckles, too."

Emily slowly pulled her bottom lip into her mouth. "I'm not interested."

Ali placed her hands on her hips. "You haven't even met him yet. And he's not a butt-grabber, I promise." Once, at a party at Noel Kahn's house earlier this year, an eighth grader had squeezed Emily's butt hard, giving her a playful wink when she'd turned around to glare at him. Emily had recounted this story to Ali with horror, not realizing that she should have taken it as a compliment.

Emily's expression still didn't change. Puzzled, Ali climbed next to her on the couch. "What's really going on?" she demanded.

Emily stared at her freshly painted nails. "I sort of like someone else."

"Really?" Ali grabbed Emily's knee. "Who?"

Emily's eyes darted back and forth. "I can't tell you."

Ali burst out laughing. She knew everything about Emily, even the embarrassing stuff: that she'd gotten her period at eleven, that she'd wet the bed at a swimming sleepover in fourth grade, that she'd accidentally grazed an older boy's erection during swim practice and hid in the locker room for the rest of the hour, terrified he thought she'd meant to do it.

"Is it someone really embarrassing?" Ali goaded. "Someone off-limits? Whoever it is, you can tell me, Em. I won't share it with anyone, I promise."

Emily grabbed a magazine and opened to a random page. "These shoes are cute, don't you think?"

"Whoever it is, I could help you get him to like you. Seriously. Just tell me, okay?" Then she leaned her head on Emily's shoulder. "I'll be your best friend?"

Emily stiffened under the weight of Ali's head. After a moment, she moved away and stood up from the couch. "I just remembered," she blurted, diving for her overnight bag and stuffing it with the pajama pants and makeup bag she'd pulled out onto the floor. "I have to do this thing for my mom."

"Now?"

"Uh-huh. I forgot." Emily slung the bag over her arm and hurried through the kitchen. She shoved her feet into her shoes, which were waiting by the front door, not even bothering to tie them. She glanced back at Ali, who was still on the couch. "See ya."

"Emily!"

But the door slammed shut, making the pots and pans hanging over the kitchen island clang together slightly. Ali blinked hard in the silence. *What the hell just happened?*

She stood up and padded into the kitchen, yanking open the fridge but not pulling anything out. A dog-of-the-month calendar on the wall caught her eye, and she looked at the thirty-one squares that represented May. She and Emily might not have had any one-on-one time since February, but it had been much, much longer than that since Ali had actually spent a Saturday night alone.

8

FAMILY THERAPY, THIS ISN'T

On Sunday morning, Ali, Jason, and the DiLaurentis parents pulled up to a familiar sign pointing to a secluded road lined by tall, thick trees. THE PRESERVE AT ADDISON-STEVENS, read the calligraphy lettering. Mr. DiLaurentis put on his blinker and steered up the drive.

"Those white trees are freaky," Ali grumbled, glancing out the window at the birches in the woods, their albino branches twisting and curling over the road. "They remind me of the people in this place."

Her mother scowled at her in the rearview mirror, but Ali pretended not to notice, slathering on an extra coat of nail polish. Her mom hated the smell, but Ali wanted to punish her. This morning, after she'd woken up and showered, her mother had walked into her bedroom without knocking and sat on her bed. "You're visiting your sister at the hospital today."

"No, I'm not." Ali had willed tears to her eyes. "It's

too hard on me, Mom. I have nightmares every time I go there."

For some reason, the pity act wasn't working. "If you don't come, you can't go to the end-of-seventh-grade sleepover with your friends," Mrs. DiLaurentis proclaimed.

Ali's mouth dropped. "You can't tell me what I can and can't do!"

Mrs. DiLaurentis stood. "I'm your mother, of course I can," she said sternly. "She's your *sister*, Alison. I know you two have a lot of bad history, but you need to get past it and try to have some sympathy. Have you thought any more about the therapist I recommended?"

Ali had flopped onto the bed and covered her head with a pillow. Her mom had mentioned a local therapist from time to time, saying it might help her deal with her issues with her twin. But what her mom didn't know was that she'd been to therapists for years—and they'd never been able to solve that problem.

Now she was a prisoner in the car. The closer they got to the hospital, the tighter the knot in her stomach cinched. As her father continued up the drive, Ali's phone beeped. She thought it might be a text from Nick—they'd sent messages back and forth all morning, and she was sure he was *this* close to asking her out. But it was from Emily instead. *I'm sorry about last night. Where are you? Can we talk now?*

Ali gazed at the building in the distance. The hospital was a big white mansion with impressive columns, looking more like someone's house than a mental institution. A nurse and a patient hobbled along the path. Another patient sat on a bench, just *staring*. An ambulance was parked in a side driveway, waiting for a disaster.

Can't right now, she wrote, then turned her phone off. She'd begun to understand why her parents kept the second twin a secret all these years: There was definitely a stigma to having a daughter or sister in a loony bin. People might assume the DiLaurentises were bad parents for putting her there. Or maybe they'd assume the rest of the family was crazy, too.

Her heart pounded fast as they pulled up to the guard's gate and gave their name to a khaki-clad man with a walkie-talkie. They circled the driveway and passed the obsessively manicured topiaries and the glassy-eyed patients on the lawn. For a moment, Ali thought she recognized one of them from the Radley, a girl who used to scream in her bed for hours on end, but she couldn't be sure.

They parked in the visitors' lot and got out. Ali lagged behind her brother and parents, staring at the names on the plaques of old patients who had passed on that were mounted beside the trees and benches. NELLY PETERSON. THOMAS RYDER. GRACE HARTLEY. That was another thing people said about the Preserve: The suicide rate was worryingly high. People must have thought death was a better option than being trapped in here.

The lobby had marble floors, a big fountain in the center, and modern white couches. After giving their name to a lab coat–wearing receptionist, they were buzzed into the patient ward, which was markedly shabbier and older than the lobby or the outside. They entered the day room, which was big and bright with several large windows, threadbare couches pushed against the walls, and an old, blinking TV playing a movie Ali didn't recognize. The room smelled of antiseptic cleaner and macaroni and cheese. A nurse listening to headphones sat behind a window in the corner. A woman Ali was almost positive was a psychiatrist was talking to a despondent girl with white-blond hair by a bookcase full of board games.

Then, the door opened, and a familiar girl walked into the room.

Ali sucked in her breath. Her sister's blond hair had been blow-dried and curled to perfection. Her skin looked flawless, despite the gross hospital food she was no doubt eating, and her boobs were still a teensy bit bigger and her waist a teensy bit smaller than Ali's. Gold earrings dangled from her ears, and she wore shimmery pink lipstick.

"Hi, everyone," her twin chirped pleasantly, giving her parents a peck on the cheek and squeezing Jason's arm. Only when she turned to Ali did her expression shift a little. Fury smoldered behind her eyes.

Everyone sat down on one of the plaid couches near the TV. Mrs. DiLaurentis scrambled around getting everyone Cokes from the vending machine. She presented her daughters with Diet Cokes, looking proud of herself. "I figured you girls didn't want real sugar."

Ali wrinkled her nose. "I don't drink Diet Coke, either. No one at school does."

Mrs. DiLaurentis looked abashed. "But I bought you a whole case last month."

"But that was before I read that fake sugar makes you just as fat." Ali pushed the can away. "I got everyone at school to drink Vitaminwater instead."

"Courtney" snorted. "It's fun being a trendsetter, isn't it, *Ali*?"

Ali flinched. *Not long ago, you* weren't *the girl who set the trends,* her sister was really saying. *You were nothing.* "Of course it is," she said confidently. "Plus, I think it's *much* healthier."

Suddenly, the despondent girl who'd been talking to the therapist in the corner made a flying leap onto the couch and engulfed Ali's sister in a huge hug. "C!" she whooped.

"Hey, I," "Courtney" said, slinging her arm around the girl's shoulder. "Everyone, this is Iris, my roommate. And Iris, this is Jason, Mom and Dad, and my sister." She looked squarely at Ali. "*Alison.*"

Iris turned her ice-blue eyes to Ali. "So you're the famous Alison. I've heard a lot about you."

Ali gave Iris an equally bitchy smile back. "Don't believe everything you hear. I'm not *nearly* as wonderful as Courtney says."

"Oh, and Courtney *does* say you're wonderful." Iris didn't blink. "But she's pretty awesome, too. We have a lot of fun here. Tuesday's our standing spa day, isn't it, C? And Thursday is yoga!"

"How nice!" Mrs. DiLaurentis clapped her hands.

Ali squinted. "You have a spa here? And yoga?" The Radley didn't have either of those.

"Uh-huh." Iris's smile showed all her teeth. "You're jealous, aren't you? I bet you want to be in here, too."

Ali flinched, a chill running up her spine. Her sister had told this girl everything. And Iris clearly believed her.

Iris stood. "Well, I'll let you guys catch up." She waggled her fingers at the family and sauntered off, her jeans hanging low on her skinny hips.

Mrs. DiLaurentis set her Coke on the coffee table. "She seems . . . nice."

"She's a skeleton," Jason mumbled.

"She's pretty cool." "Courtney" fiddled with her earrings. "She's in here for an eating disorder. But I guess she's doing a lot better—she's leaving on Wednesday. Who knows who I'll get stuck with. I liked the roommate I had before her, too—her name was Tabitha. But I feel like I can't get lucky three times."

"So how are your classes?" Mr. DiLaurentis asked. Everyone at the Preserve had a private tutor who kept them on pace with their grade level.

"They're going really well," "Courtney" answered eagerly. "I've definitely aced English. Geometry, too. I'm not so sure about history and science." Her face brightened. "But I've had a lot of help. A friend of mine, Tripp, tutored me. He's awesome."

Mrs. DiLaurentis exchanged a surprised glance with her husband, who looked just as floored. "That's so nice!" she chirped. "Is Tripp here?"

"Courtney" shook her head. "He was. But he transferred elsewhere." She ran her finger in a groove in the table. "It's a bummer, but we've been emailing a lot."

She trailed off and stared at her lap. The DiLaurentises exchanged a charged look Ali couldn't quite decipher. "You seem much happier," Mrs. DiLaurentis said.

"I've been feeling pretty good," Courtney said. "I guess it's the new meds they have me on."

"And your nurses said you've been really cooperative," Mr. DiLaurentis added.

"They've been nice to me," "Courtney" said. "They all work *so* hard."

Ali turned her head and rolled her eyes. What was with the sweet-as-pie act? And why was her twin acting so *normal*? Usually when they came here, "Courtney" was combative and angry, barely speaking to any of them.

"In fact, I've been doing so well that they've given me permission to leave campus every once in a while," "Courtney" added.

Ali flinched. "By yourself?"

"No." Her sister smiled sweetly. "With a chaperone."

"Goodness." Mrs. DiLaurentis smiled. "You *must* be improving."

Ali pulled a loose string on the upholstered couch they were sitting on so vigorously a whole row of stitches unraveled in her hands. What lunatics allowed her sister to leave campus? Didn't they realize what she was capable of?

After a while, a nurse tapped Mrs. DiLaurentis on the shoulder to say that Courtney's group session would begin soon. Everyone hugged, Ali gritting her teeth as she wrapped her arms around her sister's shoulders. Then her twin disappeared out of the day room, an odd spring in her step.

Ali excused herself to use the bathroom—she felt light-headed and needed a few seconds to herself. She pushed through the door of the visitors' bathroom in the hall, wrinkling her nose at the acrid scent of bleach and the ring of rust around one of the sinks. Then the door opened again, and two girls walked inside. One of them was Iris. Another was her twin.

"H-hi?" Ali stammered. "Don't you have group therapy?"

"Oh, don't worry about that, *sis*," "Courtney" sneered, glancing at Iris. The roommate marched to the door and stood guard in front of it, her skinny arms crossed over her chest.

Ali's heart started to pound. She glanced at the door Iris was guarding. "Mom's going to look for me soon."

"Oh, this won't take long," "Courtney" simpered, moving closer.

Ali flinched. All kinds of horrible scenarios flashed through her mind. She saw her sister pouncing on her in bed when they were seven years old, forcing her to do whatever she asked. *If you don't, you'll be sorry.* She pictured her sister pushing her into a closet and binding her wrists with a bungee cord. She remembered her snapping the head off her precious doll, the only thing her grandmother had given her. And then she saw herself snap, tackling her sister to the ground, her sister's eyes full of glee as she screamed for help. Her twin had set her up again and again and again.

"I just want to tell you something, okay?" Ali's sister stood so close to Ali that Ali could see the pores on her cheeks, the sparkly sweep of eye shadow on her lids. "I know what you've been doing. And pretty soon, you're going down."

It felt like she'd just run a cold spike through Ali's chest. "Please don't lock me up again," she blurted, twisting away from her sister's face. Then she gasped, realizing what she'd just admitted. After the switch, she'd vowed never, *ever* to reveal what had happened to anyone, not even the girl whose identity she stole.

"Courtney" smiled nastily, catching what she'd said, too. She reached down and grabbed Ali's finger, touching the silver ring with the curly *A* in the center. "Your time is running out, *Ali*," she sneered, dropping Ali's finger once more and brushing past her toward the exit. "Say your good-byes."

9

ALL FALL DOWN

"Looking good, Alison!" Mark Hadley, an eighth grader, called as Ali passed him on the track later that afternoon.

"Can I run with you?" Brian Diaz shouted next.

Ali shot a brilliant smile to them over her shoulder, but she didn't stop. The red lines on the track blurred beneath her. She pumped her arms hard, cycled her legs, and whizzed past the bleachers, trying to clear her thoughts. This was her fifth lap, and she had decided to run as long as it took to get the memory of what had just happened at the hospital out of her mind. There was only one problem: The image of her sister's sneering face was branded in her mind.

She'd considered telling her parents what her sister had said to her in the bathroom, but she'd decided against it. Mrs. DiLaurentis would ask the real Ali for the truth. Even though the real Ali had claimed *I'm Alison, I'm Alison* again and again, what if the Preserve kept surveillance tapes? Ali had blatantly said *Please don't lock me up again*. Had she sealed her doom? And what if her sister was watching her when she got to go off campus? Did she really have a chaperone? How strict was the Preserve, anyway?

There had only been one other time she'd been alone with her sister since she'd become Ali. It had been early in sixth grade, not long after the switch happened—her sister had come home for a weekend. Apparently, the girl everyone thought was Courtney was having a hard time transitioning to the Preserve; the doctors thought some time away might do her some good.

Ali had stressed about the visit to no end. They'd all be prisoners in the house while her sister was home—her parents were still keeping things a secret—and she didn't know how to explain to her friends why she was staying away from them all weekend. She couldn't say they'd gone out of town—Spencer would see their car in the driveway and the lights snapping on and off inside the house. In the end, she said she was sick and really contagious.

But the stress didn't end there. As soon as her sister entered the house, Ali watched her like a hawk. She'd even slept in the den to make sure her sister didn't go out at night and locked her bedroom door to make sure her twin didn't break in and look through her things. For the first day, the plan worked well enough: Ali managed to keep her sister inside and contained. But on the second day, when Ali had turned her back, her sister vanished. To her horror, she found her standing in the front yard. A second girl looked up at the sound of the slammed door, her eyes wide. It was Jenna Cavanaugh. And that was when Ali remembered: Jenna had met both twins years ago, during another visit home—they'd all played Barbies in the backyard one afternoon. She was the only girl in Rosewood who knew there were two of them.

A nasty smile had spread across her sister's face. "I was just talking to Jenna, *Courtney*," she said. "I was telling her all about who you really are."

Jenna's eyes had ticktocked from one twin to the other. Black spots had appeared before Ali's eyes. She'd grabbed her sister's hand and pulled her back inside.

Their parents were in the kitchen. Ali told them that her sister was talking to the neighbors. "I was just telling them the truth," "Courtney" screamed. "I told her that I was the real Alison and that I was being held prisoner!"

A vein had pulsated in Mrs. DiLaurentis's temples, and she'd sent Courtney back to the Preserve early. It was obvious their parents didn't believe her, but if they had proof—like Ali saying *Please don't lock me up again*—their minds just might change. Ali couldn't go back there—she just *couldn't*. She tried to picture those cold, bare, antiseptic beds; that joyless common room; those nurses in their scrubs handing out pills. One year at the Radley, her family hadn't visited for Christmas, taking a trip to Colorado instead. The hospital celebration had involved a pathetic plastic tree, carols no one sang along to on the out-of-tune piano, and turkey with gross, lumpy gravy. Ali was certain that every girl on the floor had gone to sleep crying in her pillow.

Now Ali ran past the back of the track, which bordered the soccer fields. In the narrow strip of grass that separated the two were small concrete blocks flush against the ground. Each one was labeled with a year and the words *Time Capsule*.

It was from the game Rosewood Day played every year. Ali thought of the Time Capsule piece she'd taken from her twin. After he discovered what she did, Jason had stormed away with the piece and never brought it back—Ali had no idea whatever happened to it. But that hardly mattered—she had used the missing piece to garner sympathy from her friends.

She wiped sweat from her forehead. *If it hadn't been for that piece of the flag, would I even be here right now?* she wondered. Perhaps her fate was that coincidental, that precarious. Perhaps it could change on a dime once again.

Unexpected tears sprang to her eyes. It felt as if all the balls in the delicate juggling act she was performing had crashed to the ground. Not only with what had happened with her sister, but everything that was going on with her friends, too. Why were they keeping so many secrets from her? Didn't they like her anymore? Didn't they want to be part of her clique? Had they forgotten how much she'd done for them? And what did her sister mean by *I know what you've been doing*? What if she could *see* her friends defying her, see her screwing up so badly?

Ali passed the bleachers once more without even realizing she'd made another lap and then, suddenly, felt the
ground go out beneath her. In seconds, she was sprawled
out on the track, her cheek hitting the pavement hard.

"Are you okay?" Mark Hadley said, standing above her.

"I'm fine." Ali tried to laugh it off as she stood.

A single tear rolled down her cheek, but she quickly
sniffed and kept the rest at bay. Alison DiLaurentis did *not*
cry. Alison DiLaurentis didn't freak over her loser sister,
nor did she stress, worry, or fear for her popularity. That
was why she was the most popular girl in school—because
she knew she deserved it. Her sister was just undermining
her like she always did. And as for her friends, maybe she
just needed to remind them how special and amazing she
was, how they'd be nothings without her. She'd kill them
with kindness, dazzle them with the sparkling magic that
drew them to her in the first place. It would be easy, really.
She already knew what all of them wanted. She could snap
her fingers, and it would be done, just like that.

Right?

10

STAR-CROSSED LOVERS

"*But soft! What light through yonder window breaks?*" Aria said dramatically, clutching her breast.

"*It is the east, and Juliet is the sun,*" Spencer continued, then collapsed onto the bench outside the People's Light & Theater Company, a few miles from Rosewood, where some of the class had come on a field trip to watch the famous play. "That is *so* romantic."

"Yeah, but don't forget they die in the end," Ali teased, kicking at a divot in the grass. "They don't even get to enjoy being in love. Lame!"

"Yes, but death is the most romantic gesture of all, don't you think?" Aria asked, her eyes sparkling. "I mean, if you're willing to *die* for someone, that means you really love them."

"Thanks, but I'd rather live and enjoy being in love," Ali said.

And she *did* feel in love these days. She and Nick had been texting nonstop for two weeks now. They hadn't gotten together yet, but their first date was the next day, and she couldn't wait. It had also been two weeks since her sister had made that threat, and nothing had come of it. Yet. Though Ali had tumultuous dreams of her sister somehow proving what she'd done, there had been no parental interventions or terrifying exposés. Her sister hadn't shown up on their doorstep or in Ali's bedroom at night, forcing Ali out of her bed so they could switch back. The DiLaurentis parents had called her both Sundays, Ali listening stealthily on the extension. "Courtney" talked about her boyfriend, Tripp. Her classes. How Iris, her roommate, was gone, but how she hadn't been assigned someone new yet. Nothing about Ali. Nothing remotely crazy at all.

Which made Ali even more nervous.

Two weeks hadn't changed the situation with her friends, though. Emily was still keeping secrets. Hanna was still socializing with Josie. Spencer still seemed wary of Ali, and Aria had shut down entirely. Every challenging remark from Ali's friends felt like a test she needed to pass—especially if her sister *was* watching, judging, gathering intel to prove she wasn't who she said she was. She was *not* going to the Preserve. She was *not* saying her good-byes. She'd die first.

Aria grabbed her purse. "I need to go to the bathroom."

"I do, too," Emily said, glancing apologetically at Ali before standing, as if she was supposed to ask permission. Ali just rolled her eyes and ignored her.

Next to her, Spencer's gaze was on the field. Near a picnic table full of the teacher chaperones were a bunch of seniors including Jason, Darren Wilden, Melissa Hastings, and Violet Keyes, who'd been after Jason for years. Ian Thomas was there, too. Spencer's eyes lit up when she saw him.

She jumped up. "I have a question for Mrs. Delancey," she said, nodding at one of the English teachers.

Ali and Hanna, the only two left, watched Spencer's ponytail bounce against her back as she ran toward the picnic table. She asked Mrs. Delancey a question, but she kept sneaking peeks at Ian out of the corner of her eye.

Ali made a disgusted noise at the back of her throat, and Hanna looked up from her sandwich. "What is it?"

"She's only over there to be near the older boys."

"We could go over, too," Hanna suggested.

"No." Ali crossed her arms over her chest. "I'm mad at Spencer."

"You are?" Hanna looked worried. "Why?"

Ali tapped her nails against the bench. *Same reason I'm mad at you*, she wanted to say. But instead she sighed. "Long, boring story."

Hanna went quiet. Ali stared out at the yellow school buses parked in the lot, which disrupted the pastoral Chester County fields and farms. Their ugliness suited her mood, though, as her friends' disobedience had just stirred up all her unsettled feelings once more. What if she *was* slipping? What if her sister *did* figure out a way to come back and take her life over again? If Ali went to the

Preserve, she'd never get to see these fields again. And she hadn't even *appreciated* them.

Sometimes, in her darkest moments, she pictured her parents finding out what she'd done and leaving her on the side of the road somewhere to rot. They'd hate her forever. Maybe they'd even throw her in jail.

She felt a teardrop on her cheek. When she looked up, Hanna was gaping at her. "Ali?" she said. "What's the matter? Are you okay?"

Ali's throat bobbed as she swallowed. For a fleeting second, she considered telling Hanna, with her poop-brown hair, braces, and earnest, yearning expression, everything. But instead she just shrugged, her insides turning to rock. "Forget it."

Laughter sounded from the other side of the picnic grounds, and Ali looked up. A group of seniors stood on the grass, pantomiming one of the duel scenes from the play. Ian wielded an imaginary sword. Eric Kahn, Noel's ninth-grade brother, laughed raucously. Spencer was gone.

Suddenly desperate to be away from Hanna, who'd witnessed a brief chink in her armor, Ali grabbed her Polaroid camera, jumped up from the table, and sauntered over to Ian and the others before Hanna could ask where she was going.

"Hey, Ee," Ali said, giving him a sly, flirty smile.

Ian paused from his pretend-duel and smiled back. "Hey." He pushed a lock of blond hair off his forehead. "I didn't know you were coming to this."

"I've been here the whole time," she said, tilting her hips.

Ian smiled and moved a little closer to her. "Oh, yeah?"

"Yep." Ali held up the camera, the knot in her gut slowly unfurling. "Can I get a picture of the two of us?"

"Sure," Ian said, and wrapped his arm around Ali's shoulders. Ali held the camera out at arm's length and snapped a photo. The machine whirred and grumbled, then spat a white photo out the bottom. Slowly, the image filled in. Ali's face looked model-perfect. And the way Ian tilted his head toward her made him look like her boyfriend.

Ian examined the picture, too. "You look gorgeous," he said.

A thrill ran through Ali. "You do, too," she answered. When she tilted her chin up, she was surprised to see Ian's face right there, almost like he wanted a kiss. But *she* didn't want Ian—that was Spencer's weird thing. Which made her think of her plan to win over her friends again. And that gave her an idea.

She pulled away and gave Ian a long look. "I know someone who likes you."

Ian's eyebrows shot up. "Who?"

"Spencer."

Ian blinked, perhaps thinking Ali was going to say it was her. "Spencer Hastings?" He laughed. "Okay."

"Would you kiss her?"

He stared at her like she was crazy. "That seems a little dangerous."

Ali wanted to snort. It was amazing how Ian didn't flat-out refuse, because he had a girlfriend. She lowered her chin and made puppy-dog eyes. "Please? She would *love* it, Ian. She has a thing for you *bad*."

A pleased smile spread across Ian's face. He pretended to think. "How about this. If I give a kiss to Spencer, then I get a kiss from you."

"Okay," Ali said, shrugging. A kiss for Ian Thomas was hardly the worst thing in the world. It would certainly be something to brag to Cassie and the others about. "But you have to really kiss Spencer, okay? Not just a little peck on the cheek. Kiss her like you mean it."

"You've got a deal," Ian said, holding out his hand to shake. When Ali did, he let his fingers touch the inside of her palm, and her insides tingled a little. Ian might have been skeevy, but he *was* gorgeous.

She started back to where her friends were sitting, feeling a million times more optimistic than before. Once Spencer knew that Ali got Ian to kiss her with a snap of her finger, she'd be so grateful and impressed that she'd never disobey Ali again. But as she passed an old oak tree, she heard an odd, high-pitched giggle. She stopped and looked around, listening. There was someone sitting on the top of one of the picnic tables, staring at her with hard, narrowed eyes.

Melissa. And by the look on her face, it seemed like she'd heard every word Ali and Ian had said.

11

BANG, BANG, YOU'RE IN LOVE

The following day, Ali stood in front of the full-length mirror in the bathroom of Henry's Paint Ball and Laser Tag, an indoor/outdoor boy extravaganza on the edge of Rosewood. Nick had wanted this to be their first date, and though Ali normally balked at the idea of paintball, she was willing to do anything to snag and keep the boy who'd spurned her twin—even put on the ugly blue paintball jumpsuit. She smoothed her hands over the baggy fabric, then tied a neon-pink J. Crew belt around her waist. That made it look a little better.

"Ali?" a voice called when she stepped out of the bathroom.

Ali's heart did a flip. Nick leaned against the check-in booth, looking gorgeous despite the fact that he was in a jumpsuit, too. His piercing blue eyes stared at her and only her. Dimples appeared at the corners of his smile. She bounded up to him as coolly as she could, resisting the urge to squeal.

"Hey," she said, grinning.

Nick gestured to the paintball area, an obstacle course of bushes and bulwarks, providing places to hide. "You ready?"

"Absolutely," Ali answered. But when Nick passed her a gun, she balked. It was *huge*.

Nick giggled. "You don't have to act like a girl around me. I remember you kicking butt on paintball day at camp."

Ali clutched the gun to her chest and stood up straighter. She'd never played paintball in her life, but Nick couldn't know that. She peered at the other kids playing in the field, shooting out from behind the bushes to tag their enemies. She'd hung out with enough boys to know that there were two teams; the object was to capture the yellow flags that hung from the fence across the wide expanse of grass. How hard could it be? "Let's rock," she said.

As they traipsed across the field, Nick leaned into her. "So what's up in Alison DiLaurentis's world?"

"Not too much," Ali said as they crouched behind a bush. She wasn't about to tell him the truth—like about her visit to the mental hospital, for example. "How about you?"

Nick peered over the top of the bush. A kid whizzed past, but he was in a blue jumpsuit like them. Globs of paint exploded toward him from all directions, and he shrieked and covered his head. "I just got a job at a new French restaurant at the King James."

"Rive Gauche?" Ali asked excitedly. "I love that place! Now I'll have to come more often."

"I hope so." Nick's eyes gleamed. Then he poked her playfully. "Of course you'd know about Rive Gauche. You're probably the type of girl who likes to shop, huh?"

"I do like to shop," Ali said. "But I'm not a *type* of girl."

"No?" Nick raised an eyebrow. "At camp you were. You had those girls in your bunk wrapped around your little finger."

"Maybe I've changed," Ali teased. "You said yourself that I'd really grown up."

Nick didn't look convinced. "So you're not a Miss Popular, gets-everything-she-wants, loves-manicures-and-pedicures, has-a-huge-group-of-friends, and is-good-at-everything-she-does kind of girl anymore?"

Ali peered over the bush, but no one was in view. That was absolutely the image she wanted to project, the perfect Alison she needed to be. But suddenly, she wanted Nick to know that she was more than that. Deeper. "For your information, I don't like mani-pedis," she admitted.

Nick widened his eyes. "Shocker!" he said in mock horror. "I'll alert the press."

Ali edged closer. "And I kind of like watching football," she whispered. "*And* eating wings instead of salads."

"No!"

She giggled. "I love animals, too."

"Oh, yeah?" He smiled at her. "Do you have any pets?"

Ali shook her head. "Not now. But I used to have a gerbil."

Nick looked surprised. "You don't seem like the gerbil type."

Ali poked him. "There you go making assumptions again." She hiked the paintball gun higher on her shoulder. "My gerbil's name was Marshmallow. She was the best—I decorated her fur, painted her nails, and put bows on her head."

"So you're okay giving a gerbil a mani-pedi, even if *you* don't like them." Nick clucked his tongue. "Animal cruelty."

"She didn't seem to mind," Ali admitted, suddenly feeling wistful. "For a while, Marshmallow was my only friend."

Nick snorted. "Yeah, right."

Ali clapped her mouth shut, realizing she'd said too much. Marshmallow had been her only friend because she'd been her pet at the Radley. It had been a big privilege to be allowed to have her as a pet, and she'd relished the responsibility, giving her lots of cuddles, making sure she got enough exercise on her wheel, putting her cage right next to her bed because hearing the *tap-tap-tap* of her claws on the side in the middle of the night comforted her.

"Well," Nick said, moving closer to Ali, "hopefully I can get to know this girl who is definitely *not* Miss Perfect."

"I'd like that," Ali said shyly. "And what about you? Any secrets I should know about?"

Nick fingered the trigger on the gun. "Not really. What you see is what you get," he said, staring into her eyes.

Tingles shot through Ali's body. Then suddenly, something red flashed before her eyes. A girl in a red jumpsuit zigzagged through the field. Ali leapt up and aimed at her, firing the paintball gun as if she really *had* been the paintball master at camp. The girl squealed and ran for cover.

Ali grabbed Nick's hand. "Come on!" She pulled him into the field toward the flags. Paint flew at them from all directions, and Ali ducked and giggled, managing to avoid every assault. The yellow flags loomed close. She ripped one from the fence and let out a whoop. Nick, who was right behind her, was so excited he picked her up and spun her around.

"You *do* rock paintball!" he cried, his smile wide. "I guess you haven't changed *completely*."

"I guess not," Ali said as he gently put her down. Her chest heaved from her sprint across the field. But standing there with Nick, grinning like crazy, she didn't notice any pain at all. *I'm the best Alison ever*, she thought.

No one, not even the real Alison, could ever take her place.

12

ALI IN THE ALLEY

A few days later, Ali sat with her friends on a bench in front of Pinkberry, which was on Rosewood's main thoroughfare a few blocks away from school. Across the street, the neon sign for Ferra's Cheesesteaks blinked off and on. Women in capri pants and big Chanel sunglasses went in and out of the Aveda salon. The bells on the door of Wordsmith's Books jingled cheerfully. Aside from the occasionally stinky exhaust from the passing cars, the whole world smelled like spring flowers and hot caramel from Pinkberry's toppings bar.

"And then, when I looked out my window, one of the workers was staring at me." Ali was telling her friends about the guys who'd come to dig the hole for the gazebo that morning. "And then he actually *whistled*! I mean, he was as gross as Toby Cavanaugh used to be. Maybe even *grosser*. I felt icky all over. What if they took pictures of me?"

Spencer dropped her spoon in her cup. "You should have closed your curtains if you didn't want them to see you."

"What does it matter?" Emily jumped in. "Those guys can't do that! You should tell your parents, Ali."

Ali made a halting motion with her hand. "It's okay. I can handle it on my own."

"Seriously." Emily was breathing heavily, which she always did when she got worked up. "That's, like, harassment! They should hire someone else! Do you want *me* to tell them for you?"

"Easy, Killer," Ali teased, using her favorite nickname for Emily. Okay, so she'd stretched the truth a *teensy* bit. The workers actually hadn't as much as cast a glance in her direction this morning, even when she walked to Jason's car.

"Okay, everyone, switch," Ali said to her friends, plopping the plastic spoon back into her cup of Pinkberry and handing it to Hanna, who was on her left. Hanna handed her pistachio to Emily, Emily gave her peanut butter–flavored frozen yogurt to Spencer, and Ali got Aria's lychee-nut with chocolate sprinkles.

Ali let the flavors melt on her tongue, feeling that all was right with the world. So far today, she'd received three texts from Ian promising her that Spencer's kiss would come soon but also wanting to know when his kiss with *her* would be. Hopefully, in time, he'd just forget—especially now that things were going so well with Nick. She was still basking in the glow of their amazing date. Part of her wanted to tell her friends about it, but part of her wanted to keep Nick to herself for a little longer. She hadn't even written about him in her diary yet; he was so special she hadn't been able to find the right words to describe him.

She suddenly felt so happy that she wanted to pass the feeling along. She rested her head on Spencer's blazer-clad shoulder. "So, girls. I think we should all find amazing crushes for the summer. And then we make a move to turn those crushes into boyfriends."

Hanna looked thrilled. "I'm in! I claim Sean!"

"Great!" Ali grinned. "What about you, Spence? Got anyone you're into?" She didn't know when Ian was going to make his move, but the sooner, the better.

Spencer stiffened and gave her a *Please don't tell anyone* look. "Uh, *no*." She stabbed her spoon into the ice cream and vigorously scooped up a bite.

"Well, *I* have a crush," Aria said proudly when Spencer didn't answer.

"We know, we know." Emily cuffed her playfully. "On Noel. You've only told us fifty times."

"Yeah, and we even bonded last week," Aria said excitedly.

Ali demurely blotted her lips with a napkin. "Why don't I ask him out for you?" she said, feeling generous.

Aria's eyes widened. "What would you *say*?"

"I'd tell him that you're the most awesome girl in the world."

Aria laughed. "And he'd *believe* you?"

"Of course, Aria. Noel listens to me. Whatever I say, goes. I can convince him that you're the only girl he should go out with." She looked around at the others. "Tell her, guys. Tell her I can convince him Aria is amazing."

"She can," Emily said. Of course she was the first to agree.

"It's true." Hanna nodded.

Even Spencer reluctantly shrugged. Aria swirled her spoon around her rapidly melting ice cream. "You would really do that for me, Ali? What's the catch?"

"No catch." Ali mussed Aria's barrel curls, which she'd helped her do that morning before school. "I just want you to be happy." *As happy as I am*, she thought.

"You're amazing." Aria gave Ali a huge hug.

After the girls finished their dessert, Spencer announced she was due at the Rosewood Memorial Hospital, where she volunteered as a candy striper. Hanna's mom was waiting for her at the Starbucks down the street. Emily and Aria mounted their bikes and headed for home, too. Ali tossed her yogurt cup in the trash and sauntered toward Wordsmith's, then spied Jason's car parked in a no-loading zone. For once, he was actually on time.

"Do you mind if we stop at the Kinko's in Hollis before we go home?" Jason asked when Ali climbed into the car. "I have to make a photocopy of my transcript for school." Then he glanced at her in the backseat. "And move to the front! I'm not your chauffeur!"

Ali grumbled, then climbed into the front seat at the next stoplight and buckled her seat belt. "Why do you have to make a copy of your transcript for Yale?" she asked.

"Because it has my final grades," Jason answered. "Yale requires all students to submit them to make sure they still want to admit us."

Ali wrinkled her nose. "I thought you were already in."

"It ensures that kids don't flunk out their last semester of high school," Jason said, hitting the gas when the light turned green.

Ali closed her eyes and thought about her brother going to college. It used to be one of the things he talked to her about when he visited her at the Radley—he wanted to major in political science, he said, and then maybe become a lawyer who specialized in child emancipation cases. *I should get emancipated from Mom and Dad*, she'd said sadly. *Then maybe I could get out of this place.* Jason had murmured in agreement.

They were quiet as the car rolled past the curlicue-lettered sign announcing Hollis College. The campus had a lot of old, brick buildings, a Big Ben–type clock tower, and a big arena that held the ice hockey rink and the fencing rings—Hollis's only Division I sports. They passed a bar called Snooker's, which had a chalkboard out front that listed that week's Phillies schedule. As Jason took a left at the next light, cruising down a street that was rife with college bars and head shops, he gave Ali a sidelong glance. "Can I ask you a question?"

Ali shrugged. "Depends what the question is."

Jason took a big swallow from his water bottle. "I know Courtney was in the bathroom with you before we left the hospital. Did she say anything?"

The smile melted off Ali's face. She didn't think anyone had seen *Courtney* go into the bathroom. When she'd emerged, the hall had been empty—Jason and the others had been waiting in the lobby. Was it possible that he'd heard what her twin had said?

"I saw her come out after you," Jason said, as if reading her mind. "Was everything okay?"

Ali flicked the string bracelet on her wrist. "It was fine. We just talked about stupid stuff."

"Are you sure?"

Ali blinked. "Why wouldn't I be sure?"

"I don't know." Jason raised his hands defensively. "I'm just asking."

Ali licked her lips and considered telling him how the real Ali had threatened her, but then her words echoed in her mind. *Please don't lock me up again*, she'd said, basically admitting everything she'd done.

Jason stopped at a crosswalk to let students pass. "Do you think Courtney seems different?"

Ali flinched. "Different how?"

"Happier, I guess. Not herself."

There was a sizzling feeling in the pit of Ali's stomach. "Does anyone know who Courtney really is? She's crazy."

"*I* know who she is."

No, you don't, Ali thought with a flare of anger. *You don't know anything.*

Jason pulled into a parking space in front of Kinko's. "I know you've never understood why I visited her all those years at the Radley," he said quietly. "I just thought she needed someone in her corner, you know?"

"So why did you stop visiting her at the Preserve?" It was a question Ali had never asked him.

Jason ran his finger over the silver BMW keychain. "I didn't mean to stop visiting her at first. I was just swamped with schoolwork and couldn't make the time. The times I did visit her, though, she seemed so . . . *strange*." He swallowed hard, then glanced at her. "She told me some weird things about you."

Ali's stomach tightened. "She's a jealous, crazy bitch."

Jason didn't look convinced. "For a while, I thought some of the things she told me were true."

Ali tried hard to keep her hands from trembling. "She's lying."

Jason opened his mouth, then closed it again. He stared at her hard, as though trying to memorize every freckle, every eyelash on her face. "Do you ever wish you could go back and change what you did?"

The words hit Ali like an icicle through the heart. *What you did.* But he meant what *Ali* did . . . to *Courtney*. Right? Not the switch. "I didn't do anything," she snapped.

Jason kept his eyes on the road. "We *all* did things we

could have done differently. We could have helped her. Been more of a family."

"That's not how I see it," Ali said sharply. "She's crazy. She needs to be locked up. End of story."

Jason bit his bottom lip and didn't say anything. After a moment, he got out of the car and slouched into Kinko's. Ali watched the door open and shut, her stomach turning over. The walls seemed to close in on her inside the car, and she suddenly felt squeezed into a seat that could no longer contain her.

She fumbled for the door handle and staggered onto the street. Cars and trucks whizzed past the busy thoroughfare. Students rushed by holding Starbucks coffee cups and textbooks. The clock tower let out four bongs. Ali took a few careful steps down the sidewalk, trying to find her balance again.

She walked to the end of the block and studied the skater-logo stickers someone had plastered to a stop sign. Then, a lilting giggle sounded from around the corner. Ali turned and cocked her ear. There it was again. It was coming from the alley.

She poked her head into the narrow strip of road between two university buildings. THESE SPACES RESERVED FOR ART HISTORY DEPARTMENT FACULTY ONLY read a placard in front of a parking spot. A Subaru was in the lot, its window cracked, two people inside. One of them had a blond ponytail and an earnest, college-girl smile. The other, the driver, had a craggy face and wild, professor-style hair.

Ali straightened up, recognizing the familiar PLANNED PARENTHOOD and VISUALIZE WHIRLED PEAS stickers on the Subaru's bumper. There was that dent in the fender, too, the one Aria's mom had made when she'd run over a decorative boulder in Ali's front yard.

It was Aria's dad who was in that car. But the other, the ponytail girl, was definitely *not* his wife.

"I love these after-class study sessions," he was saying.

"Me, too," the girl said, then pouted. "But I hate having to squeeze them into Tuesdays at four."

Mr. Montgomery touched her cheek. "This is the only time we're both around."

The girl sighed. "I know, I know, but . . ."

Mr. Montgomery put his finger to his lips to silence her. Then he cupped her chin and brought her face toward his. Ali crept behind the brick wall as Aria's father ran his hands through the girl's hair. The girl pulled Aria's dad closer and kissed his neck.

"Ali?"

The two heads shot apart. Ali whirled around. Jason stood behind her, a plastic Kinko's bag in his hand. "You ready?" he asked.

Ali blinked hard. There was a rumbling sound behind her. "Uh . . . ," she said, poking her head back into the alley.

But it was empty now. All that remained was a cloud of exhaust, like Mr. Montgomery's car—and what he'd done inside it—had never been there at all.

But Ali knew what she'd seen.

13

DR. ALISON, AT YOUR SERVICE

Ali stepped up to Hanna's front door and rang the bell. The opening strains to Beethoven's Fifth played, then all was quiet. Ali knew Hanna was home, though. She'd texted Ali only a few minutes ago.

Ali turned around and stared at Hanna's huge, elegantly manicured front yard. Ali had always liked Hanna's house the best because it stood alone on a secluded street on top of Mount Kale, which was just outside Rosewood. It was heavily wooded and didn't have that everyone-in-everyone's-business suburban feeling that Ali's neighborhood or other neighborhoods in Rosewood did. Often, when she slept over here, she'd see deer on Hanna's front lawn in the morning, and it was dark enough up on the mountain to see tons of stars at night.

Hanna flung the door open. Her brown hair was mussed around her face, her eyes were red behind her glasses, and there were bright-orange Doritos crumbs on

her shirt. Ali glanced behind her to a bunch of wrappers
on the coffee table. Ho Hos. Twinkies. There was an
empty cheese popcorn bag on the floor. A single pastry
sat on a plate, bathing in a pool of cream.

Ali stared fixedly at those crumbs. For a long time,
she'd wondered why Hanna ate the way she did, stuffing
huge portions of Doritos into her mouth as though Frito-
Lay had announced it was never making them again. She
used to lead her friends in making fun of her—*It's not a race,
Hanna*, and *Watch out, your teeth will turn orange.* That was
before they went to Annapolis a few months ago, though,
and she saw what Hanna did with Kate's toothbrush.

"Hey," Hanna said woodenly, letting Ali in and tapping the keys of the burglar alarm, which was beeping.
Whenever Hanna's mom wasn't home—which was always,
since she worked at a high-powered job in the city—she
made Hanna keep the alarm on at all times.

"What's wrong?" Ali asked.

"Nothing," Hanna said, not meeting Ali's gaze. Then
she looked down at the Doberman coffee mug in her
hands, her expression a twist of pain and sadness. Her
father used to use that cup, but Mr. Marin had moved out
months ago.

"Did you talk to Aria?" Ali asked.

"No . . ." Hanna's head whipped up. "Why? Is something going on with her?"

Ali ran her tongue over her teeth. All she could think
about since it had happened was what she'd seen Aria's

dad doing in Hollis. Did Aria know? Was that why she was acting so strange lately? She hadn't told Ali what was going on, but what if she'd told one of the others? Hanna would be a good choice—her parents had divorced last year.

But Hanna looked genuinely caught off guard, so Ali figured Aria hadn't told her. Maybe she shouldn't say anything. It was one thing for Ali to talk about an open secret behind Aria's back, but maybe it was another to tell Hanna something she didn't already know. Besides, it made Ali feel powerful to know something so awful about Aria's family.

"Um, forget it," Ali mumbled. "But you're obviously not okay. What's going on?"

Hanna slumped down in a chair at the dining room table. The place settings had been shoved aside, and her history book was splayed open to the chapter they were being tested on tomorrow. She let out a tortured sigh. "My dad sent me vacation photos of him, Kate, and Isabel on spring break."

Ali blinked, waiting for Hanna to go on. Isabel was her father's new girlfriend, and Kate was her pretty daughter. Ali had met them both in Annapolis.

She was about to ask Hanna what the big deal was, but suddenly, she remembered she was being the New Ali, the girl who killed her friends with kindness. Kate was definitely a sore spot for Hanna. Although Hanna rarely mentioned it, Mr. Marin had left for Annapolis and given Hanna's mom custody of their daughter. It was surprising because Hanna and her dad always used to be such a team before he left. They'd sing Beatles songs in the front seat during carpools, trying to get the other girls to join in. No matter how many times Ali told Hanna she was being babyish, they still brought up some imaginary friend named Cornelius Maximilian at dinner. And one time, when Hanna's dad had taken Hanna and Ali to the beach for the day, it seemed like Hanna wanted to hang out with him instead of sneaking off to the boardwalk with Ali to talk to boys. *Weirdo.*

Mr. Marin was so different from Ali's own dad, who put on a suit every day and went to work and talked to his family during meals but otherwise retreated to his office. Even though Ali would never, ever tell Hanna so, she'd felt a little relieved when Hanna's dad took off. Hanna no longer had that special, sparkly thing in her life that Ali secretly, deep down, envied.

Now Hanna was worried that Kate had taken her place. Ali had offered to come with her to Annapolis, promising that they'd outclass Kate and make her feel small and stupid. The only thing was, once they'd gotten there, something in Ali had shifted. Kate seemed sort of . . . *nice,* a lot like her, in fact. Maybe Hanna needed to suck it up. But instead, Hanna *ate* it up—all the party snacks Isabel had put out for them, that was. Ali had never seen her shovel food in so compulsively, yet Hanna had seemed surprised when her father called her a "little piggy." When Ali had followed Hanna to the bathroom and pushed open the door, she'd found Hanna hunched over the toilet bowl, a green toothbrush in her hand. Hanna had begged Ali not to tell anyone, and so far, Ali hadn't.

She touched Hanna's hand. "It really hurts to see all of them on vacation together, huh?"

A look of shock passed over Hanna's features, followed by gratitude. "Sort of," she breathed. "And, I mean, you've seen Kate."

Ali nodded. "She was really nice, though, Han."

Hanna looked pained. "Maybe she was, I don't know. But Kate's wearing one of those bikinis that goes up her butt. It's not like my dad would let *me* wear one of those."

It's not like you'd look good in one of those, either, Ali thought, but she didn't dare say it. Kate was thin, the kind of girl who could expose a bit of butt cheek and drive boys wild. While Hanna wasn't fat, she wasn't the type of girl who could pluck a pair of jeans off the rack and buy them without trying them on. And she was painfully aware of it, too—always pinching the excess flesh on her belly, always looking around at the other girls in the locker room enviously, always the last to pull off her shirt at the country club or on the beach.

Ali's gaze drifted to the food detritus on the coffee table. "Bingeing isn't the answer, Han."

Hanna shook her head vigorously. "*No.* I only did that once, Ali. I swear. Some of this was left over from my mom last night."

Ali crossed her arms over her chest. It was such a lie— Hanna's mom was stick-thin, did yoga religiously, and ate a macrobiotic diet. "You can tell me, Han. You've gone through a lot lately. Cassie was telling me about a friend who binged—she did it to regain control."

Hanna turned away and started fiddling with her pen. "I'm fine, Ali. I don't have a problem."

Ali felt annoyance rise inside her. Wasn't she good enough to confide in? She held Hanna's gaze, waiting for her to admit the truth, but Hanna just flicked the tassels on her loafers. Ali dropped her hand. "Fine," Ali said briskly. "You don't have a problem."

"You didn't tell anyone about Annapolis, did you?" Hanna asked suddenly.

A mysterious smile spread across Ali's lips. She waited a few beats, watching as panic flooded Hanna's face. Then she squeezed Hanna's hand hard. "Of course I didn't, silly. My lips are sealed—I promise."

Ali's phone rang. She broke her gaze from Hanna and reached for it in her bag. *Unknown Caller*, said the screen. Ali frowned. She answered, pressing the phone to her ear.

All she could hear was breathing on the other end. "Hello?" Ali said again. "Hel*lo*?"

Hanna lowered her brow, watching Ali carefully. Ali turned away, her heart speeding up. All at once, she had a horrible feeling who the person on the other end might be.

"Hello?" she said once more, wandering into the hall. More breathing. "Is this you?" she whispered, picturing her sister sitting on one of those ugly Preserve couches, smiling into the receiver. But patients at the Preserve weren't allowed to make phone calls, right? Had they changed the rules? Or was she out on one of her "chaperoned" visits?

There was a little sniff on the other end of the line, followed by a *click*. Ali stared at the call time flashing on the screen until her vision blurred.

"Ali?"

She jumped and whirled around. Hanna stood at the end of the hall, a crumpled-up chip bag in her hands. "Is everything okay?" she asked. "Who was that?"

Ali stared down at her phone, worried for a brief flash that Hanna might know everything. Then she straightened up and pushed her hair over her shoulder. "Just a stupid prank call," she said breezily. "Probably some kid who has a crush on me."

"Oh, definitely," Hanna said, giving Ali a quick smile.

Ali walked to the TV and flicked it on, wanting to forget what had just happened. Hanna was all too eager to plop down beside her, probably relieved to let things drop, too. But as they flipped through the channels, all Ali could see was herself lying in a spare hospital bed at the Preserve. Tied down, as they used to do at the Radley to girls who got too upset.

I know what you've been doing, her sister's voice echoed in her mind. *Say your good-byes.*

14

2 GOOD + 2 BE = 4 GOTTEN

The following day, the girls cruised up and down the aisles of Saks. The store was tastefully lit with recessed lights on signature pieces, and the walls were painted in black-and-white stripes. Dance music pumped out of hidden speakers, and thin, pretty salesgirls floated around the room with warm smiles on their faces. But Ali's favorite thing about Saks was that it always smelled like they were inside a perfume factory. No other department store smelled as good.

Hanna plucked a quilted Chanel purse from a shelf. "This. Definitely." The girls were playing their favorite game: What Would You Buy If You Had All the Money in the World?

"Really?" Ali made a face. "That's so grandmotherly."

Hanna looked horrified and dropped it. "Uh, I picked up the wrong one. I meant this." She showed her a red Louis Vuitton. Ali nodded her approval, and Hanna smiled with relief.

"I'm into this one," Emily said, holding up a Chloé satchel. "Can't you just see me carrying this to school?"

"That's gorgeous," Ali said, sighing. "I wish I'd seen it first."

Emily pushed it toward her. "You take it. I can pick something else."

Ali rolled her eyes. "It's just a *game*, Emily." She selected a Dior satchel from the wall. "I'll make do with this."

"Can I help you, girls?" a saleswoman asked behind them. She raised an eyebrow when she saw the luxury pieces in their hands. Ali glanced at the others, and they burst out laughing, then dropped everything and scampered away.

"Let's go to Contemporary," Ali announced. "I actually want to spend some money today."

They filed onto the escalators and peered at their reflections in the mirrored walls. Ali was wearing skinny jeans and a flowing hot-pink top she'd seen on the cover of *Teen Vogue*. Aria had put a blue streak in her hair and wore a silver sequined shirt, blue flare-leg jeans, and clunky wedges. Hanna had on a beautiful French Connection mini-dress that was, unfortunately, way too small on her. Spencer looked superpreppy in a Lacoste tennis dress and Tory Burch flats, and Emily wore her uniform of baggy jeans and a plain blue T-shirt. Ali made a mental note to persuade her to buy something cute today.

As they got off at Contemporary, Ali spied a skinny ice-blonde by the dresses and froze. It was Iris, her sister's old roommate at the Preserve. She was with two other girls her own age, and when she saw Ali, a malicious smile spread across her face. She waggled her fingers in a taunting wave.

Emily frowned. "Do you know her?"

"No," Ali said, guiding her friends across the sales floor, far, far away.

She took deep breaths as they headed toward the jeans. *It doesn't matter that she's here*, she told herself. *She won't say anything about the Preserve. She probably doesn't want the girls she's with to know she was committed.*

She stared intensely at the rack of jeans, pretending Iris wasn't there. Aria, Emily, and Spencer drifted over as well, and soon, all five of them were at the jeans wall, pulling out their sizes in skinny-legs and bootcut, dark wash and light. Then they trooped for the dressing rooms, squeezing into one together before the salesgirl yelled, "Only one girl per room, please."

Halfway through her massive pile of clothes to try, Ali spun around in the three-way-mirror; then noticed Emily sitting on the couch at the end of the dressing room hall with a wistful, faraway look on her face. She stopped. "Why aren't you trying anything on, Em?"

Emily shook her head. "This stuff is way too expensive. My parents would die if they saw the prices."

"We'll chip in and buy you something," Ali offered.

But Emily seemed in her own world, simply offering Ali a vague smile and a shrug. "I'll just watch you try stuff on. I don't mind."

Suddenly, Ali perked up, a thought forming in her

head. She perched on the edge of the couch. "Did something happen between you and that guy?" she asked excitedly.

Emily frowned. "What guy?"

Ali cuffed her gently. "You know! Your crush, silly!"

"Oh." Emily's mouth twitched. "No. Nothing has happened with that."

"Are you going to tell me who he is yet?" Ali asked.

"Who *who* is?" Aria asked, bursting out of another dressing room in a pair of skinny corduroys. "Do you like someone, Em? *Who?*"

Emily looked back and forth, a panicked expression rolling across her features. She suddenly reminded Ali of the cat, Kiki, her family had when she still lived at home—whenever they tried to corner Kiki to take her to the vet, she'd arch her back and widen her eyes just like Emily was doing now. "Um . . ."

"Is it that guy from swimming?" Spencer asked. "What was his name . . . Ben? He's so cute."

"I think she should like Kenneth Griggs in my art class," Aria said.

"He's gorgeous!" Hanna stepped out of a dressing room, too. "You guys would look amazing together!"

"It's not Ben," Emily said in a small voice. "Or Kenneth."

Suddenly Ali knew what she had to do. "Guys, if Em doesn't want to tell us quite yet, then we need to give her some space."

The girls nodded and stepped inside their dressing rooms once more. After the doors closed Ali grabbed Emily's hand and pulled her into the shoe area. "Sorry they overheard. But you can tell *me*, right?"

Emily looked like she really, really had to pee but was trying to hold it in. "I don't think so."

A wave of hurt coursed through Ali. Why wasn't she good enough to tell? She disguised it with a frown of disgust. "I don't understand. Why is it such a big deal?"

Emily paused and stared at the Kate Spade pumps on the wall. As Ali waited, she felt the distinct sense that someone was staring at her. Across the room, Iris had reappeared, leaning against a rack of blazers, her gaze on Ali, a strange smile on her face. Ali swallowed a lump in her throat and turned away.

"Please, Em?" Ali said softly. "Maybe I can help. Is it someone your parents wouldn't approve of? Someone older?"

Emily's big, freckly face reddened. She shook her head.

Annoyed, Ali tried a last-ditch effort. "You know my friend Cassie? She asked me to be her BFF. And I'm thinking about it."

Emily blinked with this change of subject. "Really?" She sounded crushed.

"I wasn't going to be, but if you won't trust me, then maybe we're not as close as I thought," Ali said.

Emily's eyes were wet with tears. "I can't," she

whispered. And then, swallowing hard, she ducked around a rack of Jimmy Choos and ran.

"Emily!" Ali cried, running after her.

Emily darted into the skin-cream section, but Ali lost her near the makeup. She searched for the strawberry-blond head in Accessories and Men's, but Emily was nowhere. Then she spied a small, discreet sign for a women's bathroom a few paces down and jogged over to it.

Classical music tinkled inside. The room smelled like roses and had a small basket on the sink containing hair spray, gel, spray-on deodorant, tampons, and butterscotch candies. The towel girl, who was leaning against the sink and tapping on her cell phone, smiled at Ali. One pair of sneakers was visible under the stall door. They were Emily's.

Ali spied a familiar denim backpack on the counter. She couldn't remember how many times she'd told Emily that carrying around a backpack wasn't cool, but Emily always said it was the best on her swimmer's shoulders. The flap was open, and a few of her notebooks peeked out. The doodles Emily was so fond of drawing were visible on the cover.

Ali glanced at the feet under the stall, then at the bag again. It felt like Emily had purposefully left it there for Ali to find.

When the towel girl's back turned, she pulled the bag toward her and slid the top notebook out. *Upper Main Line Swimming!* Emily had written in bubble letters on the front, the name of her year-round competitive swim club.

Below it, she listed the names of the girls on her state-champion relay team. Next to that were doodles of the dog character on *Family Guy*, which Emily wasn't allowed to watch at her house, and a large red heart with the letter *A* in the center.

A, Ali thought, her stomach jumping. She was on to something.

She lifted the cardboard cover of the notebook and looked at the first page, but there was nothing written there. She flipped through the pieces of lined paper, but they only contained notes about the Pythagorean theorem and little geometric diagrams. There was a rattling sound of toilet paper on the roll, and Ali froze and looked up. Emily's feet shifted beneath the stall. She let out a loud sniff, like she was crying.

Whose name started with *A*? Andrew Campbell? Austin Chang? That hot senior Aaron Gearheart?

Oh God, it's Aaron Gearheart, Ali thought, her stomach sinking. Aaron dated girls from Hollis—rumor had it he'd even gotten someone pregnant. He'd eat someone like Emily for breakfast.

She flipped through more pages, praying it wasn't Aaron. When she got to the very last piece of notebook paper, she spied a small red heart in the corner. It was so small, in fact, Ali could only read the handwriting if she put her face very close and squinted.

I love Ali.

15

PLAYLAND ISN'T JUST FOR KIDS

The following afternoon, Ali stood in the doorway at Rive Gauche. Bartenders in crisp white shirts flitted around pouring drinks and cleaning glasses. A waitress rushed past with a tureen of rich-smelling fondue. A few girls from school were sitting in a booth, including Melissa Hastings, who had already noticed Ali and was glowering. Ali craned her neck, looking around for Nick—he was working today and had asked if she'd stop by during his break—but she didn't see him anywhere.

She was so happy he'd texted. In some ways, she *needed* to see him, needed to confirm to the world that she liked a *guy*. Finding that heart on Emily's notebook had shaken her to her core—she'd dropped the notebook and run out of the bathroom as fast as she could, mumbling a lame excuse to Spencer and the others and begging Jason to come pick her up right away. How had she not sensed Emily's feelings? All those times Emily had defended her, all those compliments she gave. Even yesterday, Emily had been content just sitting on the couch in the dressing area watching Ali model the jeans in front of the three-way mirror. Ali had changed in front of her a zillion times, thinking nothing of it. This totally explained why Emily had watched Ali so closely when she did that sexy dance to the Justin Timberlake album a few weekends ago. And she'd made a contented little sigh when Ali was finished, like she'd dream about Ali later that night. . . .

Ali wasn't sure how she was supposed to handle it. It was clear Emily was terrified to tell Ali her feelings. She probably knew Ali would tell her she didn't feel the same way and that their friendship would crumble. Emily was too valuable of a friend for that, though—she was so easy to talk to and, more than that, so *controllable*. She did anything Ali asked—Ali would never find a sidekick like that again.

"Earth to Alison?"

Ali looked up and saw Nick in the doorway, dressed in Rive Gauche's white shirt and black pants. "Hey," she said with a big smile. Just being with him again made her suddenly feel so relaxed, as though she'd slipped into a warm bath.

A beep sounded, and Nick glanced down at his phone. After staring at the screen for a moment, he dropped it in his pants pocket. "So," he said, grinning at her, his blue eyes bright and clear. "Do you want to go on the merry-go-round with me?"

Ali almost burst out laughing. "Are you serious? The one in the kiddie playland down the hall?"

Nick smirked. "Why? Are you too cool to go on a merry-go-round?"

Normally, Ali would have said yes, but something about riding a merry-go-round with Nick seemed kind of fun. "I'll go if you go," she challenged.

"You're on." Tingles shot up Ali's spine as he grabbed her hand. Together, they walked out of the restaurant and down the long corridor, passing a cluster of stores, including Woof, the luxury pet store. When she'd first taken her sister's place in Rosewood, she'd spent hours in there, admiring the cashmere blankets, leather pet clothes, and organic treats even though her family didn't have a pet. *This is a place where even* dogs *have to wear the right clothes,* she'd thought.

Nick looked at the store. "Are you a dog person or a cat person?"

"A gerbil person, remember?" Ali teased. "But I guess I'd pick cats over dogs."

"That means you're aloof and mysterious," Nick said.

"Or that I don't like dog slobber," Ali pointed out.

"Or that you don't like watching dogs hump everything that moves."

Ali burst out laughing.

They passed Chanel, Bloomingdale's, and a high-end kids' store, chatting about school, homework, and Nick's new job—he'd already had a woman who could've been his mother hit on him today. "It was totally weird," he admitted. Then he looked at her. "Have you ever gone out with anyone older?"

Ali thought of Ian, then of her and Spencer's game to kiss as many older boys as they could. She'd made out with a few eighth graders, and once even a ninth grader, but they'd just been simple kisses, nothing more. "Not really," she admitted. "Have you?"

Nick ducked his head. "To be honest, I haven't gone out with very many people. I've only had one girlfriend, and she . . ." He trailed off. "It didn't work out."

"You're kidding," Ali blurted out. "I thought girls would be all over you."

"I haven't found the right girl, I guess." He turned his liquid-blue eyes to Ali and looked like he was going to say something else, but then he shut his mouth.

"What?" Ali asked, her heart pounding hard.

A blush rose up Nick's neck. Ali waited, a fizzy feeling of anticipation mixed with excitement swirling in her stomach. But then someone bumped her bag, and some of her Polaroids, which she kept in the front pocket, fluttered out to the floor. Ali looked up and saw a girl with short blond hair striding away. It was Spencer's sister. Ali glared at her. Had she bumped into Ali on purpose?

"Wow, cool," Nick said as he bent down to help her pick them up. "What are these?"

He held up one of Ali and Aria in art class. They'd positioned their big, bushy paintbrushes under their noses to look like mustaches. Then he looked at one of Jason lounging on the couch, a cheese curl hanging out of his mouth. She'd taken it on the sly yesterday and planned to use it as blackmail later.

"Oh, just something I do," Ali said. She rummaged through the photos. "I have one of you from the day we re-met." She found it and held it up.

"You carry around a picture of me?" Nick looked touched. "I want a picture of you, too."

Ali leafed through the photos and found one that Spencer had taken of her outside Rosewood Day. Her blond hair gleamed in the sunlight. Her smile was wide and sly, like she had a secret she wasn't telling. "Here you go," she said shyly, passing it to him. It felt significant to exchange photographs with a boy. Almost as big as friends exchanging half-heart necklaces or friendship rings.

They rounded the corner and the merry-go-round materialized, its calliope playing a circusy song. The wooden, elaborately painted horses bobbed up and down. A kid rode in the little sled behind the horses, and a father stood next to a young boy on a roaring lion.

Nick grabbed her hand. "Want to go on?"

"Sure," Ali said, not even bothering to look around to see who might be watching. Normally, a girl like her would never ride the merry-go-round. But with Nick, these sorts of things were cool.

They paid for tickets, and when the carousel stopped, the attendant lifted the chain and let them select horses.

They chose two white ponies next to each other and climbed on. As Ali put her feet in the straps, she was suddenly flooded with nostalgia and sadness. A memory flashed into her mind of the last time she'd been on a merry-go-round. It was back when she and her sister were friends, before anything terrible happened. The two of them had been dressed in identical pink skirts and white tops; they'd both asked for pink balloons from the balloon cart. The horses were so tall that their father had to boost them on, and they'd sat side by side, just as she and Nick were doing now. As the music started, they both squealed and grabbed hands across the aisle.

What had made her sister change? Why, suddenly, was she so jealous, so desperate to be the only girl in the house? It was probably an answer Ali would never know.

As she ran her fingers over the horse's molded mane, a surprising thought struck her: She *missed* her sister. Not the crazy person she'd become, not the threatening presence in the bathroom, but that little girl she once was, her old best friend. Sometimes, in the middle of the night at the Radley and even now, she found herself reaching for something in the darkness. She'd wondered more than once if it was her sister's hand.

The music started up, and the carousel began to turn. Ali smiled at Nick, wiping the thoughts from her mind. Nick gripped the pole with one hand and held her hand with the other. He didn't take his eyes off her the whole time. Ali's heart beat along with the bass drum that accompanied the carousel's old-timey song.

The merry-go-round rotated several full turns before either of them looked away from the other. As the ride slowed, Nick's phone chimed, and he pulled it out of his pocket and started texting.

"Who are you writing to?" Ali blurted, then wanted to clap a hand over her mouth. She wasn't supposed to *care* who he was texting. She was supposed to act cool and aloof. Guys couldn't stand girls who wanted to know every detail of their lives.

But Nick turned the phone screen around so Ali could see. "My buddy Jeff." He pointed to the text-message thread. A guy named Jeff G. asked him what he was up to, and he'd replied, *I'm hanging out with my new crush, Alison.*

Ali's mouth dropped open. "I'm your new crush, huh?" she said, trying to sound untouchable and apathetic. But her voice was too full of joy for that. Her fingers were shaking. There was a voice inside her screaming, *Yes!*

"I hope you are," Nick said, helping her off the horse and walking her out of the little fence that surrounded the carousel. "I want to know everything about you, Ali." He laced his fingers through hers. "I like you a lot."

"I-I like you, too," Ali heard herself saying, her voice sounding small and nervous—and thrilled.

"Good," Nick said, leaning in close. And there, beside the pipe organ and the screaming kids waiting in line and the cotton-candy kiosk, which smelled nauseatingly sugary, he edged close and touched his lips to Ali's. It was over in an instant, but Ali knew she'd remember the feeling of the kiss for a long, long time.

They smiled giddily at each other for a few seconds, but suddenly something behind Nick caught Ali's eye. A familiar figure stood just inside one of the little mall hallways that led to the bathrooms and the staff offices. Was that her *mom*?

She squinted, at first annoyed that her mom was spying. But then she saw the second figure standing next to her. A man in shadow placed his hand on Mrs. DiLaurentis's arm, talking urgently about something. It wasn't Ali's father.

Acid rose in her stomach. She breathed in sharply and pulled away from Nick. His brow furrowed. "What's the matter?"

"I . . ." Ali's gaze remained on her mother and the man. He turned and touched the side of her face in a gesture so tender it made Ali curl up inside.

"Ali?" Nick's voice was soothing, but it seemed so far away. "Are you okay?"

"No," Ali whispered, backing away. Part of her wanted to see who the man was, but another part of her was terrified to find out. Instead, she turned around and sprinted toward the exit, running faster and faster until her legs ached and her lungs burned.

16

PLAYING IT COOL

Later that night, Ali lay in an X shape on her bed, staring up at the ceiling. She'd changed the bedroom since she'd taken it from her sister—removing the pictures of Naomi and Riley and replacing them with ones of Aria, Spencer, Emily, and Hanna; reorganizing her sister's messy closet and throwing out the items she didn't like; rearranging the desk so that it was by the big picture window that looked out onto the backyard; and hanging a big poster that said FREEDOM over her bed. It was a little inside joke with herself.

The one thing she kept of her sister's was the ceiling lamp above her head, a mobile of several bright yellow stars and a silvery moon. Back when she was Courtney, she'd given this to her sister as a birthday present, and she was surprised her sister had held on to it. Deep down, did her sister regret what she'd done? Or did she just like the design?

Beep.

She opened her eyes and looked at her phone, nerves streaking through her stomach. But it was only a new text from Nick: *Is everything okay? I'm worried about you.*

Ali didn't know how to answer. Nick had caught up with her in the parking garage; she'd leaned against one of the concrete pillars and taken deep breaths, trying to calm down. He'd asked her over and over what she'd seen, but she just shook her head and said she couldn't talk about it. She didn't know *how* to talk about it. She was Alison DiLaurentis: This didn't happen in her perfect family. Her mother didn't canoodle in public places with strange men. And who *was* that guy, anyway? What was he saying so urgently to her? Was her mom going to leave them for him?

It was something that happened to other families, sure—like Aria's. Even like Hanna's. But it didn't happen to *hers*.

I'll tell you later, she finally wrote. *I promise.*

Whenever you're ready, he wrote back.

A door slammed outside, and then there was a laugh. Ali rolled off her bed, walked to the window, and peered at the Hastingses' house next door. Spencer stood on her driveway in an old plaid field hockey skirt, a cutoff T-shirt, and bare feet. Her blond hair was pulled back off her head, and her lips were lined in pink gloss. Her cheeks flushed, but not from blush. She was chatting with Ian Thomas, who was leaning against his SUV.

Ali raised her eyebrows, having temporarily forgotten about her deal with Ian.

Ian spoke, and Spencer giggled. When he touched Spencer's arm, Spencer didn't pull away. She leaned forward and kissed his cheek. Then, Ian grabbed her, pulled her closer, and kissed her on the lips. Ali widened her eyes. Even though she'd told Ian to do it, his passion surprised her.

After they pulled apart, Ian turned and climbed into his car. Spencer remained on the grass, her hands in her skirt pockets, a goofy smile on her face. One of her dogs, Beatrice, nosed Spencer's hand, and she began to absently pet him.

Ali shoved her feet into her flip-flops and ran down the stairs. She could just imagine how this would go down: Spencer would confess that she'd just kissed Ian, her voice full of wonder. Ali would say that *she* had helped make that happen—see? She can do anything! And Spencer would look at Ali with such gratitude, thanking her profusely. She'd be under Ali's thumb forever.

Spencer was still in the exact spot when Ali crossed the lawn. When she saw Ali, she jumped as if coming out of a trance. "Oh." Her voice cracked. "H-how long have you been out here?"

"Not long," Ali said, playing dumb. "Whatcha doing?"

Spencer fiddled with the end of her blond ponytail. "Nothing."

"You're standing in the middle of your yard for no reason?" she teased.

Spencer shrugged. "I was getting the mail."

Ali snorted, looking at Spencer's empty hands. "Then where is it?"

"It's . . ." Spencer trailed off. Her brow furrowed. "I didn't get it yet, okay? God."

Ali placed her hands on her hips. Why was Spencer acting so irritated? And why wasn't she fessing up about her big kiss? She decided to try a different tack. "I had a really great day," she lied. "What about you?"

Spencer poked her fingers under Beatrice's mesh collar. "It was okay."

"Nothing interesting happened?"

One shoulder rose. "Not really."

Ali blinked. Did Spencer really think Ian had kissed her because he *liked* her? Was she *that* out of touch with reality? In this situation, some girls might just admit they'd seen everything, but to Ali, that felt cheap and desperate. She wanted Spencer to offer the information to her, to *want* to tell her.

She turned on her heel. "I have to go."

"You *do*?" Spencer asked.

Ali didn't answer. She stomped back through the hedges, gritting her teeth so forcefully that they made a horrible squeaking sound as they slid against one another. Halfway across her lawn, she heard a rustling sound behind her and thought it might be Spencer, coming to tell her everything. They could salvage things, Ali decided. She'd forgive Spencer for hiding it, even, as long as Spencer begged.

But when she turned, it wasn't Spencer. It was Jenna Cavanaugh. A shiver ran up Ali's spine. Jenna's black sunglasses obscured most of her face except for her naturally red lips and her pointed chin. Her black hair cascaded down her shoulders, and her legs and arms looked even more model-thin than they'd been last fall before she starting going to her special school. Her German shepherd guide dog stood by her side, his long, pink tongue dripping with saliva. It seemed like Jenna was staring right at Ali, really *seeing* her, but of course that was impossible. Ali ducked behind a tree anyway.

"Ali?" Jenna called out. "Is that you?"

Ali shrank back further. Even though she wanted to tell Jenna that it was, she didn't want to start a conversation—not with Spencer still in her yard. What if Jenna said something about her twin?

"Ali?" Jenna called again.

A screen door banged across the street, and Toby Cavanaugh stepped onto the porch. Ali froze. What was *he* doing home? Hadn't he been sent away forever?

Toby stepped off the porch and crossed the yard. "Jenna, what are you doing over there?"

His haunted voice made Ali flinch. That horrible moment in sixth grade all came back to her in an instant: the angry way Toby had said *I saw you* that night, the horror in his eyes when she'd thrown what she knew about him back in his face. Not long before that, she'd come upon Jenna in tears. Even though she tormented Jenna in school, Jenna knew more about Ali than any-one else—and she never told anyone. All of a sudden, she wanted to atone for how nasty she'd been. She wanted to make it up to her.

What's wrong? she asked Jenna. She squeezed her hand. *You can tell me. You know I won't tell a soul.*

Jenna raised her head. It took her a long time to speak. *It's my brother*, she began.

When she was finished, Ali gave her a hug. *You know that I have sibling problems, too. I can help you. We should come up with something to make him go away forever.*

And they had.

"Jenna," Toby said again, more sternly this time. When he reached the curb where Jenna was standing, he paused, as if sensing Ali was there, too. His eyes narrowed into two iron-cold slits. Ali's heart thudded in her throat.

Finally, he took Jenna's arm. "Come on," he said. "Let's go in."

Jenna pulled on her dog's harness. Tapping her white cane, her dog walking at her side, she disappeared inside the house, not saying another word.

17

LIKE GETTING WATER FROM A STONE

There was no sound as beautiful, Ali thought as the twangy guitar-note ringtone that announced she had a new text message from Nick.

What's your favorite subject in school? was the latest one. Ali, who was sitting on her front porch swing waiting for Aria, tapped the keyboard with her reply. *It used to be English*, she wrote, *but now we have to read so many boring books that I guess it's study hall. LOL.* She didn't want to list her *real* favorite class—science—for fear that she'd look like a nerd.

Mine too, Nick wrote back, and Ali smiled.

Her phone beeped again. *Hey, remember that counselor at camp who got stung by all those bees?* Nick wrote. *What was his name?*

Ali bit down hard on the inside of her cheek. *I know who you mean*, she typed after a moment. *Can't remember though.*

A familiar Subaru rolled up, and Aria got out of the back, carrying Pigtunia under her arm. *We'll talk later*, Ali wrote to him. *I'll be here*, Nick wrote back.

She glanced at Aria's father behind the wheel. He wore a ripped T-shirt with printing so faded on the front that it wasn't even legible anymore. His thinning hair stood up every which way, and he had that half-beard scruff going that some girls thought was sexy but Ali thought just looked dirty. She couldn't even look him in the eye.

Byron looked away, too, as if he knew Ali knew. Which meant Aria had to know, too, right? If Aria admitted something, then maybe Ali would tell her that she knew how it felt. That she'd seen her mom and that random guy at the mall. The secret felt like a shaken-up can of Coke inside her, its contents fizzing and pressing against her sides. It would feel good to tell someone, especially someone who could commiserate.

Aria walked up the porch steps and sat down on the swing next to Ali. "What's up?"

"Not much," Ali said. "What's up with you?"

Aria pushed off the porch rails to give the swing a bit more momentum. "So I have to talk to you about something."

Ali's heart lifted. "What?" she asked innocently.

Aria spun the beaded bracelet around her wrist. "You know the drama class I'm taking after school?" Aria asked. "Well, we had a new student today. Toby Cavanaugh."

On instinct, Ali gazed across the yard, half expecting

Toby still to be standing there, as he had been last night. "He's back," she stated, not exactly like a question.

"Yeah." Aria bit her pointer finger. "He kept staring at me, too. And then we had to do this speech exercise, and we were partnered together. I had to say a phrase, and he had to repeat it back to me until the phrase changed. I picked *It never snows in the summer.* And we said it back and forth, back and forth, until Toby started saying *I know what you did last summer.*" She widened her eyes dramatically. "Do you think Toby knows something?"

Ali touched a rusty spot on the swing's chain. Only Spencer had been there for her confrontation with Toby, and Ali had made her promise to not tell the others. It seemed safer to keep it between them.

"Toby doesn't know what we did," she said definitively. "And anyway, The Jenna Thing happened last spring, not summer. He's just mental." Then she looked at Aria. "*That's* what you had to tell me?"

"Well, yeah." Aria frowned. "Don't you think that's a big deal? Toby's *weird.*"

Ali shrugged. "Yeah, but that's not exactly *news.*"

She rested her head on Aria's shoulder, thinking for a moment how she could get Aria to talk. She decided to use her last-ditch plan. She cleared her throat. "Something weird happened to me, too, and I really need someone to talk to about it." She stared at the lawn. "I think my parents are breaking up." Just saying the words made a lump form in her throat.

Aria twisted around to stare at her head-on. "Why would you say that?"

"They've been arguing a lot." Ali stared at her palms. "And they've said they have something to tell me and Jason—I just know it's about that." There was no way she was telling her about her mom, though. Not yet.

"I'm sorry."

Aria looked genuinely sympathetic. It felt good for a moment, but then Ali realized it wasn't enough. "I don't know what I'd do if my parents weren't together," she said. "It would be even weirder if they were with someone else. Have you ever thought about that?"

Aria folded in her shoulders. "Not really."

"Your mom's beautiful, though—and she's around all those art dealers. Your dad is surrounded by students twenty-four-seven. It's possible, don't you think?"

Several expressions—awkwardness, humiliation, shame—crossed Aria's face at once. "Anything's possible, I guess."

Her lips parted, perhaps to spill it all. But then her gaze landed on something just past Ali, and she stood up from the swing so quickly that Ali went careening backward. "Oh! Jason!"

Jason walked up the front steps, his backpack slung over one shoulder. "Hey," he said gruffly.

"How are you?" Aria's voice was high-pitched and strange. "Are you excited to graduate?"

"Not really," Jason said, opening the door and banging it shut again.

Aria sank back into the swing, looking disappointed. Ali pressed her fingernails into the meatiest part of her palm, feeling humiliated. Had Aria just changed the subject on purpose? Did she know . . . and *not* want to tell? Ali had just told Aria something true and scary and terrible. Didn't Aria have the decency to reciprocate? Wasn't that what friends did?

Nastiness settled over her like a heavy black cloak, and she poked Aria hard. "Do you still like Noel?"

Aria's eyes lit up. "Of course! Did you talk to him about me?"

"I did, in fact," Ali lied.

"And?"

Ali allowed a slight pause, then laid her hand on Aria's knee and squeezed. "Well, I went over to his house. But something kind of . . . *weird* happened. I told him about you, and he said he likes you as a friend."

The corners of Aria's mouth turned down. "Oh."

"And then he said he likes me. And I think I like him back."

Aria sat back. "Oh!" Her voice was unnaturally bright. "Okay. Wow."

"But I won't go out with him if you don't want me to."

The pain was obvious in Aria's face. "Um, okay," she said after a moment.

For a moment, Ali almost regretted the lie. Noel probably *would* have gone for Aria if Ali had asked. And she really *had* planned to talk to him about her. But why should she put herself out for a friend who wouldn't even tell her what was going on in her life? Friendships were tit for tat—what was *she* getting out of this?

The corners of Aria's mouth wobbled. She looked at her phone screen urgently, even though it hadn't chimed. "Um, I have to go," she said. "My mom needs me."

"Trouble at home?" Ali asked as a final attempt. *If she admits it now, I'll tell her I made it all up*, she decided. *I'll tell her I'll talk to Noel for real.*

But Aria just scrambled down the porch. "No," she said, breaking Ali's heart just a little. And then she sprang up and headed across the backyard. Ali watched her disappear into the woods on her way to her development. Her head was down, her shoulders hunched, and, after a moment, Ali was sure she heard a low, uncontrolled sob emanating from the pines.

Ali pressed her lips together and tried to swallow her regret. It wasn't sad. It was *good.*

18

NOTHING LIKE HEARING YOUR
BFF SING YOUR PRAISES!

A few days later, the last bell of the day rang, and all the students in Ali's English class leapt to their feet and headed to the door. "Don't forget, people!" Mrs. Lowry, their English teacher, bellowed. "Your Hemingway parodies are due on Monday! I'm not taking any lates!"

"Have you started yours yet?" Spencer asked Ali as they walked through the door and into the hall, which was crowded with kids at their lockers.

"Nope," Ali answered, shaking her head. "Wanna do it for me?"

Spencer sniffed. "I have a huge history paper, Ali. Sorry."

Ali crossed her arms over her chest. Not long ago, Spencer would have done Ali's homework in a heartbeat without complaint. *I saw you, you know,* she wanted to say. *I know what you did with Ian.* Every day that passed without Spencer saying anything made the betrayal seem worse and worse.

Ali's phone rang. She dove for it inside her bag. *Unknown Caller.* She was about to hit IGNORE when Spencer cleared her throat beside her.

"I hate when I get calls from blocked numbers," she said. "Usually it's my mom checking up on me, but she doesn't want me to know it's her calling."

The phone rang again. Ali glanced at Spencer. "Can you block any number?"

"I think certain phones don't allow it." Spencer stopped at her locker and began to spin the dial. "Pay phones are usually good for it. Cell phones, too."

Ali nodded. She remembered seeing a bank of pay phones in the Preserve lobby—maybe her sister had somehow gotten to one of them without the nurses noticing. Or maybe she'd borrowed someone's cell phone.

Spencer gave Ali a suspicious look. "Why do you want to know how to block calls?"

Ali opened her mouth, then shut it again. Spencer sniffed. "Fine," she said sharply, facing her locker again. "*Don't* tell me."

Finally, the phone went to voicemail. Ali stared at the screen, waiting for the little message icon to appear, but it didn't. Suddenly, she felt like she had to get away from Spencer, and fast. She pushed through the crowd of kids to the double doors that opened out onto a small courtyard that connected the middle school to the high school. It was mostly high-schooler territory; junior high kids were ostracized if they sat on the courtyard's three benches or lingered there after school. Ali got a pass, though, especially if Cassie or any of the others were around, but she didn't see them anywhere. She did see, however, a petite, slightly chubby girl standing in the corner of the courtyard, talking animatedly with her hands. She stood up straighter. Was that *Hanna*?

Josie stood next to Hanna, nodding sympathetically. Ali crept closer, ducking behind a potted tree so that Hanna didn't see her. When she was only a few feet away, she caught strains of Hanna's conversation over the din of the other students.

". . . And she's, like, so *manipulative*," Hanna was saying. "There are some things she knows about me that I don't want *anyone* to know, and I'm so afraid she's going to tell someone if I screw up at all. It's driving me crazy. And she's acting even weirder than usual lately, keeping all these secrets, getting these weird phone calls—she probably hates me."

"You have to cut her loose before she ditches *you*," Josie answered.

Hanna pulled her bottom lip into her mouth. "But she's been my friend for two years now. We've been through a lot together."

Ali's eyes widened. Was Hanna talking about *her*?

"She might have been a good friend to you before, but she isn't a good friend now," Josie said firmly. "You're super cool, Hanna. You'll be fine."

Ali clapped her hand over her mouth. Was Josie *high*?

Hanna wouldn't be fine without her—not at all.

She couldn't take it anymore. She stepped from behind the tree and rushed past Hanna as though she hadn't seen her. "Oh!" she said, feigning surprise just after reaching her. "Hi, Han! Hi . . . Josie, was it?"

Hanna paled. Josie's smile wavered. "H-hi," Hanna said, her eyes darting back and forth. "How long have you been out here, Ali?"

Ali put her hands on her hips and blinked.

Her silence seemed to unnerve Hanna even more. Hanna glanced at Josie. "I should go."

"Of course," Josie said. She raised a palm to Ali, then walked to her side of the school.

Ali whipped around and marched back into Rosewood Day, her shoulders tight, her jaw clenched. Hanna scrambled to catch up with her. "I hope you don't think I was talking about you, Ali," she said. "I was talking about Kate. I swear."

Ali approached her locker and pretended to concentrate on the combination. "Mm-hmm."

"Josie has a stepsister, too," Hanna said, her voice not particularly convincing. "She's sort of . . . been there, you know?"

Ali faced her, her eyes narrowed. "And you've been Kate's friend for two years? Since when?"

Hanna's mouth dropped open. No sound came out.

Ali wrenched her locker open and shoved a bunch of textbooks in her bag without paying attention to which subjects they were for. "You should be careful who you talk to, Hanna. You don't know Josie. She might not keep your secrets as well as I do."

Hanna nodded obediently. "O-okay."

Ali started for the parking lot, where she was to wait for Jason. "But she *does* seem really nice," she said after a moment. "You know what I'm thinking? Maybe I'll have a party. We should invite her."

Hanna twisted her mouth. "Really?"

"Uh-huh," Ali said.

"Th-that would be great," Hanna mumbled.

"Glad you think so," Ali answered. Since it was clear that Hanna wasn't getting the message that Josie wasn't necessary, maybe it was time to try a different tack: stealing Josie away. Proving to Hanna that everyone wanted Ali as a friend more than they wanted Hanna.

They were at the front walk by then, right next to the big, bubbling fountain. Hanna's mom pulled up to the curb, and Hanna waved good-bye as she climbed in. Ali continued toward the flagpole, passing girls carrying economy-size boxes of Toblerone chocolates to sell for a French field trip, and a group of boys bounding toward one of the back buses. She scanned the parking lot for Jason all the while, but she didn't see him. She took a left and walked to the main drag of shops right down the road. Pinkberry's happy sign seemed garish and annoying. The Italian flag flapping in front of Ferra's Cheesesteaks made her dizzy. She needed to get a grip.

But then something materialized in front of her eyes. A gold Mercedes was parked at the end of the block. The engine wasn't running, but a person sat in the driver's seat. Ali would recognize that shiny blond hair anywhere. It was her mother.

She crept closer. Her mother held a cell phone to her ear, and there was something about her posture and ducked head that made Ali want to listen. The window was open, and once Ali was only a few cars away, she could hear some of her words. *We just need a little more cash, honey. Just to pay the rest of her hospital bills.* Then she shifted. *I know, I know. But she's your daughter, too.*

Ali shifted. Why would her mom be begging her father for cash?

Mrs. DiLaurentis made a kissing sound into the phone, then hung up. A split second later, the phone rang again. "Oh, hello, Kenneth," Ali's mom said with a sigh. Kenneth was Ali's father's name. Her mom's tone of voice was totally different from the one on the last call. Bored. Exasperated. *Over it.*

Ali's heart picked up speed. She ducked into Wordsmith's Books before her mother could spot her. Even though she had no proof, she knew that her mother had just now been talking to two different people—two different *men.* She'd asked the first one for money, presumably for Ali's sister's hospital bills. But then she'd said, *She's your daughter, too.* Which made no sense.

Unless . . .

The room suddenly started to spin. Ali listed backward, nearly crashing into a wire rack full of novelty greeting cards. Unless the first man her mother was talking to on the phone was her twin's real father.

Which made him *her* real father, too.

19

ON THIN ICE

Two days later, just as Ali was leaving the house, Jason stepped in her path and opened the door for her. "You going somewhere?" he asked.

"Why do you care?" Ali asked, feeling prickly.

Jason winced at Ali's tone of voice. "I just thought I could give you a ride." He shifted uncomfortably. "I thought maybe we could . . . talk."

Ali wrapped her hand around the doorjamb, staring at her brother's Vans. What did he want to talk about? The last time they'd really talked, she'd voiced her concern about her parents getting divorced. That was even before she'd found out about her mom's affair. All of a sudden, the desire to tell him about her mother and that strange man pulsed inside her. The *old* her would have. They would have sat in the Radley's common room and dissected the thing to death, trying to figure out why Mom was doing it, who the man could be, what was going to happen next.

It was way too hard to keep it to herself. With every passing day, she felt like she was going to burst.

"Ali?" Jason prompted.

She shuddered and jerked up, coming back to reality. She *wasn't* her old self, and she could never be again. Alison DiLaurentis didn't have that kind of relationship with her brother—he was too moody and weird to care about. She stepped off the porch. "I can get there myself," she called over her shoulder. "I doubt we're going the same direction, anyway."

Ten minutes later, Ali parked her bike in front of the Orvis Hollis Memorial Ice Rink at Hollis College, where she was meeting Emily. HOME OF THE HOLLIS PENGUINS, said a placard by the sidewalk. Boys with ice-hockey skates slung over their shoulders and long sticks with boomerang-shaped ends sauntered out of the double doors. Even from the street, Ali could smell the rink's freshly popped popcorn and concession-stand hot dogs.

"Alison DiLaurentis *ice-skates*?"

Ali turned. A black Escalade had pulled up to the curb, and Ian Thomas's tanned, handsome face leaned out the window.

Ali walked over to him. "Are you following me, stalker?" she teased.

"You got me." Ian got out of the car and walked over to her, stopping so close that they were almost touching. "I just wanted to let you know that I kissed Spencer, just like you asked. So when are you going to hold up *your* end of the bargain?"

Ali removed a tube of gloss and eased it across her lips. The last thing she wanted was to kiss him, but something about the way he was looking at her made her feel superhero-powerful, like she could spin cars over her head or bend bars of steel with her mind. A second later, though, it hit her: Cheating on Nick with Ian made her no better than her mother.

A chill shot through her. Could someone *else* really be her true father, some random, awful man she didn't know? It made no sense. Her father had taken her and her sister sledding when they were small. He'd come to her dance recitals. He knew that she liked orange juice without pulp and Wawa French vanilla coffee. Whatever had happened, *if* something had happened, she was almost certain he didn't know about it.

And maybe something had happened. Mr. DiLaurentis and Jason had identical toes, the second one larger than the first. And Ali had her mother's blond hair and ice-blue eyes. But she didn't have either of their noses—not her mother's pert little button or her father's ugly hook. For the longest time, she'd been grateful that she hadn't inherited her father's nose, but now she regretted it. And where had her bow lips and sarcastic smile come from? She had stared at her father for so long at dinner last night that he'd asked her twice if there was something wrong.

Ian moved his hand toward Ali's arm, but Ali stepped

away before he could stroke her wrist. "You know what? I've changed my mind. I'll only give you a kiss if you break up with your girlfriend."

Ian's brow furrowed. "Melissa?"

Ali barked out a laugh. "No, *Spencer.* Of course Melissa. I'm not the type who goes for guys who are already taken."

Ian crossed his arms over his chest. "It's just a kiss."

"My deal is final." She spun around and sauntered toward the entrance to the ice rink.

The inside of the ice rink was dark and chilly. Team pennants and championship plaques hung on the walls, and eighties New Wave music blared from the speakers. A Zamboni groaned back and forth on the ice, clearing away all the nicks. Several little kids stood impatiently against the Plexiglas walls, their skate-clad ankles wobbling.

Ali spied Emily at the rental desk. When Emily turned and smiled, Ali's stomach flipped over. This was the first time she'd been alone with Emily since she'd discovered the heart on Emily's notebook. Even though she was almost positive Emily had no idea Ali knew about it, she still felt shaky, like Emily might guess that she knew.

And how could she *not* know? Ali had run out of the dressing room so fast. She hadn't even tried to hide it, which wasn't like her at all. It made her paranoid about all the other secrets in her life. What if people found out about those?

"Hey," Emily said softly as she approached. There were two pairs of white ice skates looped over her wrist, and she wore a heavy cable-knit sweater and jeans. She handed Ali a pair of size-seven skates and sat down on the bench. "Thanks for meeting me. This is going to be so fun."

"If you like dodging little kids," Ali said, watching as kids in Girl Scouts uniforms and brown rental skates spilled out of the bathroom. "*And* falling on your butt. I haven't skated since I was little."

"Don't worry," Emily said softly. "I'll help you."

Ali looked at her friend, thinking about that heart again. *I love Ali*, it had said. Ali loved her, too, but not like *that*. She still didn't know whether to be flattered or just completely weirded-out.

Ali shoved her heel into the skate boot and pulled the laces tight. She'd just finished tying a bow when the Zamboni rolled off the ice and the guards opened the gates again. The little kids dashed for the center. Disco lights dazzled the newly shiny ice. A Flo Rida song started to play.

Ali's ankles wobbled as soon as they stepped on the ice. Emily extended her arm. "Grab on. I got you."

Ali clung to Emily's sleeve. Her feet zigzagged under her, and she thrust out her other arm to get her balance. When a boy in ice-hockey skates and a Flyers jersey whizzed past, almost clipping her side, Ali listed to the left, but her feet veered right. Suddenly, she was on her butt on the cold ice.

"Oops!" Emily said, helping Ali up. She navigated both of them toward the wall and instructed Ali to hold on for a moment. "Move your feet like this, in a glide," she explained, demonstrating. Her skate cut a perfect line in the ice. "Keep your ankles stiff. And don't stare at your feet—that'll definitely make you fall."

"I'm not falling ever again," Ali muttered. But she tentatively pushed off the wall and tried to copy Emily's movements. Her ankles wanted to turn, and her thighs burned even more than they did after running up and down the field hockey field, but after two laps around the rink, she started to get the hang of it. Actually, it was almost *fun*.

"See?" Emily said. "You love it, don't you?"

"Don't tell anyone," Ali said, winking.

"Promise," Emily said, giving Ali another heart-twisting smile. Ali smiled back, but then jerkily turned away.

They wove around a bunch of Girl Scouts skating in a clump and ogled the figure skaters who were doing complicated jumps in the center. Then Emily cleared her throat. "Are you excited for graduation?"

"Definitely," Ali said. The ceremony was coming up, and they all got to wear official-looking gowns and caps, just like the seniors. "In fact, I'm going to have a little get-together the weekend before. I'll probably invite Cassie and some of the other girls, so it will be mixed grades. Hanna is going to invite her friend Josie, too."

"Oh." Emily's disconcerted expression didn't quite match her chipper tone of voice. "Are we still having an end-of-seventh-grade sleepover?"

"As far as I know," Ali said. "Why?"

"I just wasn't sure." Two pink spots appeared on Emily's cheeks. "I mean, I haven't seen you much lately. You haven't, like, texted. I thought you were mad at me."

Ali stared at the big Pepsi clock on the wall. "I've just been busy."

"Okay." Emily's voice shook. "So . . . you're *not* mad?"

Ali looked at her challengingly. "What would I be mad about?"

For a split second, she almost wanted Emily to say it. *I know you saw what I wrote about you on my notebook.* Maybe it would be better to get it out in the open.

"Nothing!" Emily said quickly. For a moment, *she* almost lost her balance, her skates slipping in opposite directions and her arms wheeling in a circle.

Ali grabbed a loop of her jeans to keep her upright. For a moment, she held Emily's gaze, daring her to look away. Suddenly, she pictured Emily losing interest in her, Ali becoming just another friend, the generous, awestruck compliments coming to an end. Even though she didn't return Emily's feeling, there was something about it that made her feel just as powerful as what she was doing with Ian.

She cleared her throat. "You look cute today, Em."

A bewildered look fluttered across Emily's features. "I *do*?"

"Uh-huh. Your hair looks nice. And I didn't realize how tiny your butt was from swimming."

"Oh my God, my butt is huge." Emily looked like she was about to faint. "Well, you *always* look nice, Ali."

"Well, then I guess we're *both* gorgeous," Ali said, nudging her playfully.

Emily's mouth twitched with excitement. "You're definitely the prettiest girl in this rink. In *Rosewood*. Sometimes I can't even believe I know you."

Ali felt heat rush to her face, tears dot her eyes—she hadn't known how much she'd *needed* that sort of stuff said to her. Embarrassed, she turned away and swallowed it down. "I can't believe I know you, either, Em." She meant it in more ways than one: If she hadn't switched with her sister, she *wouldn't* know Emily.

The lights in the rink suddenly dimmed, and a slow song began to play. The little kids hurried off the ice, and the remaining couples glided toward each other to slow-dance skate.

"Couples skate only," an announcer's voice said over the loudspeaker. "Grab the one you love."

A disco ball snapped on, sending shards of sparkling light all around the glassy rink. Ali turned to Emily, her heart thudding fast. "Wanna dance?"

Emily's lips parted, and her eyes widened. "With *you*?" she said, shocked.

Ali smiled lazily, trying to control her jumping heart. "Sure, with me. Girls can skate with girls, can't they?"

She placed her hands on Emily's waist. She tried to ignore Emily's shaking fingers as Emily wrapped them around Ali's neck. After a moment, Emily shut her eyes. A tiny smile appeared on her face. They swayed back and forth to the beat.

"This feels good, doesn't it?" Ali whispered in Emily's ear.

Emily nodded nervously. When Ali pulled her even closer, Emily let out the tiniest sigh. The disco lights dappled against their faces. Ali could feel Emily's lungs rapidly expand and contract.

Bzzzz.

Ali's back pocket vibrated. She reached for it and pulled out her phone. *Call from anonymous*, it said.

Reality came tumbling back, and Ali pulled away. "Hello?" she demanded into the phone, stopping short on the ice. A couple almost collided with her, but she didn't care.

No answer, just breathing. "Say something!" Ali screamed. "I know who this is!"

Her sister didn't speak, only let out a small, high-pitched giggle.

"Ali?"

Emily touched her arm. Ali stared at her, the phone limp in her hand. Emily's eyes flicked to it. "Who is it?" she asked worriedly.

Ali shook her head quickly. "It's just Cassie," she said, pulling the first name she could think of out of her mind. "We've been pranking each other all week. No biggie."

Emily pulled her bottom lip into her mouth. "Are you . . . *sure?*"

"Uh-huh," Ali chirped, shoving her phone back into her pocket. It vibrated again, but she ignored it.

Another slow song started up, and Emily reached for Ali's hand once more. But Ali pulled away, feeling sweaty and flustered and way, way too visible. What if her sister was somehow watching right now? What if she saw Ali doing this and thought she was dancing with Emily for real?

"I think one slow dance is enough for today, don't you, Em?" she asked, trying to make her voice teasing, even though she was exhausted and frazzled.

Emily's cheeks turned pink. "O-of course! I didn't want to dance! I just wanted to get a hot dog—and I wanted to see if you wanted one, too!"

But the devoted smile lingered in Ali's mind, and as they glided toward the exit, a sour feeling welled in her stomach. Saying nice things hit Emily in her sweetest, squishiest, most vulnerable spot. And while teasing out vulnerability was usually Ali's specialty, something about this made her feel especially guilty.

Perhaps it was because Emily was her best friend. Or perhaps it was because, deep down, the things Emily said back sometimes made Ali feel squishy and vulnerable, too.

20

THE BOMB

"How many brothers and sisters do you have?" Nick asked Ali on the phone the following afternoon.

"One," Ali said automatically, propping her feet against the wall of her bedroom and staring at the ceiling. "You?"

"I'm an only child. It was tough growing up. I was always playing by myself."

"Yeah, but you got all the attention," Ali pointed out.

Nick groaned. "Everyone who has siblings always says that. But it wasn't that much fun."

"I would have loved to be an only child," Ali murmured, more to herself than to Nick.

She rolled over onto her stomach. She'd been on the phone with Nick for forty-five minutes and thirty-six seconds—not that she was counting. This was the longest conversation she'd ever had with a boy, and they still hadn't run out of things to talk about.

"How about friends?" Nick asked. "You got a best friend, or a group, or what?"

"I have a group—they're all my best friends." Ali picked at her nail polish. "I'm not sure about things between us right now, though."

He paused. "Are you in a fight?"

"Not exactly. They just . . . well, some of them aren't the people I thought they were. Has that ever happened to you?"

Nick thought for a moment. "I had this friend a while ago. She was awesome—really sweet, really funny—but it turned out she had this dark side."

Ali raised an eyebrow. "Was this a girlfriend?"

"Not exactly," Nick said. "She was a girlfriend's friend. A real psycho."

The word *psycho* ripped through Ali's body like a gunshot. "How did your girlfriend know her?"

"Hang on," Nick said, and there was a pause. "Sorry," he said, getting back on the line. "I thought my mom was calling me."

Jackhammers started up in the backyard, and Ali groaned. "What's that?" Nick asked.

Ali sighed. "Workers are digging this hole in my backyard to make way for a gazebo. It's the longest process *ever*."

"Why would workers need to dig a hole to build a gazebo?"

"That's the question *I've* been asking," Ali said,

laughing. "Who knows? Maybe we're putting in a bomb shelter instead. Or maybe this gazebo needs a basement." She moved the phone to the other ear. "So I'm going to have a party before graduation. Just a small group of friends, but I'd love for you to come." Her heart pounded unexpectedly. It surprised her how nervous she was asking Nick out. This was the first time since she'd become Alison that she worried about a boy saying no.

"When is it?" Nick asked.

"Friday," Ali said. "Just at my house. Totally casual."

"Um . . ."

There was a creak behind her, and Ali turned. Her mother was standing in the hall, a nervous expression on her face. It was the kind of look one didn't ignore.

Ali clutched the phone to her ear. "I have to go. To be continued." Then she pushed END.

Mrs. DiLaurentis took a few steps into the room. "Can you come downstairs for a sec? Your dad and I want to talk to you and Jason about something."

For a moment, Ali's legs felt glued to the bedspread. Her mind flashed instantly to her mom and whoever that guy from the mall was the other day. The way that guy had touched her mom's cheek. Maybe it would be better not to go downstairs at all.

"Come on," Mrs. DiLaurentis said, offering her hand.

Ali didn't know what else to do but follow her. Her heart thudded loudly as she trudged down the stairs and made the turn into the kitchen. Mr. DiLaurentis sat at the table, and Jason leaned against the counter, snacking on an open box of Cheez-Its. Ali tried to make eye contact with him, but he looked away.

She sat down at the table and stared at the floral centerpiece.

Mrs. DiLaurentis broke the silence. "Honey, we have some news about Courtney."

Ali's head shot up.

"She's been doing really well lately. She isn't calling herself Ali anymore. She's taking her meds and getting along with the other patients and the staff. You saw it yourself at the hospital a few weeks ago—she seemed happy."

"She seemed crazy," Ali interrupted sharply.

Her mother held up a finger. "Just let me finish, okay? We had a long talk with her doctors, and they've recommended that we try her out at home for a while. She'll be here next week, and then we'll go from there."

Ali understood each word individually, but together they made no sense. "Next *week*?" she asked, then scooted the chair backward. "But what about my end-of-school party? I invited lots of boys, kids from Rosewood Day."

"We'll pick her up the Tuesday after—how does that sound?"

Ali just blinked. "But she'll be here for graduation? The sleepover? She's not *coming* to graduation, is she?" And she *definitely* wasn't coming to the sleepover.

"Oh, no, one of us will stay with her." Mr. DiLaurentis

placed a hand on her arm. "It'll be okay, honey. We promise."

"No, it *won't*." Ali's voice cracked. "This is a terrible idea."

"I know it's a lot to take in," Mrs. DiLaurentis said gently. "And we'll be here to help you through it. But, honey, we really think she's not going to hurt you anymore. Try to look at this compassionately—if it were you in the hospital, wouldn't you want us to get you out of there?"

Yes! Ali wanted to scream. *I wanted that so badly, and you never did!*

She looked around the room. Everything seemed different somehow, the walls closer together, the clock bigger, the oven too shiny. Outside, a huge crow perched on top of the tree house, looking ominous. "She's not calling herself Ali anymore?" she croaked.

"That's right," Mrs. DiLaurentis said. "That's a really good thing, don't you think?"

Ali wasn't so sure. Unless she really *had* gone insane, the most logical reason her sister had for not calling herself Ali anymore was so that doctors would deem her sane and send her home. And *then* what would happen? Would she take her rightful place as the real Ali and force Courtney to keep quiet or else? Or—more likely—would she figure out a way to get *Courtney* to go back to the hospital so she'd be the one-and-only DiLaurentis girl again?

"Are you going to tell everyone who she is?" Ali asked. "Will I have to tell my friends? Everyone at school? What are people going to *think*?"

"Let's take this one step at a time," Mrs. DiLaurentis said. "Right now, we'll just try her at home for a few days. We'll keep Courtney inside like we did the last time she was here."

"Except she *didn't* stay inside," Ali snapped. "She went out and talked to Jenna Cavanaugh. She practically exposed all of us."

"We'll watch her more carefully this time," Mr. DiLaurentis insisted, setting down his mug. "We hope that you girls talk a little, too. We've scheduled a counselor to come out here and help us through the transition. We really need to start dealing with some of these issues instead of avoiding them."

"But I don't want to *talk* with her!" Ali screamed. She knew she sounded wild, but she couldn't help it. Then she looked at Jason. There was a little smile on his face, like he was actually happy. "Did you *know* about this?"

Jason nodded. "They told me last night. I think it's a good idea, too."

"You *would*," Ali snapped. She leapt up from the table and stormed out the door.

"Alison, where are you going?" Mrs. DiLaurentis cried.

"Out," Ali snapped, her voice making an embarrassing crack.

"We're not done talking!"

Ali just waved them away, but Mrs. DiLaurentis started after her, reaching out to grab the back of Ali's shirt. Ali twisted away and broke free, but instead of continuing on, she whirled around and stared her mother down. Her eyes burned. Her nostrils flared. All of a sudden, Ali was filled with rage for the woman standing across from her. Her limbs literally contorted with hate.

"I know what you're doing," she spit out. "I've seen you with . . . *him*. I know the truth."

At first, Mrs. DiLaurentis's brow creased, but then her face went very pale. She looked nervously at her husband, then at Jason. Ali's skin prickled. So it *was* true. Maybe all of it.

Ali whipped around and fled out the door. "Alison!" Mr. DiLaurentis called after her. "Damn it! Come back!"

But Ali was already halfway across the yard toward the trees in the back. Tears streamed down her face. Her throat felt clogged with screams. Suddenly, it felt like everything she was desperately trying to hold together was now a big ball of unraveled yarn. She pictured it lying in a tangled mess of impossible knots on the ground. No matter how much she tried to work out the kinks, it would never, ever be the same again.

What if they sent her to the Preserve? What if there was a bed waiting for her *right now*? She thought of the stack of Polaroids in her top drawer, all her mementos from the past year and a half. They would be all she had left of this life. Of *any* life. She would die before she had to go back. She would literally kill herself.

"Alison!" her mother called from the porch, but Ali

kept going. Only when she came to the gazebo hole did she stop and glare into its dark abyss. It had to be a ten-foot drop. If her parents found out, if "Courtney" somehow masterminded sending Ali to the Preserve in her place, she would jump in the hole and never come out. What would her parents do? Would they try to save her? Would they miss her? Would they even *care*?

"Ali!" her mom called one more time, and Ali raised her middle finger up high. She kicked at a pile of dirt and watched little pebbles cascade down, down, down, filling up the empty bottom, and then continued on into the woods, where she could cry without anyone hearing.

21

AN OFFER SHE CAN'T REFUSE

Two afternoons later, Ali and Spencer sat at Spencer's big dining room table, watching the rain stream down the windows. They'd cleared some of the china plates, napkins, and candlesticks off the table—Mrs. Hastings was the type who always had the table set so she could wine-and-dine a guest at a moment's notice—to make way for Ali's laptop and a stack of index cards. They were using Ali's iTunes to pick a playlist for the impromptu end-of-school party Ali had put together for Friday. The flash cards contained vocabulary words for their English final tomorrow.

"Okay, *megalomaniac*," Spencer said.

Ali tipped the chair back. "Is that a band or a vocab word?"

Spencer giggled. "Vocab, silly."

Ali threw up her hands. "You got me."

Spencer flipped the card over. "Someone who has

delusional fantasies of power, relevance, and omni-potence."

"Got it," Ali said, turning away. That definition reminded her of someone: her psychotic sister. Wanting to be the only DiLaurentis girl. Pushing her out of the family by any means possible. And now they were bringing her *back*.

It was six days, one hour, and twenty-three minutes—roughly—until her sister returned, and Ali had no idea what to do about it. Worse, her family had thrown themselves into preparing for her twin's return: getting a new quilt for the guest bedroom, buying her a laptop and a desk, inquiring about membership for her at the Rosewood Country Club, setting up an account at the Rosewood pharmacy so they could easily refill her meds. Mrs. DiLaurentis had even had the balls to ask Ali if she had any clothes that she wouldn't mind giving up—"Courtney" probably needed a few things to start her off. As if Ali was really going to let her wear her jeans and T-shirts! It was incredible: Even though her parents believed the girl in the hospital was the real Courtney, they were *still* treating her better than they'd ever treated Ali when she was there.

She'd tossed and turned all night, having nightmares about the corridors of the Preserve and the moans she used to hear at the Radley. Could her sister prove, unequivo-cally, that Ali had lied for all these years—and forced her to take her place in the Preserve? And what could Ali do if she did? It was true, after all.

"Ali?"

Spencer was staring at her, a pencil hovering halfway between her mouth and the paper. Her blue eyes were wide, and strands of hair had come loose from her ponytail. "I asked if you thought Nas would work for the playlist."

"Oh." Ali spun her initial ring around her finger. "That sounds good."

Spencer cocked her head. "Are you okay?"

"Of course!" Ali blurted. Then she shrugged. "I just had a crappy night's sleep last night. Jason was playing his awful music again; you know how that goes."

Spencer flipped a page of the textbook. The grandfather clock in the hall bonged out the hour. Just as Ali's mind started to wander into that wasteland of hysteria once more, Spencer slapped the book shut and looked at her phone. "*Yes*," she whispered, tapping the screen.

Ali looked up. "What is it?"

Spencer smiled slyly. "Nothing."

Ali shifted her chair over to get a peek, but Spencer hid the screen with her hand. Not before Ali could see Ian Thomas's name at the top of a text message, though. "You're texting Ian," Ali stated.

Spencer placed her phone facedown on the table. "Maybe I am."

Ali stared at her, shocked by the snarky, haughty tone of voice Spencer was using. That tone was reserved for her and only her. She held Spencer's gaze for several beats.

She was *not* going to ask Spencer about this. She was not stooping so low that she had to beg.

Just as she thought, after a few seconds, Spencer's tough exterior cracked. "Okay, okay. You know how I've had that crush on Ian? He and I kissed on my driveway a little while ago." She cuffed Ali's arm playfully. "Which puts me ahead in the older boy–kissing competition."

Ali kept her features composed. "Hmm," she said tepidly.

Spencer twirled the pencil in her hands. "I think he wants me bad. He was all over me." She gave Ali a smug little smile. "So now I'm wondering what to do. Should I call him? Wait for him to come to me? It's going to happen again–I just know it. But I don't know how to play things. Maybe I should invite him to your party? What do you think?"

Ali's mouth fell open. Was Spencer serious? Did she honestly think the Ian thing was for real, that it was going to continue? He was dating her *sister*. She glanced at an old school picture of Melissa on the wall, for a moment feeling bad for her. Then she pictured that man reaching across and touching her mom's face. That man who was possibly her *father*, some asshole not even big enough to admit that she was his. How dare her mother never tell her this! How dare she keep it a secret from the entire family! What if Ali wanted to meet this guy, wanted to know where she truly came from? Did *she* matter in all this? She felt just like she did at Radley–forgotten, second-best, an impediment instead of something to nurture and cherish. *Bitch.*

She felt that same black, gummy nastiness she'd felt with Aria the other day ooze over her. She turned to the row of photographs along the wall instead, grabbing the big frame of Melissa's senior picture. "That's a pretty foul thing to do to your sister, Spence," she said. "He's your sister's boyfriend."

Spencer squinted. "So?"

Ali looked into Melissa's eyes in the photograph. They were the same blue as her own. "I know you hate her, but that's low, even for you."

"But you told me to go for him!" Spencer bellowed, her voice cracking.

Ali frowned. "No, I didn't."

Now Spencer was on her feet. "Yes, you did! Don't you remember Melissa's party? You said, *You should totally go for him. All's fair in love and war.*"

Ali crossed her arms over her chest. "Well, I've changed my mind. And anyway, I didn't think you'd actually do it."

Spencer stomped over to the corner of the room and aimlessly stared out the window. The view was of Melissa's barn. There was a light on inside; Melissa must have been home. "I really *like* him," she said tremulously, her eyes suddenly glistening with tears. "I thought you'd be happy for me."

Ali sighed and stood up. "I'd be happier if you liked someone else."

Realization washed across Spencer's face. "Do *you* like him?"

Ali shook her head sharply. "*No.* I just think it's wrong. And I think you should tell Melissa what you did."

"I can't!"

Ali sank into one hip. "Yes, you can, Spence. And if you don't, I will."

Spencer's eyes searched Ali's face as if she'd never seen her before. After a moment, she turned to the side and let out a small shriek. "Maybe I don't need you as a friend anymore," she growled through gritted teeth.

Ali laughed. "C'mon, Spence. You'd be nothing without me."

"That's not friendship. I'm tired of you always trying to be better than me."

Ali snorted but didn't take the bait. "Besides, if we're no longer friends, then I have absolutely no reason not to tell Melissa what happened. I'm only keeping my mouth shut because I care about you *so very much*." She blinked innocently.

Spencer ran a hand down her forehead. Her mouth opened, but no words came out. She walked over to her books, gathered them up in her arms, and marched angrily out of the room, dropping a few index cards as she went. She didn't come back to pick them up, and Ali stared at her neat, even handwriting. *Svengali*, it said. *Definition: person who, with evil intent, controls another person by persuasion or deceit. The Svengali may feign kindness and use manipulation to get the other person to yield his or her autonomy.*

That's me, Ali thought grimly. *It's who my family has turned me into.*

She walked through the bushes and into her yard. But just as she was about to open the front door to her house, her skin prickled. It felt like there was someone standing behind her, watching, but when she turned, the street was empty. She narrowed her eyes at the Cavanaughs' house across the street. The blinds were drawn. No lights were on.

Something fluttered out of the doorjamb and fell to her feet. She bent down, picked it up, and frowned at the Polaroid photo before her. It was the picture she'd taken of herself and Ian at *Romeo and Juliet* a few weeks before. Only now there was red-lipsticked writing over her and Ian's smiling faces. Ali drew in a breath as she read the message, then looked around once more.

"Hello?" she said quietly, her voice cracking. "Ali?" No answer.

Swallowing hard, she looked down at the message once more. *You're dead, bitch*, it said, in handwriting that looked eerily like her sister's.

22

DADDY'S LITTLE GIRL

On Thursday afternoon, Ali and Aria stood in the aisles of Sparrow, a dusty record store in the heart of Hollis's shopping district. Cut Copy played over the speakers, and a couple of unwashed-looking college kids stood at the registers, bopping to the music with their eyes closed. Sparrow was one of the only stores left in the Philadelphia area that sold actual record albums. Even though Ali's family didn't even *own* a record player, it was fun to flip through the stacks, looking at the album covers.

"I'm really excited for this party," Aria said as she rifled through the dance records. "That was nice of you to throw it, Ali."

"I'm looking forward to it," Ali said calmly. Then she looked down at her beeping phone. For once, it wasn't a call from an anonymous number, but a text from Spencer. *Took the history final today*, it said. *Do you want the answer key?*

That's okay, Ali wrote back, feeling a ripple of satisfaction. This was the third bargaining text she'd received from Spencer today, all to keep Ali from saying anything to Melissa. In the first text, Spencer had said Ali could *have* her Burberry tote instead of just borrow it. In the second, she'd said she was working her hardest to get the barn for the sleepover. Ali could probably ask for the moon right now and Spencer would offer to pull it down with a lasso. It felt good to have Spencer back in her control. "Maybe I should get into DJing," Aria murmured, her bangle bracelets clanging together as she picked up a big pair of plastic headphones and clapped them over her ears. "Do I look cool? Maybe a college boy would be into it."

"You look like an air-traffic controller," Ali said, ripping them off her. "Big headphones screw up your hair."

Aria pouted, then shrugged and put the headphones back on the shelf. She held up an old Rolling Stones record. "You should get this for Noel. He really likes classic rock."

Ali blinked. "Why would I get it for Noel?"

Aria looked surprised. "Because you're going out with him?"

Ali stared pointedly at a dust bunny in the corner; it was the type of store that had probably never seen a Swiffer. She'd almost forgotten that she'd told Aria that Noel was into her instead. She'd even told her they'd gone out on two dates, even though they hadn't. "Right," she said tepidly. "You must be really hurt about Noel, though, huh?"

Aria strolled into the rare-records room, which had a couple of listening booths in the back and aqueous, neon-colored lava lamps on tables in the corners. "I don't know," she murmured. "I got some news today that lessens the sting a little."

Ali looked up at her. "What kind of news?" She worried, suddenly, that there was an innocent excuse for what happened between Mr. Montgomery and that girl. That Aria's family was fine—it was only *her* family that was messed up.

Aria picked up a Fleet Foxes album, then set it down again. "My dad got an offer to teach at the University of Iceland next year. We might all go."

Ali blinked. "*Iceland?* I thought only penguins lived there."

"That's Greenland," Aria said knowingly. "Iceland is lush and beautiful. We looked at pictures of it on the Internet last night, and it looks awesome—it's full of volcanoes and glaciers and has amazing snowboarding. There's a great music scene there, too, and apparently all the guys are tall and gorgeous."

Ali stared at her. Just picturing Aria's family happily sitting around a computer made her light-headed. The last DiLaurentis family gathering was when her parents had told her that her sister was coming home, and look how well *that* had gone. "Isn't Iceland the place that, like, stays light out all the time in the summer and dark in the winter? That would suck!"

Aria shrugged. "I guess you get used to it."

"And what if they don't speak English there?"

"They do. We checked. Everyone speaks perfect English. And the literacy rate is a hundred percent."

Ali sniffed, unconvinced. "What if they make you learn how to yodel?"

"I think that's Sweden," Aria said. "Or Norway."

"It sounds like an awful idea," Ali decided. "Didn't you read last month's *Teen Vogue*? They listed the coolest places to visit, and Iceland didn't make the cut."

Aria cocked her head. "If you're jealous, you can come visit. I'd love that."

"I'm not jealous!" Ali snapped.

But maybe she *was* kind of jealous. Plus, Aria didn't even seem to care that she was leaving Rosewood, leaving *her*. In fact, it seemed like she *wanted* to get the hell out of here, like her friends weren't worth anything to her. Aria hadn't even said yet how much she'd miss anyone. She hadn't mentioned how sad she'd be to leave.

The feeling made Ali hot and itchy, like she'd just been bitten by ants. Suddenly, she was hit with a thought. It was around this time when she'd made her discovery in the alley. Maybe there was something to discover there today, too. She suddenly wanted Aria to suffer as much as she was.

She looked up at Aria. "Did you say your *dad* got this offer?"

"Yep." Aria smiled. "They are going to make him

the head of the department. He's thinking of doing his research on trolls. Crazy, huh?"

Ali sniffed. "Your dad isn't going to leave Hollis."

Aria squinted. "Why not?"

Ali rocked back and forth in her heels. She searched Aria's expression for any sign of recognition, but Aria just stared at her with narrowed eyes. Shrugging, Ali whipped around and started out of the store. Aria followed as she sauntered down the sidewalk. "Where are you going?" she called. "Are you mad?"

"I'm not mad," Ali said breezily. "I just needed some air. Walk with me."

"I'm sorry, Ali." Aria sounded defensive. "But I thought you'd be happy. It's an amazing opportunity for my dad—for all of us."

"Uh-huh," Ali chirped. "I'm *very* happy for you, Aria. Your life is going to be truly perfect." *That's what you think*, she added in her head.

They passed the familiar Kinko's, then the place at the curb where she and Jason had parked a few weeks back. When Ali turned down the alleyway that butted up to the art history building, lo and behold, there was the battered Subaru in its regular faculty-only parking spot. *Yes.*

Aria rounded the corner behind her. "Ali, why are we . . ." She trailed off, looking at her dad's car. "Oh, hey! Let's leave my dad a note."

Aria reached into her bag, perhaps looking for a notepad and a pen, when something in the car caught her eye.

Her brow furrowed when she saw her father's head pop up over the seats. She was about to call out, but then the girl's head appeared as well. Ali saw the exact moment Aria realized what was happening. Her purse dropped from her hand. She took a big step back, stumbling over a sewer grate. Byron Montgomery leaned toward the girl and kissed her on the mouth.

"*Dad?*" Aria blurted.

The figures in the car shot apart. Mr. Montgomery turned and looked at Aria, the color draining from his face. The girl, who was blond and pretty and most definitely a grad student, stared at Aria impassively, a whisper of a smile on her lips.

"Aria!" Mr. Montgomery said, kicking open his door.

Aria took another step back. She glanced at Ali, her eyes round. Her expression conveyed all kinds of questions. *Did you see that? Is this happening?* And maybe, just maybe, *Did you know they were here?* And then, before her father could reach her, she turned around and ran.

23

THE TANGLED WEB

That evening, Ali lay on her stomach on her bed, her diary splayed out before her. She had a lot to write; plenty had happened. These days, she was writing more about her friends' lives and transgressions than she was writing about her own. It was kind of like writing a juicy novel but not having to work for any of the details, since all of them were there in her memory. She wrote a final sentence about Aria spying her philandering father in the car, then laid down her pen, picked up her cell phone, and composed a text to Aria herself.

How are you doing? she wrote. *Wanna talk?*

There was no response. Ali ran her tongue over her teeth. This wasn't how it was supposed to go. Aria was supposed to break down to her, *need* her, and then Ali would confess what she was going through in turn. Instead, Aria was being so silent, almost like this was Ali's fault.

Her phone beeped, and for a second, Ali thought Aria had written back. But the text was from Nick. *Miss you.*

Ali's heart flipped over. *Miss you back*, she responded. *Are you coming to the party?*

Not sure if I can, Nick responded. *I might have to work that night.*

No! Ali replied. *Try to get the night off!*

A knock sounded on her door, startling her into dropping her phone to the carpet. Her mother stood in the doorway. "It's so nice out," she said softly. "Why don't we sit on the deck?"

Ali scooped up her phone and met her mother's gaze with a stony stare. "Are you asking me to sit on the deck, or telling me?"

Mrs. DiLaurentis looked tormented. "Please?"

Ali chewed on the inside of her lip as she followed her mother down to the huge wood deck at the back of the house. Her mother had set up a pitcher of lemonade and two glasses with several sprigs of mint propped on the lip, an old tradition from when the girls were small. At their old house, wild mint had grown in the side yard; Ali and Courtney used to love picking it and pressing it close to their noses to inhale the fresh scent. They drank their lemonades like sophisticated ladies, pretending they were cocktails. She smiled at the memory and then, seconds later, coughed to conceal a small whimper.

"Are you okay?" Mrs. DiLaurentis asked, pouring lemonade into her glass.

Ali shrugged and stared out at the lawn. It was immaculately green and manicured, thanks to weekly landscapers. Only the ugly hole at the back marred the pastoral scene. "Whatever."

"Looking forward to your party?" Mrs. DiLaurentis asked.

"Uh-huh." She took a sip of lemonade.

"Your dad set up the speakers on the deck. And the workers will be gone by then, but there's going to be a big hole. Just make sure no one goes out there, okay? We don't want anyone falling in."

"Okay." If she gave one-word answers, maybe her mom would leave her alone.

Mrs. DiLaurentis folded her hands. The sun streamed across her face, lighting up one cheek and casting the other in shadow. "You really seem like something's bothering you."

Ali slammed down her lemonade glass hard, the ice clinking. Was her mom that much of an idiot? Of *course* something was bothering her. Several somethings. And her mother knew exactly what those various things were.

She looked at the half-dug hole instead. "When are they going to finish that thing?" she asked sharply. "They're taking forever. By the time they're done, the opportunity to have fabulous summer parties will be over."

Mrs. DiLaurentis didn't glance toward the hole, her eyes still on Ali. "Do you have anyone to talk to, honey? About . . . things?"

Ali stared down at her flip-flops. "If you mean *her*, we were keeping that a secret, remember? I *can't* talk to anyone."

"Well, if you'd like to talk to your friends about it, that's okay with us."

Ali sucked in her stomach. "No, thanks."

Mrs. DiLaurentis brushed an invisible mess of leaves off the surface of the patio table. "Perhaps a counselor, then. They can help."

Ali glowered at her. "You've got the wrong twin. I'm not the crazy one. I don't need a shrink."

Mrs. DiLaurentis shut her eyes. "That's not what I meant. But the way you reacted the other day when I said Courtney was coming home—you seemed very disturbed."

Ali shifted her chair around so that she wasn't facing her mother. "What do you expect? You just dropped it on me! Even Jason knew before I did! And I don't *want* her home, Mom. It's a terrible idea."

"She's part of the family. And sometimes, in families, you have to do things you don't want to do."

"And what happens if she tries to hurt me again?"

A car grumbled on the street. A mourning dove cooed from the trees. Mrs. DiLaurentis pursed her lips. "That won't happen."

The incident in the bathroom at the Preserve flashed in Ali's mind. "How do *you* know?"

"I just do, okay?" Then Ali's mom stared at the half-dug hole, then at the shrubs that separated their yard from the Hastingses'. "We should talk, too, about what you said to me. About . . . *him*."

Ali stood and headed for the sliding door. "No, thanks."

Mrs. DiLaurentis caught her arm. "It's not what you think, Alison."

Ali yanked the door open. "Yes, it is."

"It isn't, and you shouldn't have confronted me with it. Now your father is asking questions. I'm not having an affair with anyone, and it was rude of you to say so."

Ali's head whipped up. All sounds—the swishing of the wind, the neighbor's Weedwacker, the steady hum of the heating unit—seemed to cease all at once. "Are you seriously going to sit here and deny it?"

Mrs. DiLaurentis's eyes darted back and forth, searching her face. "What do you think you saw, exactly?"

"I saw some guy touching your cheek at the mall. And I *heard* you," Ali hissed. "I heard you talking to someone in a sugary voice—someone who wasn't dad. It sounded like whoever it was knew about Courtney."

A muscle by Mrs. DiLaurentis's mouth twitched. Her eyes had darkened to a deeper blue, which they always did when she became serious or enraged. "Yes, there is someone who knows about Courtney besides us. But it's someone who has kept things an absolute secret, I promise. There are a lot of things you don't understand, Alison. Things you don't need to know."

Ali ran her hand down the length of her face. Rage

bubbled up inside her, then geysered out. "Things I don't need to know?" she growled, her voice sounding feral. She yanked her hand away from her mother, her head spinning faster and faster. "When are you going to tell the truth, Mom? When are you going to tell me where I really come from?"

Mrs. DiLaurentis jerked her head back and frowned. "What are you talking about?"

"I *heard* you!" Ali screamed. "I heard you say, *She's your daughter, too!* So this *does* concern me, Mom. Knowing who my real father is concerns me a *lot.*"

The color drained from Mrs. DiLaurentis's cheeks. "*Alison,*" she hissed. And then she rose to her feet and slapped Ali across the face.

It came so fast, so out of nowhere, that Ali didn't feel the sting until a few seconds after it was over. Tears welled up in her eyes. Her mouth dropped open, but she was too stunned to speak.

Mrs. DiLaurentis settled back into her chair. Calmly, evenly, she picked up the overturned glass. There was a long pause. Ali's heart pounded; her cheek stung. It felt like everything hinged on what her mother would say next.

"There will be no more of that," Mrs. DiLaurentis announced in a deep voice. And then her gaze shifted to the half-dug hole at the back of the yard. "The workers are set to pour the concrete for the gazebo the weekend your sister is home," she said in the clipped, perfunctory voice Ali was used to, the voice that got things done. She squeezed Ali's shoulder twice. "Just in time for your fabulous summer parties."

And with that, she was gone.

24

HANNA LETS IT ALL GO

The following evening, Ali placed the last bowl of chips on the table and stood back for the effect. "Do people even eat Doritos anymore?" she asked aloud, then spun around and glanced at her friends. Too bad Hanna wasn't among them; otherwise, she would have made a snarky comment.

"It looks great, Ali," Emily said, adjusting the daisy behind her ear, which she'd picked from Ali's side yard. Emily had dressed up for the party—for her, anyway—wearing a pair of crisp jeans without any holes in them and an almost-tight T-shirt she'd borrowed from Aria that said *Irish Girls Do It Better*. Ali was sure that if Emily's mom caught her wearing it she'd be in huge trouble.

"The Christmas lights were a nice touch," Spencer said. She still had her eye on her house next door, probably waiting for Ian, who had a date with Melissa tonight, to show up.

"Thanks," Ali said. Her dad had brought up a box of Christmas lights from the basement this morning and strung them all over the patio—Ali had first seen the effect at a restaurant in Little Italy in New York City. After that, her dad had offered to pick up any guests who didn't have rides and grill burgers for them. *Guilty much?* Ali had wanted to snap, not taking the bait. It was obvious he was trying to atone for her twin's arrival the following Tuesday, but nothing could make up for that.

She lit a few more candles and placed them on the tables, then checked to make sure the stereo was cued up to a peppy, dance-friendly playlist and that the deck had been swept clean so everyone could dance. She touched Aria, who was standing in the corner, looking at the texts on her phone. "Everything okay at home?"

Aria paled, glancing around at the other girls on the deck. "Fine." She almost sounded annoyed. "I was just texting my mom what time I'd be back."

Ali flinched. That was what she got for trying to be nice? Fury welled up inside her. Fine. If Aria thought Ali was a bitch, then she *would* be a bitch. "So do you know who that girl was?" Ali asked, easing closer, barely recognizing her own voice.

Aria's mouth snapped into a tight line. "I don't know what you're talking about."

"Do you think your mom knows? Everyone at Hollis?"

Aria gave Ali a pleading look, then shoved her phone in her pocket and walked away. Ali watched her go, grinding her teeth. She wasn't sure if it was Aria she was really angry at—all she saw, when she shut her eyes, was her mother's hand reaching out to give her that slap. But the meanness felt good, right. She felt in control.

She tipped her head to the sky, admiring an airplane flying high above. The night was clear and cloudless, with just a hint of a chill, which was perfect for couples who wanted to snuggle up. But that was the only bummer: Even though Nick had asked, he hadn't been able to get the night off work. Maybe it was better that way, though. It wasn't as if Ali had told anyone about him yet—she still wasn't sure where they stood, and she didn't want to tell her friends about him prematurely. And anyway, tonight she had work to do.

The doorbell rang, and Ali darted back into the house and yanked it open. Hanna and Josie stood on the porch, both in similar print dresses that Ali had seen hanging on the racks at Otter. "Welcome!" she said coolly, pushing her disgust and jealousy down deep. Hanna had never been twinsies with *her*.

She stepped aside to let Josie and Hanna in when more guests appeared at the curb. James Freed and the new boy, Mason Byers, spilled out of James's dad's BMW. Kirsten Cullen and Lanie Iler, who were always on the fringes of coolness, started up the path next, followed by Sean Ackard. For a few moments, everyone convened in the foyer, Mason meeting Lanie, James giving Kirsten an I-like-you-but-I'm-going-to-pretend-I-hate-you poke, and

Hanna skittering away, mortified to be in the same room as her crush. Josie, however, lingered and shook Sean's hand. "What grade are you in?" Ali heard her ask him.

"Going into eighth," Sean answered.

Josie frowned. "Really? You look older than that."

Sean blushed. "People tell me that sometimes. I guess it's because I'm tall."

Ali watched as Josie giggled and pushed a lock of hair behind her ear. Did she . . . *like* him? She glanced over at Hanna, who was now talking to Spencer and eating a handful of Doritos, perhaps not noticing that Josie and Sean were talking. Ali steered Hanna to the patio and got her in a conversation with a couple of girls from the junior high field hockey team. Then she went back inside. Josie was still talking to Sean. This was almost too easy.

James cuffed Sean on the shoulder and led him toward the patio, where someone had turned on the stereo. Ali used the opportunity to sidle over to Josie. "It was so nice of you to come," she simpered. "Any friend of Hanna's is a friend of mine."

Josie gave Ali a circumspect look but then shrugged. "It was nice of you to invite me. I don't really know so many people around here yet, but everyone seems really nice."

"Like Brayden, right?"

Josie blinked. "Who?"

"That guy you were just talking to. Brayden." Ali chose a name at random in case Hanna had told Josie about her crush. It was doubtful Hanna had actually pointed him out, as Josie had been flirting, and clearly Sean hadn't told her his name, either. "I think he was into you."

Josie bit the edge of her thumbnail, looking intrigued. "You think?" she asked reluctantly.

Ali nodded. "I've been friends with him for a long time. I can tell."

Josie's eyes flicked back and forth. "He *was* really cute."

"Do you want to get to know him better?" Ali asked.

Josie smiled. "Sure."

Ali nodded. "You know what I'll do? I'll send him back into the sunroom with some drinks so you guys can talk in private." She winked knowingly.

Josie stared at Ali for a few long beats. "Thanks."

"Go in there and settle yourself on the couch," Ali said, gesturing toward the sunroom. To her delight, Josie did exactly as she was told. Then Ali scuttled back to the patio, which was suddenly filled with kids. Spencer and Kirsten were dancing. Aria and Emily were at one of the tables, talking to Joanna Kirby, who would have been perfect for Ali's clique except for the fact that she was way too obsessed with horses—rumor had it she still played with the figurines. Ali spied Sean across the patio with James Freed. Hanna was standing close to him, gnawing on her fingernail, probably contemplating talking to him. Ali swept him up before she could.

And after that, it was easy. Sean, always the gentleman, immediately got two cups of punch and headed for the sunroom. Hanna watched him, confused, but stayed glued to her spot next to the hanging basket of impatiens.

Five minutes passed. Then ten. Hanna wriggled as though she had bugs in her undies. She plunged her hand into the Doritos bowl again and again until there were only crumbs. Finally, Ali joined her at the railing. "What happened to Josie?"

"I don't know," Hanna said anxiously. "I haven't seen her since she came in. What if she thought this was lame and left?"

Ali ignored the fact that Hanna had more or less insulted her to her face and linked her elbow in hers. "Let's look for her in the house."

They walked into the kitchen, where the silence was shocking in comparison to the loud voices outside. Ali poked her head into a bathroom, then peered up the steps. "I don't know, Han."

When Hanna wandered toward the sunroom, Ali didn't join her. She didn't have to. She watched as Hanna stopped short in the doorway, the color draining from her face.

"What is it?" Ali asked, coming up next to Hanna.

Hanna took a big step back. Tears were in her eyes. Ali peeked in and saw Josie and Sean cuddled up on the couch, clearly almost kissing. "Oh my God," Ali said, grabbing Hanna's hand.

All kinds of expressions crossed Hanna's face. She shook her head, then fled toward the bathroom. The door slammed hard. Ali rattled the knob, but it was locked. "Hanna?" she called out. "Han, please let me in!"

A small, dry cough emerged from inside. Water splashed. The toilet flushed. Ali cupped her palm around the knob. It was déjà vu of what had happened in Annapolis in February. She suddenly felt a pang. *She* had made this happen today. Then again, she had sort of made the Annapolis thing happen, too.

Ali twisted the knob, and it gave—it was almost like Hanna *wanted* her to come in. The door opened to a familiar scene: Hanna crouched over the toilet bowl, her eyes red. She looked up at Ali not with horror but with defeat. Ali slipped inside and shut the door again.

"I'm really not doing it that much," Hanna blurted.

"I know," Ali soothed. "And seeing what you just saw . . . oh my God, Han. It's awful."

Hanna nodded. "I *told* her I liked him. I *told* her he was going to be here. And she went right for him!"

"Some girls are just like that," Ali said, stroking Hanna's hair. "You know what you need to do? Never talk to that bitch again, starting now. If she tries to talk to you, freeze her out. She's dead to us."

Hanna swallowed a sob. "But she was so cool. And fun. And—"

"You can't let her get away with this," Ali interrupted. "Girls like that will walk all over you if you let them, Han. And if Sean doesn't realize how special you are, that's his problem. I'll make sure that Josie's reputation is trashed at

Rosewood Day, okay? I'll even make sure no one shops at Otter. I'm texting Spencer right now to ask her and Sean to leave. And we'll find another boy for you this summer—someone way better than Sean, anyway. I promise."

Hanna wiped away a tear. "You will?"

"Absolutely." Ali slicked Hanna's hair off her face. "No offense, Han, but Sean's too straitlaced for you. You need a guy who's wilder, cooler, a little more fun. I know tons of boys like that."

"Okay," Hanna murmured. And when she looked at Ali, Ali could tell that she wouldn't speak to Josie again. She would do anything Ali asked, especially now.

Then Hanna cleared her throat. "And you won't tell anyone about . . . *this*, will you?" She gestured to the toilet.

Ali shifted her weight against the sink. "Hanna, don't you think you *should* tell someone?"

"No!"

"Not even your mom?"

Hanna shook her head, her hair flopping back and forth. "Please," she begged.

Ali crossed her arms over her chest, pretending to think about it. "Okay," she said. "Best friends have each other's backs—I have yours if you have mine."

"Definitely," Hanna said eagerly. "I'll do whatever you want."

"Perfect," Ali said, and patted Hanna on the head. "That's all I ask."

She got Hanna a cup of water and told her to wash her

face. Then she helped her out of the bathroom, Hanna's girth leaning heavily on her shoulder. Even though Ali's clothes now smelled as pukey as Hanna's, she didn't complain.

That was what good friends were for, after all.

25

TREE HOUSES MAKE
GREAT FIRST DATES

By eleven o' clock, the party had wound down and almost everyone had gone home. Aria said she was tired, Hanna said she was sick, and Spencer had a field hockey camp orientation the following morning, so Emily was the only one who stayed over. The next morning, the two of them sat on the patio, staring at the rising sun and then the gaping hole in the backyard. A tarp flapped on top of it. A few tools had been left on the grass nearby.

"Have the workers said anything else to you?" Emily whispered.

"Here and there," Ali said, pretending to be upset.

"That is so wrong." Emily clucked her tongue.

Ali pulled her legs underneath her on the chair. The truth was, even when she'd paraded in front of the workers in a bikini, they'd barely looked at her. She wondered if her dad had warned them or something.

She stretched out her legs. "Did you have fun last night?"

"It was okay." Emily shrugged. "Hanna seemed really upset about Sean, though."

"Yeah." Ali inspected her fingernails, hoping Emily hadn't seen any of the machinations of that. But even if she had, she might not ask.

"Aria seemed quiet," Emily went on. "So did Spencer."

"Sort of," Ali said.

"Do you know what's going on with them?"

The overhead light seemed to make a halo over Emily's head. She was flicking the loose threads of her Jenna Thing bracelet again and again. "I think they should probably tell you themselves," she said.

Her phone beeped, startling both of them. Ali grabbed for it, hoping it was Nick, but the call came up as *Unknown*. She turned the phone over.

"Do you need to get that?" Emily asked.

"Not right now." Ali gave her a tight smile.

The phone stopped, but immediately started ringing again. Ali groaned and kicked it under the table with her foot, then stood. "Come on," she said to Emily. "Let's walk around."

They wandered over to the half-dug hole and looked inside. The workers had dug down several feet more than the last time she'd checked it out, exposing more twisted roots and loamy dark soil. Several banged-up shovels lay in the bottom, and a Swiss Army knife lay abandoned by the edge.

Ali scooped up the knife and stared into the bottom. "I dare you to jump in the hole."

Emily looked worried. "What if I can't get out?"

"You could," Ali said, but when she looked into the hole again, she wasn't so sure. It seemed deeper, suddenly, than it had even a moment ago. "On second thought, forget it," she decided. "I'd get too dirty pulling you out."

Emily turned and eyed the tree house at the back of the property. Suddenly, she grabbed the Swiss Army knife from Ali's hand and walked toward the solid trunk. After a moment, Ali heard scratching sounds. Emily was cutting something into the bark.

"Are you cutting down my tree?" she asked, walking over to her.

"Nope." Emily stepped away from the tree and showed off the trunk. Carved into the bark was EF + AD. "Do you like?"

A dizzy feeling swept across Ali's body as unexpectedly as a pop-up thunderstorm might come upon a town. "Cute," she said, her voice cracking.

"I'm just so happy we're friends," Emily gushed. "I wanted to . . . I don't know. Show you, I guess."

"Uh-huh." Ali's throat suddenly felt dry.

Emily dropped the Swiss Army knife on the grass and peered up at the tree house. "It's been ages since we've been up there."

"Let's go," Ali said, eager to change the subject.

She grabbed the threadbare rope and placed her feet on the planks her dad had nailed to the trunk as steps sometime in the many years she'd been locked in the hospital. It was an easy climb into the tree house, which was basically just several boards for a floor, pieces of plywood for the walls and roof, and cutouts for windows. Dried leaves and dead bugs littered the floor. Spiderwebs had taken residence in the corners. Ali brushed everything aside with her hands and sat down, her butt bones digging into the wood.

Emily climbed up next and sat beside her. They'd grown so much that there was barely room for both of them; their forearms just touched. They stared out the little window, which offered a good view of the Hastingses' barn. Melissa Hastings moved back and forth in front of the window. It seemed like she was talking to someone on the phone.

Then Ali turned around and looked at her house. The light was on in her bedroom window, but the guest room's window was dark. It had been the first window she'd peered out of in Rosewood. In a few days, her sister would be staying in that room, looking out that window instead. Or would she be in her old bedroom again? Would she have convinced her parents the truth about what happened?

Ali's insides twisted.

"It's so nice up here," Emily breathed, bringing Ali back to the moment. "So . . . quiet. It feels like we're not in Rosewood anymore."

"It would be nice to get out of Rosewood, wouldn't it?" Ali murmured. "I'm definitely not living here when I'm older."

"Me, neither," Emily agreed. "I don't even want to live here *now*."

Ali looked at her for a moment. She wanted to ask why not. Her parents? Her zillions of brothers and sisters? She wondered if it had something to do with her burgeoning crush. Rosewood wasn't exactly the most tolerant place of people who were different.

"A tropical island would be nice," Ali said after a moment.

Emily's eyes lit up. "I would love to live on a beach. Swimming every single day? Amazing."

"Why don't we go right now?" Ali said. "I could book us tickets with my dad's points. We could run away and never come back."

"Really?" Emily sounded astonished. "You'd want to go with me?"

"Sure, Em." Ali shifted her weight. "It would be fun to go with you." Maybe running away was the answer, she thought suddenly. She could avoid her sister forever. She'd never have to face what was to come.

"It would be really fun to go with you, too, Ali," Emily said breathlessly. Her fingers were trembling a little, but Ali pretended not to notice. "When I say how happy I am we're friends, I really mean it. This is . . . *amazing*."

"Definitely," Ali said, staring at Emily's thigh. It had shifted closer so that it was now touching Ali's knee.

Emily looked up and met Ali's gaze. "Wasn't the ice rink fun?"

"Sure," Ali said, a strange feeling settling over her. "We'll have to do it again sometime."

A heartbreaking smile appeared on Emily's face. "Really? I would *love* that!" Now her thigh was definitely touching Ali's knee. Emily placed a hand over Ali's and then pulled it away, seeming embarrassed. "I've been thinking about that day a lot, Ali."

Suddenly, all Ali could see in her mind's eye were those tiny letters spelling out *I love Ali* on Emily's notebook. The air seemed charged—Emily seemed eager to get something off her chest. Ali was afraid she knew what it was, too. She moved her knee away in one clean jerk and touched Emily's shoulder. "I have something to tell you," she blurted. "It's a secret."

Emily pressed her lips together. Her eyes shone.

Ali licked her lips and took a deep breath. "Well, I'm sort of seeing someone. This older guy. He's absolutely amazing."

For a moment, the tree house was utterly silent. "O-oh," Emily stammered. Her eyes darted in a lot of directions.

"I wanted you to know because you're my favorite, Em. You always have been."

Emily swallowed audibly. "Th-that's great. What's his name?"

"It's . . . well, I don't want to tell you yet. Soon though, okay?"

"Okay," Emily said.

They were silent again. Static electricity hung in the

air, as scratchy as a dryer sheet. The birds chirped. Far in the distance, someone barked out a laugh. And then, suddenly, Emily twisted her body toward Ali. Before Ali knew what was happening, Emily's lips were touching hers. They felt soft, *normal*, just like a guy's lips, really, and for a split second, Ali shut her eyes and let the sensation wash over her. In many ways, it felt good to be adored so purely. It felt good to give someone exactly what she wanted.

But then she came back to herself and pulled back. This wasn't what *she* wanted. And people would think it was weird. How dare Emily just assume Ali would be into this?

All Ali could see were the whites of Emily's eyes. Ali felt a nasty smile settle across her lips. "Well," she heard herself say, her voice taut and mean, "I guess that's why you get so quiet when we're changing for gym."

Emily flinched. A horrible, tortured, fake laugh leaked from her mouth. "God, sorry," she said. "I don't know what happened to me just then. I guess I was thinking about the guy I like and got confused."

Ali laughed crudely. "I don't think you like anyone at all, Em. I think you're lying to me."

Emily's eyes widened. "I *do* like someone."

"A guy?" Ali teased.

Tears gleamed in Emily's eyes. She shot up and lunged for the rope ladder. "I have to go."

Ali didn't say another word as Emily climbed down

and started across the yard. She watched her from the tree house as she mounted her bike and wobbled down the street, her ponytail bouncing. Emily didn't look back once.

For a split second, Ali could feel Emily's hair in her hands again, her soft skin against her face. And then she bit down hard on her lip, the emotions too jumbled inside her to make sense. On one hand, she felt disgusted. On another, she felt restored. And on another . . . well, even more than what she'd done to Hanna, she knew that she'd just altered things with her best friend for good.

And although Emily was probably even more in her power than ever, it felt sort of . . . *awful*.

26

OVER THE EDGE

"We're getting close," Nick whispered in Ali's ear.

"Where are we going?" Ali stifled a nervous giggle. Grass prickled under her feet. The scents of honeysuckle and lilacs drifted through the air. In the distance, she could hear water rushing and birds chirping.

"It's a surprise," Nick said, squeezing her hand. "But I promise it's good."

It was later that afternoon, and Ali was out with Nick. They'd met at the King James, and Ali had assumed they were going to do some shopping, but then Nick had wrapped a blindfold around her and said that where he was taking her next was something she couldn't see until they got there. As far as she knew, they'd gotten into a taxi, Nick whispering the directions so Ali wouldn't hear. The drive had been about fifteen minutes, and gravel had crunched under the tires when they arrived.

"You know, I must really trust you," Ali said now. "I wouldn't let just anyone lead me around blindfolded."

"I'm honored," Nick said. "I just hope you like where we are."

After a few more steps, Nick stopped and pulled the cloth from her eyes. "*Ta-da.*"

The first thing Ali saw was Nick's heartbreakingly cute face—those soulful eyes, those pink kissable lips, those cute locks of hair that curled over his ears. Behind him was a field full of flowers, and behind that was what looked like a rocky cliff. Water spilled over the sides and gushed into a gulley far below. Several kids splayed out on the big black rocks in varying degrees of nakedness. A plaid picnic blanket had been set up a few paces away, complete with a bottle of sparkling cider on ice, a long loaf of French bread, a wheel of cheese, and some grapes. A portable iPod stereo sat on the blanket, too, and hip-hop tinkled out of the speakers.

"Where is this?" she asked.

"Floating Man Quarry." Nick looked surprised. "You've never been here?"

Ali stared into the big, clear lake at the bottom of the cliff and shook her head. Spencer used to urge them to come here, but Ali had always refused, worried that everyone would like this place *too* much, which might make Spencer think she was cooler than Ali.

"The cliff-diving is amazing." Nick walked to the blanket. "People are always trying to shut this place down because they say it's dangerous, but no one's gotten hurt yet."

Ali sat down on the blanket next to him, noting the grass nearby was wet with dew and flecked with clover. Then Nick turned to her and kissed her softly on the lips. Her stomach swooped, and her head felt faint. Nick's hands brushed her shoulders. Then he pulled away and smiled bashfully at her.

"You're so amazing," he whispered.

"You, too," Ali said back.

Then Ali flopped onto the blanket and stared at the sky. Nick cut off a piece of bread for her and slathered it with cheese. As she took it from him, he squeezed her hand again. "I'm serious, you know. This is, like, the best. I'm glad you came here with me today. I hope it makes up for missing the party last night."

"I'm glad I came, too," Ali said. But suddenly, for reasons she couldn't exactly explain, a sob rose into her throat. This was almost *too* nice. She turned away.

Nick paused from pouring two glasses of sparkling cider, lowering the large bottle to the blanket. "What is it?"

Ali shook her head. "Nothing. Sorry. I'm just being an idiot."

"Are you sure?"

A Jeep pulled up, and a few kids got out, stripped off their clothes, and walked to the edge of the cliff. Ali watched as they jumped off without even looking down first. Everything that had happened recently bubbled inside her, ready to spill over. Her sister. Her friends. It was more than she could take. Her problems felt like one of those snakes-in-a-can toys that had been at her grandmother's house: No matter how hard she tried to fit the lid back on, it kept popping off, the snakes jumping free.

She looked over the cliff, trying to shove everything down deep. "How long is the drop?"

"I don't know, but not far enough for it to be danger-ous," Nick guessed. Then he turned to Ali and gave her a very serious look. "You don't have to change the subject with me, you know. I do it, too, when there's something I'm dealing with but don't know how to talk about. But whatever you're worried about, whatever you think you can't say, you totally can."

Ali swallowed hard. She glanced at Nick, then cut her eyes away. "I shouldn't," she said. "It's not usually some-thing I talk about."

"I can't promise I can help. But at least I'll listen. You strike me as someone who tries really, really hard to hold things together because everyone else in your life can't. I'm the same way."

Ali glanced at him gratefully. "Really?"

"Uh-huh. It gets me in trouble sometimes, especially when I am dealing with some really serious stuff and I have no one to turn to. But we all *need* someone to turn to. And maybe you and I should turn to each other."

Ali nodded. Suddenly, she felt brave. She took a breath. "I have a twin sister," she admitted. "No one knows about her."

Just saying the words out loud made her dizzy. She looked around, certain a bolt of lightning would zoom down from the sky or a plague of locusts would descend on the quarry—something to prove that the world had truly altered for good. Instead, a butterfly flapped past and the clouds shifted overhead. Nick reached for her hands.

"And?" he said.

"At first, when we were little, we got along great." Ali pulled up a handful of grass and let it blow away in the wind. "But then, suddenly . . . well, I don't know. Something happened. And then she hated me. Wanted me gone. She did terrible things to me."

Nick squeezed her hand. "I'm really sorry."

A lump formed in her throat. "My parents sent her away. She's been gone a long time. But I just found out she's coming back to live with us again."

Nick blinked, his expression stunned, as if she'd just slapped him. "She *is*?"

"Well, yeah. My parents want us to try to be a family, but we're *not* a family—not with her. She's going to ruin everything. I can just feel it."

"When did you find out she was coming back?"

Ali twisted the stud earring in her earlobe. "A few days ago." She felt the tears rising. "Everything else is a mess, too. My parents . . . who *knows* what's going on with them. And my friends—I don't even know them anymore. I would be able to handle that stuff on its own, but with my sister coming back, it's just like . . ."

"It's too much," Nick finished for her.

Ali nodded. "Exactly."

Then he opened his arms and pulled Ali in. She nestled into his chest, allowing herself exactly one full sob. It felt so good to be hugged ridiculously tight. She pressed her ear to his ribs and heard his heart beating, its rhythm unusually fast.

He leaned back and stared into Ali's eyes. "Whatever happens, just keep your head about you, you know? You'll get through it—I'll help you. Don't let her bring you down. And whenever you want to vent, you can call me. I just want to make sure you're safe."

Ali attempted a wobbly smile. "Okay," she said shyly. Then she lowered her eyes. "I've never told anyone that, you know."

"Well, I'm glad you told me," Nick answered.

"I'm glad I told you, too."

There was a growl, and several ATVs pulled up. Three boys dismounted, pulled off their helmets, and took running leaps off the cliff. A different group of kids climbed up the hill toward their parked car, all of them looking tanned and tired. Ali placed a wedge of cheese in her mouth and chewed thoughtfully. She *was* glad she'd told

Nick. She felt lighter somehow, like everything would be okay.

After a while, Ali stood up, heading for the little concrete bathroom pavilion across the parking lot. Inside the ladies' room, she smiled at her reflection in the warped mirror. "He's amazing," she whispered to her image.

"Boo," said a voice.

Ali shrieked as two hands clapped over her eyes. Whoever it was yanked his hands away and guffawed loudly. When Ali turned, she saw Ian Thomas doubled over laughing. His breath smelled sourly of booze. His Ray-Bans fell off the perch on his head and clunked to the concrete floor.

She stepped away from him. "What are you doing in here? This is the girls' bathroom."

"So?" Ian gave her a bad-boy smile. He slurred his words a little. "I saw you and I thought I'd come in for that kiss."

"Did you *follow* me to the quarry?"

"*Someone* sure thinks she's important," Ian teased. "For your information, I love to cliff-dive. I had no idea you were going to be here, too. Who's that guy you're with? He looks like a wuss."

"He's not a wuss!" Ali turned to face the sink again, pumping the soap into her hands.

"He doesn't look like your type at all." Ian came up behind her and touched her shoulders. "So? How about that kiss?"

Ali wriggled away and faced him. "I'm with someone now. The deal is off."

Ian raised an eyebrow. "So it's serious with you and Mr. Wuss, huh?"

"That's none of your business."

He pressed his palm against the wall, looking unconvinced. Suddenly, before Ali knew it, his lips were touching hers. Ali stood stock-still, shocked, letting the sensation of his mouth against hers wash over her. His lips were soft, and his movements were confident. And then a second emotion crashed in her head: She was kissing someone even though she had a boyfriend. She was no better than her mom.

"*Alison?*"

When Ali opened her eyes, her heart dropped to the floor. Standing in the hall, peering through the propped-open door, was Nick. His mouth hung open. His eyes blazed. He glanced from Ian to Ali, then to Ian's hand, which was firmly entwined in hers.

Ali pulled away. "Nick!"

Nick glared. His head shook ever-so-slightly, and he took a big step back.

Ali glanced helplessly from him to Ian, who was now standing against the wall, his arms crossed over his chest, a smirk on his face. "This wasn't . . . I didn't . . . It wasn't anything."

Nick blinked at her. "I know what I saw." He looked at Ian. "What the hell, man? She's my girlfriend."

Ian smiled smugly, then drew himself up to full height. He was at least four inches taller than Nick. "She wasn't trying to stop me."

Nick's eyes blazed. He stepped toward Ian, his arms outstretched. "Please!" Ali screamed, inserting herself between them. And then Nick twisted, hurling the empty bottle of sparkling cider onto the ground. It shattered into pieces, the glass flying everywhere. Ali shrieked. Ian held up his arms to protect his face.

Nick stared at Ali, shaking his head slowly. "Have a nice life, Alison." He started to turn away.

Ali caught his arm. "W-what are you talking about?"

"What do you mean?" He let out an incredulous half laugh. "It's *over*. We're done."

"No!" Ali cried, reaching for him. "I'm sorry! Please!"

But Nick had already broken away from her. He headed across the parking lot. She followed him, calling his name, but he just kept going, his shoulders tense, his gaze staring straight ahead.

"Nick!" Ali screamed. "Please let me explain!" But even as she said it, despair filled her. *How* would she explain this? *I promised him a kiss if he kissed my best friend? And, oh yeah, he's cheating on his girlfriend, my best friend's sister, something I knew about all along?* Any way you sliced it, she sounded like a heartless bitch.

Nick started to run. Ali scampered after him, alarmed at the blind, careless way he was heading toward the cliff's edge. Something about his movements seemed dangerous and irrational. It was clear Nick's heart was broken. But what was he going to *do*?

He was now just a few feet from the cliff. Ali sprinted for him, reaching out and touching his T-shirt with the tips of her fingers. "Wait!" she pleaded.

But instead of stopping at the edge and looking over at the water, he kept going. One second he was on firm ground, the next he was suspended in midair, and the next he was just . . . *gone*.

27

NASTINESS HEALS ALL WOUNDS

Sunday afternoon, Ali lay on her bed, listening to the sound of the jackhammers in the backyard. Every time she considered getting up and doing something, her limbs wouldn't move. She couldn't imagine taking a shower. She couldn't imagine brushing her teeth. All she wanted was to look at the artifacts of her short courtship with Nick. The ticket stub from riding the merry-go-round. A receipt from the paintball place. It was barely anything.

She flopped back down on the pillow, only wanting to sleep. The last time she'd felt like this was when her parents had first sent her to the Radley. She'd remained in her room, shocked and mute and horrified. *What just happened?* she'd thought over and over again. Her parents had let her bring a family album, and she'd turned the gummy, crackling pages so many times that the binding wore out. Nurses had tried to encourage her to join in group activities like singing, and music or art classes. A therapist had sat on the side of her bed and tried to get her to talk, to move—*anything*—but she'd felt like there was a huge shovel hovering above her, pouring sand on her until only her eyes could be seen from above.

Her phone beeped, and she pounced on it, but it was just a text from Spencer: *We're getting together at my house. Please come over!*

Out the window, Spencer, Aria, Emily, and Hanna sat in bathing suits on Spencer's patio. She flopped back down on the pillow, feeling tears prick her eyes. They'd take one look at her and know. Emily had probably told the others that Ali was seeing someone older; maybe they'd ask if he was why her eyes were so red. And how could she fake it?

They'd see the weakness in her eyes. They'd see what sort of messed-up life she had. They would prey on her like she'd preyed on them. That was what best friends did, wasn't it? They ate each other alive. They would give Ali a taste of her own medicine.

She scrolled through her texts, making sure she hadn't missed any from Nick, but she hadn't. What was he doing right now? Eating lunch, happily going on with his life? Would he *ever* take her back?

And even worse than that, she'd told him about her sister, something she'd sworn to keep a secret forever. Now, she felt naked, exposed.

Her phone pinged again. *You coming?* Spencer asked. *I see the light on in your bedroom.*

"God," Ali said through her teeth, tossing the phone toward the closet. It hit the wall hard, knocking off a photograph of Ali and her friends on a boat in Newport Harbor. After a moment, Ali slid off her bed, slithered toward her phone, and composed a text to Spencer.

Not feeling up to it.

Another text arrived immediately. *Why not? Are you sick? Can we help?*

Ali shut her eyes and didn't answer. The last thing she wanted was their pity.

Another *ping*. *We're going to come over*, Spencer wrote. *Whatever you need, we can help.*

"No!" Ali screamed, but she already knew it was too late. And when she stood, Spencer, Aria, Hanna, and Emily had already left Spencer's patio and were heading for the side yard. In seconds, they would be here.

Suddenly, her arms and legs could move again. She slipped on a pair of flip-flops, pulled her hair in a ponytail, and barreled down the stairs. She almost crashed into the console table in the hall as she wheeled toward the garage, but she had to get out of here—fast.

Mrs. DiLaurentis, who had her head in the fridge, looked up as she passed. "Ali? Are you okay?"

"Fine," Ali snapped, reaching for the handle to the sliding-glass door.

"Can we talk?" Bottles of salad dressing rattled as the fridge door slammed shut.

"I'm busy," Ali barked.

Outside, the sun seemed almost alien, way too bright. A lawn mower buzzed in the distance, and bees flitted around the newly sprung daffodils. Ali's nose twitched with the scent of something close and sour, and after a moment, she realized it was herself. She hadn't taken off the shirt she'd worn on her date with Nick yesterday.

She took a step off the patio, then paused. The trees at the edge of the property whispered and hissed. Ali froze. It felt like someone was watching. She looked back and forth, almost expecting to see a pair of eyes gazing out from the woods. A shiver darted up her back.

"Ali?"

She jumped, jerking her hand to the side and hitting it hard against the bricks. Standing at the edge of the yard were Spencer and the others, all of them looking sheepish and worried.

Spencer took a small step forward. "Are you sick? You *look* sick."

"I could make you chicken soup," Hanna offered. "Or brownies. My dad always used to do that for me when *I* was sick."

"Maybe you should go back to bed?" Emily asked in a small voice.

Ali ran her hand through her greasy hair and wished she'd changed her shirt. "I'm fine, just a little bug," she said, sighing. "I suppose I could tan for a while."

"Oh." Spencer pushed a lock of hair behind her ear. "Well, okay. Let's go."

They headed back to Spencer's yard. Spencer started chattering about a party next week that they were all invited to, and Hanna suggested they all go shopping for dresses after school on Monday. But with every step they took, Ali could feel their concern. That familiar thick, goopy nastiness filled her, and suddenly she wanted to shake something hard. She wanted everyone to feel as horrible as she did.

Aria glanced over her shoulder, giving Ali a worried look, and Ali felt a fire burn inside of her. She grabbed Aria's arm. "Do you want to talk about anything?" she whispered in a fake concerned tone.

Aria paled and stared straight ahead. "No. I'm fine."

Ali clucked her tongue. "It's not good to hold things in, Aria—I've seen it on *Dr. Phil* all the time. You need to vent about this. Get it out. Otherwise you'll be, like, sexually repressed or something when you get older."

Aria squirmed. "Really?"

Ali laid her hand on her shoulder. "Yep. So, tell Dr. Ali what you're going to do."

Aria kicked at a clump of cut grass that the mowing service had forgotten to bag. "I can't do anything about it," she whispered.

"Do you think they're, like, dating?" Ali's voice rose with a mix of horror and excitement. "She was so *young!*"

Aria shoved her hands in her pockets and just shrugged. But her eyes were wet, as though she was about to cry. Ali turned away. At least *she* wasn't crying right now. At least her mom was having an affair with someone her own age.

Hanna looked over her shoulder and frowned at Aria's injured expression. "What are you guys talking about back there?" She lagged behind so that Ali and Aria could catch up. "Is everything okay?"

"Of course," Aria said quickly.

"Everything's great," Ali answered. "Right, Aria?"

Aria flinched. She shot Ali a desperate, please-don't-say-anything look back. Hanna shifted, looking conflicted. Emily and Spencer stopped, too, peering curiously at them from next to the raspberry bushes.

"And everything is great with you, right, Hanna?" Ali asked. "Well, except for Sean."

Hanna twisted her mouth. The others looked at her curiously. "Hanna caught her new BFF, Josie, making out with Sean at my party the other night," Ali explained.

The girls gasped. "Oh, Hanna, that's awful!" Emily cried, placing a hand on Hanna's shoulder.

"Why didn't you say anything?" Aria asked.

Hanna shrugged. "It seemed stupid to talk about it. Sean's not for me, anyway. I'm over it."

Ali heard herself snicker. "That's for sure, Han. You definitely have your own way of getting things *out of your system*."

Hanna's head snapped up. The look on her face was one of both horror and betrayal. *What are you* doing? her expression said. Ali didn't meet her gaze. She'd meant it when she'd promised Hanna she wouldn't tell about the bingeing. But that was then. Dancing around it now felt almost fun. Her heartbreak was way worse than Hanna's. And Ali wasn't moronic enough to think bingeing was the way to deal with it.

They'd reached the pool area by then. Spencer plopped down on one of the chaise lounges and crossed her legs. The other girls sat, too, though they all seemed shaken. Aria stared blankly at the water. Hanna nervously plunged her hand into the bowl of popcorn on the table. Ali, on the other hand, felt a vaguely nuclear glow inside her. Her nastiness felt like a runaway train she couldn't stop if she tried. But she didn't exactly want to. Every time her friends squirmed, she felt like it restored just a teensy bit of her life source.

Emily picked up a *People* magazine and opened it randomly to a page. Ali glanced at the spread. On the left-hand side was a picture of a bronzed, bikini-clad girl advertising beer.

Ali nudged her. "I wonder if *she* likes tree houses."

The magazine fell from Emily's hands, and the look on her face was that of a trapped, tortured animal. Emily opened her mouth, but no sound came out.

Hanna leaned forward. "What does *that* mean?"

Ali smiled and laid her hands in her lap. "Oh, just an inside joke between me and Em. It's a funny one, too, right, Em?"

Emily just blinked, not saying yes or no. Ali tried hard not to stare at her pink lips or think about the way the kiss had felt. She also tried to ignore the little wiggle of remorse she felt inside.

The other girls stared at Emily, then Ali. All of them looked like they wanted to say something, but it seemed like none of them knew what.

Then, as if on cue, the screen door slid open, and Melissa Hastings, dressed in a green string-bikini top and a printed sarong, stuck her head out. "Oh," she said sullenly when she saw the girls. "I didn't know the patio was being used."

"*Hi*, Melissa!" Ali said emphatically, jumping to her feet. "How are you?"

Melissa paused and examined Ali, her lips twitching. "I'm fine."

Ali tapped Spencer's arm. "I think Spencer has something to tell you—a big surprise. What do you say, Spence?"

Spencer's mouth dropped open. She shook her head fast. "No, I don't."

Melissa placed her hands on her hips. "What is it, Spence?"

"*Nothing.*"

Melissa turned back to Ali, but Ali just gave Melissa a closed-mouth smile. *It's not my story to tell*, her look said. Finally, Melissa sighed and turned back into the house. The sliding door swished closed.

Spencer whirled around and glared at Ali. "What are you *doing*?"

"What are *you* doing?" Ali shot back.

Aria blinked. "What is going *on* with everyone?"

Ali glanced at her. "I don't know, Aria. What *is* going on?"

There was another painful silence. The birds tweeted obliviously in the trees. Then Spencer looked at her phone. "I have to go, okay? I just realized." She stood up and strode into the house without even saying good-bye.

The other girls watched the sliding door, perhaps thinking Spencer was going to come back. When she didn't, Aria stood up. "That reminds me, I need to get going."

"Me, too," Hanna said quickly.

Emily gave Ali a long, conflicted look, then stood as well. They peeled away and mounted their bikes or headed toward the woods. Ali let out a long, contented sigh. It had been a good idea to come out here after all. In fact, she felt so much stronger—there was no need to go back to bed anymore.

And best of all, she hadn't thought of Nick once.

28

DEAR ALI, BE MINE

After school the following day, Ali leaned toward the front window of Cassie's Jeep as Cassie made a screeching turn into her neighborhood. Her neighbor on the corner was out on his riding mower, making perfect stripes on the lawn. The little kids across the street were playing basketball at the lowered hoop. And at Mona Vanderwaal's house, Mona, Phi, and Chassey were strutting up and down the driveway in some sort of ugly-girl fashion show. Ali wrinkled her nose.

As Cassie rolled toward Ali's house, she turned to her and smiled. "I'm glad you took me up on the ride today. Was your brother busy?"

Ali shrugged. "Jason and I aren't exactly speaking right now."

Cassie's lip curled into a smile. "Want me to run interference?"

Ali pretended to laugh, not wanting to get into exactly

why they were fighting. She hadn't said a word to Jason since he'd told her that he thought it was a good idea the family was bringing her twin home, and it just seemed easier not to accept rides from him, too.

Cassie then turned and peered at the curb in front of Ali's house. "Do you have plans?"

Ali followed her gaze. Emily was standing at Ali's mailbox, putting something inside. But when she saw Ali, she quickly closed the box and stepped away from it as though it were on fire.

"Not that I was aware of," Ali murmured, a little annoyed at Emily's presence. Before, when Em showed up unannounced, it was welcome. But now, after everything that had happened, it felt sort of . . . intrusive. Clingy.

Cassie pulled to the curb. Emily stood with her arms at her sides, a timid smile on her face. She made no move to approach Cassie's Jeep, perhaps waiting for Ali's permission or introduction. Ali just turned to Cassie and gave her a huge hug. "This was so much fun," she said. Then she eyed Cassie's pack of Marlboro Lights. "Can I have one more for the road?"

Cassie raised her eyebrows. "Naughty girl, smoking on your own property! What if your parents see?"

"I don't care," Ali said.

Cassie lit the cigarette for Ali, and Ali took a big puff, trying her hardest not to cough. Then Cassie gave her a spritz of Dior perfume and took off. Ali stood with her back to Emily as Cassie turned the corner out of the development. Then, finally, she turned back to her mailbox.

"H-hey," Emily blurted. "I'm sorry."

Ali sank into her hip. "Sorry for what?"

"Interrupting. It seemed like you and Cassie were having fun."

"Uh-huh." Ali flicked the ash. "She's awesome."

Emily's gaze fell to the cigarette. "You guys *smoke*?"

Ali shrugged. "So?" She exhaled.

Emily swished the smoke away, then looked embarrassed by the gesture. "I just thought . . . I mean . . ."

Ali tapped the mailbox. It made a hollow, metal sound. "So were you stealing my mail, Em?"

Emily's mouth fell open. "No! Absolutely not! Actually, I–"

"Because that's a federal crime, you know," Ali interrupted. "You know what else is a federal crime in some states? Kissing people in tree houses."

Emily's eyes widened. She took a small step back.

Ali breathed out. "I'm *kidding*."

"Oh." Emily licked her lips. "I knew that."

She turned back to the mailbox, running her fingers over the plastic red flag. A plaintive look settled over her features, and she took a deep breath as if she was about to say something important. All of a sudden, Ali had a horrible thought: What if Emily wanted to *talk* about things? What if she wanted to, like, get all touchy-feely–*literally*?

"You know what would be awesome?" Ali cut her off

before she could speak. She pointed to the girls down the street. "If you told Mona to stop catwalking. She's giving fashion a bad name."

Emily frowned, then gazed at the girls, too. *"Now?"*

"Uh-huh."

A pained look crossed Emily's face. "Ali, I really don't want to."

Ali lowered her chin, anger at Emily's disobedience curling through her veins. *"Oh, Mona!"* she called, sotto voce. *"Guess what Emily likes to do in trees?"*

Emily's eyelashes fluttered. She opened her mouth, but no sounds came out. "Okay," she squeaked, ducking her head and trudging down the sidewalk.

Ali trailed behind her, watching as Emily intercepted the girls. At first, Chassey's, Phi's, and Mona's eyes lit up when they saw Emily coming. They closed in around her in the same way the alpacas at the garden center Ali's mom always dragged her to flocked around people at the fence. Even though Ali was standing some distance away, she could see the precise moment when Emily delivered the blow. Mona's mouth clamped shut. Phi puffed out her cheeks. The corners of Chassey's mouth turned down. She almost looked like she was going to cry.

Emily stormed back to Ali. "Well, I don't think they're going to be catwalking anymore."

"Thank *God*," Ali said. "They were totally bringing down the whole neighborhood, don't you think? Good work, Em."

Emily glanced up at her, her chin wobbling. "How's it going between you and that guy?"

"What guy?"

"You know. The one you told me about. In the tree house. The boy you like."

Ali pressed her lips together. She'd refrained from sending Nick too many begging texts because she didn't want to sound desperate, hoping that he'd come to his senses instead. Only, he hadn't. And when she tried to send him an IM last night, he blocked her from his list.

"Things are going great," she said, smiling broadly.

Emily's throat bobbed. Her gaze darted to the mailbox again. She lunged for it and opened the little door, the metal squeaking. Ali put a hand on her arm. "What are you doing?"

Emily blinked. "I . . ."

"Tampering with mail is a federal offense, Em," Ali said in a saccharine voice.

Emily nodded, then wheeled around and walk-jogged to her tipped-over bike and threw her leg over the bar. "I should go." Her gaze didn't leave the mailbox, which she hadn't closed properly. A single letter sat inside. "I'll see you later, Ali."

Ali watched her pedal down the street, then turned toward the mailbox. Her fingers curled around the long, thin envelope. It had Ali's name on the front in Emily's handwriting. She waited until Emily's reddish-gold hair disappeared around the corner, then tore it open. It was all one paragraph, the writing on both sides of the page.

Emily's print seemed more harried than usual, as if she had written it quickly, before she lost her nerve.

Dear Ali,
I need to get something off my chest. I know I told you that
the kiss we shared in the tree house was a joke. But it really
wasn't. I meant it for you and only you.

Ali lowered the letter to her waist for a moment, a strange taste in her mouth. She had a weird feeling Emily might have wanted her to read this in front of her so she could explain it, line by line.

She scanned the rest of the letter.

I'm so thrilled that we're friends. I love staring at the back
of your head in class, I love how you chew gum when-
ever we're talking on the phone together, and I love that
when you jiggle your Skechers during class when Mrs.
Hat starts talking about famous American court cases, I
know you're totally bored. I don't want anything to come
between us, but I don't think it will. You felt something,
too, didn't you? I could tell.

Ali shut her eyes and took a few deep breaths. When she opened them one more time, she read the rest.

. . . and I've done a lot of thinking about why I kissed you
the other day. I realized: It wasn't a joke, Ali. I think I

love you. I can understand if you never want to speak to
me again, but I just had to tell you.
—Em

When she finished, she folded the letter in half and pressed it deep into her pocket. But then, because that felt too intimate, she pulled it out and shoved it into the bottom of her bag, under her math book. She pulled out her phone, ready to compose a text to Emily saying something like, *I found your letter, weirdo. Ha ha, funny joke.* Except maybe it would be better just to not acknowledge it at all.

She threw back her shoulders and walked into the house. As soon as she stepped through the foyer, the hair on her neck rose. Something felt different. The knick-knacks on the table in the hall were the same. There were two caps and gowns hanging on the banister, a blue one that was Jason's, and a white one for her own seventh-grade graduation. Her gaze fell to a flowered suitcase on the ground. It was *her* suitcase—from back when she was Courtney.

She smelled freshly brewed coffee and baked cinnamon rolls, the thing her mom always made for her when she was little and needed cheering up. It was what she would make for *her*, not her sister. Her sister, in fact, used to complain that cinnamon rolls made her teeth hurt.

All at once, Ali knew what had happened. But this *couldn't* be happening. This wasn't supposed to happen until tomorrow. And then she thought about Mona and the others hanging out in the driveway, Emily lurking near the mailbox. When had she gotten here? Had anyone seen?

Her first instinct was to run up to her bedroom and never come out, but then her mother stuck her head around the corner and smiled. "Ali?" she said gently. "Your sister's home."

29

SHE'S BA-ACK

Mrs. DiLaurentis set a pan of zucchini lasagna on the table. "Careful, it's hot," she warned, and then proceeded to pour lemonade into everyone's glasses. "It's fresh-squeezed," she crowed. "It tastes better that way, don't you think?"

It was a few hours later, and the family was sitting in the dining room, which was usually used only for Thanksgiving and Christmas. Each seat had a gold place-mat, and they were drinking out of the good crystal goblets. Mrs. DiLaurentis had even lit candles, and the light made eerie shapes against their faces. And there they all sat: Mr. and Mrs. DiLaurentis at the heads of the table, then Jason, then Ali . . . and then the third daughter. The twin. "Courtney."

"So dig in," Mrs. DiLaurentis announced as she took the oven mitts off. "The lasagna's nothing fancy, but the ingredients are all fresh."

"It looks superb," Mr. DiLaurentis said, reaching for his fork.

"Absolutely," Jason agreed, taking a hearty sip of lemonade.

Ali shot him a look, but Jason didn't glance her way. Jason had actually set the table today. And offered to get the bread out of the oven. *And* volunteered to bring her sister's stuff upstairs, to which "Courtney" had smiled and said that would be great. All traces of Elliot Smith were gone.

Then Ali turned to Courtney. Her sister was politely waiting as their father spooned a rectangle of lasagna onto her plate. Her parents had picked her up while Ali and Jason were at school, saying today worked better for Mr. DiLaurentis's work schedule. She'd arrived home just before the buses pulled out of the Rosewood Day parking lot, which meant it was fairly unlikely that anyone Ali's age had seen her. Not that it made her feel much better.

Courtney's hair, which was just about the same length as Ali's, was swept back from her face with little bobby pins that had tiny stars on the ends. She wore a striped halter with a ruffled neck that Ali had never seen before, one neither from her closet now nor her packed things from a year ago, and black skinny jeans. Away from the harsh light of the hospital, her sister's skin had an extra healthy glow, as if she'd just gone on a hike. And she seemed to be *smiling* a lot, which set Ali on edge. She'd even smiled at Ali when she'd walked in the door, stepping forward and giving her a huge hug and saying how *good* it was to see her. But when her lips were close to Ali's ear, she'd whispered it again: *Say your good-byes.*

"Thank you so much," Courtney said now, in a gracious tone. "This is all *so* nice of you." She raised a modern-day Polaroid camera to her eyes and took a picture of her mother. "Say cheese!"

"Cheese!" Mrs. DiLaurentis said, smiling. The camera made a *whirr* sound, and a photo spit out. At first, Ali had thought it was *her* Polaroid camera, but Mrs. DiLaurentis had quickly said that Courtney had noticed Ali's in the kitchen and had seemed interested in it, so they'd gotten her one today, too.

Ali cleared her throat. "Funny you're interested in photography, Courtney. That's my favorite hobby, too."

Courtney blinked innocently. "Don't worry, sis. I'm not going to pretend I'm you."

She tilted her chin down and winked. Ali curled her toes inside her shoes. What if that was *exactly* what her sister had planned?

Mrs. DiLaurentis took a square of lasagna. "Lots of people can like photography, girls."

Courtney smiled bashfully, then reached for the Parmesan, which was in a little silver bowl Ali had never seen—usually, they just used the shaker.

"Oh, I'll do that for you," Mr. DiLaurentis said, spooning a bit of cheese onto Courtney's lasagna. As if she was an invalid and couldn't do it herself.

"So we had a very nice chat with the doctors today," Mrs. DiLaurentis said between bites, staring at Ali as she spoke. "Courtney was a model patient this past year at the Preserve. She made a lot of friends, really participated in the group programs, did great at her studies. . . ." She clapped a hand on Courtney's shoulder.

"They even let you play on an intramural field hockey team that met close by, didn't they, honey?" Mr. DiLaurentis piped up, smiling at his daughter.

Ali sat up straighter. "You left the grounds for *whole* practices?"

Courtney offered her a grin that probably looked genuine to everyone else but to Ali looked absolutely sinister. "Yes. Isn't that great?"

"Did you go anywhere else?" Ali blurted.

Her sister lowered her chin. "Why? Did you think you *saw* me somewhere?"

Ali flinched. So her fears weren't unfounded. Her sister *had* been watching.

But then Courtney sniffed and gave her parents a reassuring head-shake. "Please. The supervisors were on my butt the whole time. I played intramurals, went to a local ice cream parlor a couple of times, and that's it."

"But you don't like ice cream," Ali pointed out, hoping to catch her sister in a lie.

Courtney speared a piece of zucchini with her fork. "You don't know everything about me."

There was a long pause. It felt like the temperature in

the room had dropped about twenty degrees. Jason reached for more bread, chewing obliviously. Mr. DiLaurentis sipped his wine.

"Ali?" Mrs. DiLaurentis's voice broke the silence. "Aren't you hungry?"

Ali stared down at the lasagna, then felt her sister's gaze on her, as sizzling as a heat lamp. The last thing she could think of was eating right now, but if she didn't, her sister might sense just how anxious she was feeling. She cut a tiny square, her fingers shaking, and pushed it into her mouth. It tasted like sawdust. Courtney held up the camera again, pointing it to Ali as she might a barrel of a gun. Ali threw a hand in front of her face and turned away, but Courtney snapped a shot anyway.

Mrs. DiLaurentis wiped her mouth. "On the drive home, we all were talking. We were thinking that perhaps we would introduce Courtney to a few people around Rosewood, see how that goes."

The bite Ali had just swallowed rose back up her throat. "Like *who*?"

"Well, the neighbors, for starters." Mrs. DiLaurentis stabbed a tomato from the salad. "I mean, we can't keep her cooped up like we did before—Courtney said that might have been part of the problem."

"Definitely," Courtney said, nodding emphatically.

"Letting her *out* is part of the problem," Ali squeaked. She peeked at her sister. Courtney's head was lowered, but she was trying to hide a smile.

"We were just thinking people on the block," Mrs. DiLaurentis went on, ignoring her. "We think it would be a little much to bring Courtney to, say, graduation, but letting a few people know might not be a bad thing."

"So you're going to tell the Hastingses?" Ali practically shrieked. There was no way Spencer could know about this. Absolutely. No. Way.

"Well, naturally." Mrs. DiLaurentis dabbed at her mouth with her cloth napkin. "But we thought you might like to tell Spencer yourself, Ali. Maybe at your sleep-over." She turned to Courtney. "Your sister is having an end-of-seventh-grade sleepover with her friends on Thursday night."

Ali gaped at her family. They were all smiling at her like they'd been brainwashed. "Telling Spencer at the sleepover means, basically, that I'm telling *all* my friends. And personally, I don't want to tell any of them. Courtney isn't really a family member I'm proud of having."

"Alison!" Mr. DiLaurentis lowered his fork. "Your sister is sitting right here."

All eyes darted to Courtney, who was hiding yet another smile. She straightened up and folded her hands in her lap. "It's okay, really. I was ready for some . . . animosity. Honest. I can't imagine what this is like for Ali to have me back." Her voice cracked, and she turned to Ali and gave her a big, doe-eyed, starving-puppy stare. "I know it's going to take some time to heal, but I really, *really* hope we can. You know, I used to be really angry, but now I understand that that anger came from jealousy. You were totally right for wanting me in the hospital, Ali. You saved my life."

Ali's mouth fell open, but no words came out. There were actual tears in her sister's eyes. Yet again, to everyone else, she probably seemed dead sincere, but to Ali, her words were chilling. Threatening.

"Courtney!" Mrs. DiLaurentis blurted, clasping her hands at her breastbone. "That is so wonderful of you to say."

Mrs. DiLaurentis looked at Ali encouragingly, but Ali stared down at the ridges on her plate. She could feel her sister's laughing eyes upon her. All at once, she felt suffocated.

"I'm done," she blurted, carrying her plate into the kitchen and nearly breaking it as she banged it against the garbage can to dispose of her uneaten piece of lasagna. And then she ran upstairs and slammed her bedroom door hard, taking heaving breaths.

This couldn't be happening. And yet, it *was* . . . and it was worse than she'd thought.

Silverware clinked downstairs. Voices murmured. That damn camera whirred again, regurgitating more pictures. Ali looked around her bedroom, feeling her heart thud in her chest. Her sister had a plan, pure and simple. Soon enough, her sister was going to find a way to expose exactly what she'd done. Maybe she had proof, somehow. Maybe she'd make up the proof. And maybe, just maybe, their parents would believe her. After all, it *was* the truth.

Ali shifted onto the bed, laying her head on the pillow. Something sharp poked into her skull, and she shot back up. There, on the pillowcase, lay a tiny silver bobby pin. Ali picked it up and held it in her palm. There was a sparkly star on the very tip. She knew just whose it was.

She stood up, glancing around the rest of the room for signs of drawers that had been rifled through, closet doors that had been opened. Everything looked in its place. But still, a feeling of terror settled over her like a down-filled duvet. The dropped bobby pin felt like an omen. Her sister was going to take her life back—starting with her room—one dropped bobby pin at a time.

30

THE DOPPELGANGER

The following day after school, Ali stood in front of a long table in the lobby and watched as kids gave their names to Mrs. Ulster, the art teacher who was also in charge of the seventh-grade graduation. "Yes, of course, Andrew," Mrs. Ulster said, searching through a box on the floor and unveiling a long white graduation gown and matching cap for Andrew Campbell, one of the class nerds. His cap had a special medal on it because he'd gotten all A's that year. So did Spencer's, Ali guessed.

"Thanks," Andrew gathered the gown and beret in his arms. When he passed Ali, he smiled hopefully, like they were friends. She snorted and turned away.

Ali had picked up her gown the other day, so it was already at home, but she'd just retrieved her seat assignment and the two tickets each family was allowed for the event. All around her, kids were chattering excitedly about the ceremony that night. Rebecca Culpepper stated she was going to wear high-heeled sandals under her gown. Jordyn Wellsley announced he was going to break-dance his way to the podium. Chassey Bledsoe asked who their speaker was going to be, but Ali just rolled her eyes as she passed. "We don't have a speaker, loser," she teased. "That's only for seniors."

Chassey looked cowed, like she was supposed to have known that. But as Ali walked toward the parking lot, she felt a swirl of anger. She'd been excited to walk in graduation all year, and now that it was here, now that her sister was home, it all felt so tarnished. Today had been the first full day that Courtney was home, and Ali hadn't been able to sit still through her classes, fearful that her sister might burst into her classroom any minute, blurting out the truth.

A Jeep honked in the parking lot, and Ali looked up and waved. Cassie turned the ignition when Ali climbed in and pulled toward the exit. As they wound through the parking lots, she raised her eyes and pointed with her chin toward a couple climbing the hill toward the senior lot, dark gowns swinging from their hands. "I can't believe he hasn't broken up with her yet."

Ali craned her neck. It was Ian and Melissa. They held hands, and when they approached Ian's SUV, he grabbed Melissa around the waist and gave her a big kiss on the neck, to which she squealed and twisted away.

"I can't believe it, either," she mumbled, feeling a surprising stab of jealousy. It wasn't fair that Ian's relationship was all well and good after he'd screwed up hers. She wanted him to pay for it—and she thought she knew how. She pulled out her cell phone and hunted for Ian's number. *Want that kiss?* she typed in a text. *Meet me Thursday night. My yard. Nine PM sharp.*

There was a *ping* within thirty seconds. *You got it,* Ian wrote back. Ali tried to muster up a flare of excitement—after all, kissing a hot boy was kissing a hot boy. But she felt nothing.

At Ali's curb, Cassie leaned on the steering wheel. "Do you mind if I come in for a sec? I really, *really* have to pee."

"No!" Ali practically shouted.

Cassie drew back, giving Ali a strange look. "Um, we're having problems with the septic system," Ali blurted, realizing how insane she'd just sounded. "It really smells." She looked hard at the house. Had a curtain just fluttered? Could Cassie *tell* her twin was in there, just by looking at the place?

Cassie made a sympathetic face, then said goodbye. Ali shot out of the car and darted toward the door, relieved when Cassie pulled away from the curb. But just as she was twisting the knob, she heard voices inside.

"I didn't mean anything by it," her sister wailed.

"You should know better!" her mother answered sternly.

Ali's skin prickled. What had happened? And then, suddenly, she heard different voices, this time from the backyard. "Why would she be in trouble?" someone whispered. "She didn't do anything wrong."

Ali drew away from the door. Was that . . . *Emily?*

"Not that *we* know of," another familiar voice said. Ali almost choked on her gum. *Spencer.*

Her mind swirled. She hadn't invited them over. What were they *doing* here? Had her sister invited them? Or—worse—her *mother*, wanting Ali to break the news?

They could *not* know. If they did, what if they slowly figured out the rest of it—that Ali wasn't who she said she was? Maybe they'd always secretly wondered about Ali abruptly taking them on as friends. Dropping Naomi and Riley without explanation. That time Ali had gotten lost in Rosewood Day at the beginning of sixth grade. Maybe it was all cataloged in their brains, little niggling puzzle pieces that didn't quite make up a whole picture. With the introduction of a twin, it would. And if her parents figured out, they'd send her to the Preserve to punish her.

She stood on the front porch, terrified to go around the side and face the music. Suddenly, there was a loud *slam.* Her mother's voice keened out from the patio. "I just want to make sure you have the dimensions right," she yelled toward the workers in the back.

Ali stepped off the porch and tiptoed into the side yard just as her mother barreled across the back toward the gazebo workers, who were sitting around, seemingly doing nothing. "I'm not paying you to loaf," Mrs.

DiLaurentis snapped, hands on hips. "Can't this get done any faster?"

One of the workers raised one shoulder. "We're waiting for the concrete to dry."

"When is this hole going to be filled?" Ali's mother demanded. "Tomorrow?"

The same worker shook his head, his floppy hair bouncing. "Friday. That's the earliest we could get the truck."

Mrs. DiLaurentis rolled her eyes and continued to chastise them. Ali took another step closer, her friends coming into view. They were *all* there, sitting on the back patio, looking nonplussed. Blessedly, Courtney wasn't with them. So maybe they didn't know.

She took a deep breath and climbed up the patio stairs. "Uh . . . hi?" she said.

Spencer stood up. A big, nervous smile spread across Emily's face. Aria stared at Ali impassively, and Hanna squirmed in her seat. They looked guilty, and Ali's fears rushed to the surface once more.

"What did she bust you for?" Spencer demanded.

Ali cocked her head, not sure if she should answer.

"Are you getting in trouble without us?" Aria went on, her light, easy tone of voice forced. "And why did you change? That halter you had on was so cute."

Ali blinked hard. *Halter.* Her sister had worn a halter the day before. Perhaps she'd put it on this morning, too, as it was probably the cutest thing she owned.

Her knees went weak. They *had* seen her twin . . .
maybe even talked to them, but it wasn't because of their
mother. Where had she been? In the house? *Outside?*

But then it hit Ali. She bet she knew exactly where
they'd seen her sister. Ali's *room.*

That bitch, she thought, fury rising in her body like
mercury inside a thermometer. How *dare* she! Was this
phase one of her master plan? Was she trying to pass herself off as Ali and try to switch back? What was even worse
was that her friends had believed that "Courtney" was Ali.
If her sister could convince them, she could convince
anyone.

Emily cleared her throat, bringing Ali back to herself.
"Do you want us to . . . *go?*"

Ali shook her head quickly, realizing she had no idea
what sorts of expressions had just crossed her face. "Of
course I don't want you to go," she mustered, trying to
regain control. "My mom was mad at me because I . . . I
threw my hockey clothes in with her delicates again." She
rolled her eyes. "But don't worry, girls—I'm not grounded
or anything. Our sleepover extravaganza can proceed as
planned!"

The girls looked relieved, though something still seemed
to hang over them. For a moment, Ali worried if they were
looking at her and realizing there was something *different*
about her, something they hadn't seen in the girl in the
striped halter just moments ago. But then Spencer added
that she had exciting news: They could have their sleepover

in the Hastingses' backyard barn after all. Unexpectedly, Melissa was going to Prague Thursday night after graduation, so they would have the place to themselves.

"Sweet," Ali said loudly, hoping that Courtney, wherever she was, heard. She wasn't going to let her sister get in the way of her fun. Let her *try* to switch. It was never going to happen.

Suddenly, she noticed a flash of blue across the Hastingses' yard. Melissa was on her way to the barn, her gown swinging from a hanger in her hand. She'd already slung the school's valedictorian mantle over her shoulders. *Show-off.*

Suddenly, Ali had to make everyone see how powerful she was, how crushing she could be. She wasn't sure if it was for her friends' benefit, exactly . . . or for the girl watching from within the house.

Ali stood up. "Hey, Melissa!"

Melissa stopped and turned around. "Oh. Hey, guys."

"Excited to go to Prague?" Ali smiled sweetly. "Is *Ian* going?"

Spencer reached across the table and dug her nails into Ali's arm. *"Ali."*

"No," Melissa answered after a pause. "Ian's not."

"Oh!" Ali heard her own voice say. "Are you sure that's a good idea—leaving him alone? He might get another girlfriend!"

She gave Spencer a meaningful glance. "Alison. Stop it. *Now.*"

But Ali couldn't stop.

"Spencer?" Aria asked. "What's going on?"

"Nothing," Spencer said quickly.

Ali watched as the other girls exchanged an uncertain look. But none of them said anything. Then, Melissa adjusted the mantle around her neck and strode toward the barn. She glanced long and hard at the hole in Ali's yard but said nothing.

Spencer glared at Ali after Melissa was gone, but Ali didn't reply. She barely got through the rest of the visit, and when the girls left, she sprinted back into the house and made a beeline for her bedroom. Everything was in its place. Next she found her mother, who was standing at the sink, washing a few glasses.

"Did you let my friends in when I wasn't here?" she demanded.

Mrs. DiLaurentis wheeled around, looking guilty. "Honey, I thought you were home. But then I saw you pull up with your field hockey friend and realized my mistake."

Ali's body started to shake. "So they talked to her?"

"Well, yes. But then I grabbed her."

"Were they in my room?"

Mrs. DiLaurentis's gaze fell to her feet. "She's just curious. The therapist explained everything to us: She hasn't lived a normal life. We've deprived her of that. Think of yourself as a role model."

The words hurt: It was *her* they were really talking about, *her* they thought was still in the hospital, rotting away, becoming weirder and more feral by the day. "Where is she?" Ali said, her voice low and tense.

Mrs. DiLaurentis placed a warning hand on Ali's arm. "Honey, don't start a scene. I'm sure she didn't mean anything by it."

"Where. Is. She?" Ali's emotions felt like a kite whose string had gotten away from her. It was the same way she used to feel when her sister would push and push and push until she snapped. It was amazing how, after all this time, the feeling could just come back as urgent and fresh as the day she'd first felt it.

The dish towel went limp in Mrs. DiLaurentis's hands. "Look, we'll be more careful, okay? We'll keep her inside from now on, just until we're sure she's not backsliding. She'll be inside for graduation, your sleepover. Okay?"

"Do you promise?" Ali demanded. Mrs. DiLaurentis nodded almost fearfully.

But it wasn't enough. Ali turned and stormed up the steps, passing her bedroom once more. The guest room door was closed. She banged on it so hard that her knuckles ached. "Courtney?" she bellowed.

But the door didn't open. "Courtney!" Ali screeched.

"Alison, *please*," Mrs. DiLaurentis said, standing at the foot of the stairs.

"Open the door!" Ali screamed. The bedsprings inside the room squeaked. A drawer slid open, then closed. And then, distinctly, she heard a high-pitched giggle. It kind of sounded like a witch's cackle and sent a shiver down her spine.

"I know what you're doing!" Ali said, pressing her cheek against the door. "You can't get away with this!"

She heard footsteps, and the door flung open. Her sister was wearing the striped halter again, just as Ali feared. Her hair was in a high ponytail, her new Polaroid was on a strap around her neck, and she had a big smile on her face. She held Ali's gaze for so long that Ali began to feel nervous.

"Why not?" Courtney finally asked, her voice full of mirth. "*You* did."

31

THE ULTIMATE POWER

Thursday evening after graduation, a battered Subaru pulled up to Ali's front curb. Ali watched through the window as Aria spilled out from the backseat, pirouetted onto the lawn, and buried her face in the grass. "Delicious," Ali heard her murmur.

Mrs. DiLaurentis touched Ali's arm. "Aren't you going to go out there?"

Ali whipped around and looked at her mother. Her heart was pounding as though she'd run a zillion laps around the hockey field. Every sound from upstairs, where her sister had been kept during graduation, made her tense up. "Are you *sure* you'll keep her inside?" she asked, glancing toward the stairs.

A guilty look crossed her mother's face. It was clear she felt terrible for letting Ali's sister into her room to fool her friends, and she'd been trying for the past forty-eight hours to make it up to Ali. They'd ordered takeout from

Ali's favorite sushi place as a graduation dinner. She'd slipped Ali a pair of diamond stud earrings before the ceremony that afternoon, a graduation gift. But it didn't fix what had happened. Courtney had fooled her friends. Courtney had been *seen*.

What if there *had* been something different about Courtney, something telling that her friends had noticed? She imagined them going home Tuesday night and discussing it on a four-way phone call. *Her eyes looked a little different on the patio, don't you think?* Aria might have said. And then Hanna would have piped up with, *And Ali wouldn't wear a halter top like that.* And then Spencer: *You know, I've seen a light on in the guest room. And I've heard rumors over the years.*

But no. There hadn't been any rumors, had there? This had been a contained secret. Then, Ali thought of Jenna. What if she'd said something? Maybe just an innocent comment to Spencer once, something Spencer refused to believe. Or what about the man her mother had told? Maybe *he'd* said something. Her friends could have had an inkling all along.

What if they were slowly figuring it out? Everything, even the switch?

"You have nothing to worry about," Mrs. DiLaurentis said softly, breaking Ali from her thoughts. She pulled her bottom lip into her mouth. "Although honestly, honey, I wish you'd just *tell* them."

"*No,*" Ali almost shrieked.

"Why not? They'll understand. They won't care that

you kept this from them, if that's what you're worried about. People keep things from people all the time."

"Yeah, you know *that* all too well," Ali snapped.

Mrs. DiLaurentis flinched. Reflexively, she raised her hand to Ali, and Ali thought she was going to slap her again, but she only used it to push a strand of hair out of her eyes. "Let's not get into that again," she said in an even tone.

Ali gritted her teeth. Did her mother just expect her to forget everything? There was a man out there who was her real father—she was sure of it—someone her mother was keeping from her. She was determined to find out who it was. She'd considered telling Mr. DiLaurentis, but then she'd decided that it was more powerful to wait until she uncovered the man's identity.

When she turned back to the window, Emily was in the yard now, too, wearing a pair of baggy jeans and a nondescript blue T-shirt. She and Aria were joking around near Ali's flower bushes. And then Ali had another thought: If she didn't go out soon, her friends would ring the doorbell. Maybe they'd insist on coming in the house. What if Courtney appeared at the top of the stairs? What if the girls wanted to *go* upstairs, into Ali's room, and Courtney loomed in the doorway?

She nudged open the front door with her toe and flounced out to greet them. The hem of her field hockey skirt, which she'd worn to the team's end-of-the-year party this afternoon, fluttered in the breeze.

"You guys!" she crowed in the happiest voice she could muster.

Her friends looked up at her. For a moment, Ali was sure they knew everything. A split second later, though, they were all smiling as though nothing was amiss. Maybe they really *didn't* know something was amiss. Emily perked up visibly, the other day's transgressions seemingly forgotten—at least for now. Spencer and Hanna, who had just arrived in the yard, too, came toward them, and the girls convened in a group hug. But as Ali clung tightly to her friends, she glanced over her shoulder just in time to see a curtain on the second floor of her house flutter. It was the guest room. A figure stood at the window, staring at them.

"Your barn," she said to Spencer, breaking away and steering them through the hedges. She needed to get off this property, *fast*.

Blessedly, the girls followed behind her like good little sheep. But her sister's face haunted her as the five of them moaned about how long the school year had been. And when she heard someone calling "Hey, Alison! Hey, Spencer!" her stomach seized. It sounded, for a moment, like her sister's voice.

She turned around and saw Mona Vanderwaal and her band of geeks coming toward them. Part of her wanted to throw her arms around Mona in relief. Instead, she blurted, "Not it!"

"Not it," her friends said milliseconds after.

Mona rolled up on her scooter. Chassey Bledsoe and Phi Templeton followed behind, Chassey on a mountain bike, Phi on foot with her trusty, ridiculous yo-yo.

"You guys want to come over and watch *Fear Factor*?" Mona asked.

"Sorry," Ali simpered, dredging up the appropriate level of nastiness. "We're kind of busy."

Then she whipped around and trotted off. Her friends followed. When she rolled her eyes, they rolled theirs, too. *They don't know*, she thought, her heartbeat slowing down. *They don't suspect anything.* But then she peeked toward her house again. The light was still on in the guest room, and that face was still at the window. To Ali's horror, Hanna was squinting at the window, too.

Ali yanked her arm. "C'mon," she said.

They walked the line between Ali's backyard and Spencer's. A huge, garishly yellow bulldozer was parked at the back next to a cone-shaped pile of dirt. "I'm so happy the workers aren't here right now," Ali said loudly, making sure everyone's attention was on her—and not on the window.

Emily stiffened. "Are they saying stuff to you again?"

"Easy, there, Killer," Ali joked, and the girls giggled. She glanced over her shoulder once more. The light in the window was off now. The face was gone. But was her sister going to sit idly by in her room all night like a good little girl? It seemed impossible.

The barn was just ahead. Ali led the others toward it,

praying that her sister wasn't watching from the kitchen to see where they were going. What if their mother took her eyes off her? What if she got out?

Giggles sounded from inside the barn. "I said, *stop* it!" a voice squealed. It was definitely Melissa.

Spencer stopped short. "Oh God. What is *she* doing here?"

Ali looked at Spencer sharply. "I thought you said your sister was in Prague."

"I *did*." Spencer flung the door open to reveal Melissa and Ian lounging on the couch, several bottles of beer between them. Melissa shot up and adjusted her head-band. Ian's eyes canvassed the girls, his smile lazy and beguiling.

"Were you spying on us?" Ian teased.

Spencer looked horrified. "It's just . . . I didn't mean to barge in. . . . We're supposed to have this place tonight."

Ian playfully hit Spencer's arm. "I was just messing with you."

A spark seemed to pass between them, which, in turn, sent a rush of possessiveness through Ali's body. "Wow," she said loudly. "You two make the kuh-*yoo*-test couple. Don't you agree, Spence?"

Spencer blinked hard. Melissa gave Ali a strange look, then tugged on Ian's shoulder. "Can I talk to you outside for a sec?"

Ian drained the last of his Corona and rose from the couch. "*Adieu*, ladies."

He swept past Ali and shot her a covert smile. She nodded ever-so-slightly in return. They were on for meeting in her yard at 9 PM. She knew he'd be there. All she had to do now was send a text to Melissa just before their kiss. And then Melissa would see everything.

After they were gone, Ali turned back to the girls. "Ian is so hot," Hanna was saying. "Even hotter than Sean." A tiny, conflicted look fluttered across her face. She was probably thinking about Josie and Sean at the party.

"You know what I think?" Ali said to Hanna, her nastiness oozing over. "Sean really likes girls who have good appetites."

Hanna looked surprised. "Really?"

"*No*," Ali blurted. The laugh that came out of her mouth was subconscious, but when she noticed the hurt look on Hanna's face, she clamped her mouth shut. She felt crackly tonight, unbridled, totally out of control. She felt like she needed to be the most extreme Alison she could be, not only to show her sister, but to show her friends, too. *No one can replace me. No one is better than I am. Don't you dare suspect a thing.*

Suddenly, she had an idea. Maybe there was a way to get her friends in her ultimate power for real. Even if they did see her sister again, they'd always side with Ali, doing whatever she wanted, which meant the two of them could never switch back. It might also be a way to erase what they'd seen for good.

"I know the perfect thing we can do," she suggested. "I learned how to hypnotize people."

Spencer looked worried. "Hypnotize?"

"Matt's sister taught me," Ali said, her excitement growing. This was perfect. She could hypnotize them and demand that they bow down to her and only her. She could also extract the memory of her sister in her bedroom from their minds. "Want to see if it works?" she asked, trying not to beg.

Everyone shifted uncomfortably. "I don't know," Aria murmured. "Doesn't hypnosis make you say things you don't want to say?"

Ali gritted her teeth. "Why?" she teased. "Is there something you don't want to tell us?" She pointed at Pigtunia. "And why are you still carrying that everywhere? Didn't your *dad* give it to you?"

Aria paled, and again, Ali felt a remorseful twinge. Perhaps it had been *too* mean. Hanna looked sharply at her, her brow furrowed, and Spencer paused, a bite of popcorn halfway to her mouth. Ali could tell they were all working through what Ali had said in their minds. Why was Aria upset? What had Ali said? What didn't *they* know?

"Being hypnotized, um, *does* sound sort of sketch," Spencer blurted.

"*You* don't know anything about it," Ali insisted urgently. "C'mon. I can do all of you at once."

She watched as they shifted their weight. A long silence prevailed. *Please*, she repeated silently. *Please, please, please.*

"I'll do it," Hanna piped up.

"Me, too," Emily said.

Spencer and Aria begrudgingly shrugged, too. Ali let out a huge mental sigh.

"Okay," she said excitedly. "Everyone sit in a circle." She rushed around the room, shut off the lights, and lit a few votive candles sitting on the coffee table. Then she took her place at the head of the room, shut her eyes, and let out an *om*-like hum that sounded vaguely spiritual.

Her friends closed their eyes, too, and Ali felt even better. Maybe hypnosis really *was* going to work. Maybe she would be able to say some words and they'd forget. "Okay, just relax," she said. "I'm going to count backward from one hundred. As soon as I touch all of you, you'll be in my power."

Emily laughed shakily. "Spooky."

Ali began to count, padding around the room and looking at the crowns of her friends' heads. Her voice filled the space, the numbers dropping from ninety to sixty to forty-five. At thirty, she saw a flash at the window and turned. Something black disappeared from view. Her heart skipped a beat.

"Twenty-nine . . . ," she said, moving toward the window. Then there was another flash. She shielded her face, spots forming in front of her eyes. When her vision cleared, a figure stood on the other side of the glass, a modern-day Polaroid camera at her side. Ali almost screamed.

It was her sister.

"Twenty-eight . . . ," Ali said with only a slight hiccup,

her mind scattering in a million directions. *No.* She would never, *ever* forgive her mother for letting her sister out. What should she do now? Run out of the barn, tell her parents Courtney was loose? But then her friends would open their eyes and see the two identical twins, one on the outside, one on the inside. They'd exchange knowing glances. *See? Everything we suspected was right.* And what if they liked her twin *more*?

Should she pretend nothing was wrong, then? That didn't seem right, either. Her sister might barge inside the barn. She might tell the truth. And then what?

Ali glanced at her friends, but they were still sitting with their eyes closed. She twisted the window blinds shut, then pulled the curtains tight, then counted through the twenties, then through the teens. She pictured her sister crouched at the window, not seeing inside anymore, but still listening. She checked the door to make sure it was bolted tight. It was. But what if Courtney got in some other way?

"Ten, nine . . ." Swallowing a lump in her throat, Ali touched her friends' foreheads. First Aria, then Hanna, then Emily. "Three . . . two . . . ," she incanted.

Suddenly, Spencer's eyes sprang open. To Ali's horror, she leapt across the room and lunged for the window. Ali whipped around, her heart jumping into her throat. "What are you doing?"

"It's too dark in here," Spencer said, reaching for the dowel that would twist open the blinds. She opened them, and Ali winced. Her twin was gone, though.

"It's got to be dark," Ali demanded, rushing toward her. She had no idea if Courtney would reappear, but she wasn't taking any chances. "That's how it works."

Spencer paused, her hand on the rod. "No, it doesn't."

"It *does*," Ali growled, her heart beating fast. There was no way Spencer was opening that window. Her sister would be on the other side, like a perverse reflection in a mirror.

Spencer turned from the window and placed her hands on her hips. "It doesn't always have to be the way you want it, you know."

"Close them!" Ali roared, trying to control the desperation in her voice.

Spencer rolled her eyes. "God, take a pill."

"*You* take a pill!"

Ali stared at her. Something suddenly hit her: What if Spencer *knew*? Maybe she'd figured it all out—she was the smartest of all of them. Maybe she'd even seen Courtney at the window just now and had put all the pieces together. She was messing with Ali because she could; she knew exactly what Ali was afraid of.

In one defiant gesture, Spencer reached across, yanked the string, and pulled every single slat up, revealing the outside world. Ali let out a yelp and hid her eyes, preparing for the worst. She peeked through her fingers. The view was only of the thick woods behind the barn.

Ali turned to Spencer. Spencer stared out the window blankly, but perhaps there was a tiny hint of disappointment on her face. Spencer pointed to the door. "Leave."

"Fine," Ali said. And it *was* fine. She needed to tell her parents what was happening. Spencer had given her the perfect excuse.

Throwing back her shoulders, she strode for the exit, twisted the lock, and stepped into the evening twilight. The ground was wet with dew. The sky was navy blue. The cars swished on the distant highway.

"Wait a second!" Spencer called behind her. "Alison!"

But Ali kept going, swiveling her head from side to side to check for signs of her sister. Lights blazed in the Hastingses' house as well as the DiLaurentises'. The guest room window was lit up again. She didn't see her sister anywhere.

But Ali doubted she was inside. Courtney was out here somewhere. She just had to find her and drag her back to her parents. That bitch was going back to the Preserve once and for all.

32

THE LOST PUZZLE PIECES

Ali ran down the slippery slate path, looking right and left for a familiar shape in the darkness. Her sister had to be close, but where?

A horrible vision appeared in her mind: a stark, antiseptic hospital bed. Being shoved into a tiny room, the door slamming. *We're never letting you out again*, a voice taunted. She pictured herself pressing her hands against a window at the Preserve, watching her parents—and Courtney—drive away.

It couldn't happen.

A whiff of something stopped her, and she cocked her head. It smelled like a cigarette. But before she could figure out where it was coming from, the smell was gone.

"Ali!" a voice cut through the night. "Ali, come back!"

Ali paused on the slate path and looked over her shoulder. The pagoda-shaped lanterns on the footpath didn't provide much in the way of light, but she could just make out Spencer coming toward her. A new fire sparked in her stomach. Spencer wasn't supposed to be outside. She might see something—or, more accurately, some*one*.

She squared her shoulders, waiting as Spencer caught up with her. Spencer's cheeks were flushed, and there was a guilty expression on her face. "Where are you going?" she asked in a wounded voice.

Ali blinked. All of a sudden, it seemed like Spencer maybe *didn't* know. She looked so worried right then, like she was afraid Ali was going to ditch her forever. But Spencer couldn't be out here right now, not with her twin hanging around. Ali said the first thing she could think of that would make Spencer turn around and go back into the barn. "I'm going somewhere way cooler than hanging out with you guys."

Spencer's features hardened. "Fine. Go." And yet she didn't move.

Ali gritted her teeth, scrambling to think of something else. Something rustled in the woods, and her eyes flicked toward the trees. Ian? Her sister? Spencer needed to get out of here. *Now.*

"You try to steal everything away from me, Spence," she teased, trying to keep the desperation out of her voice. "But you can't have this."

Spencer squinted. "Can't have what?"

Ali laughed nastily. "*You* know."

Spencer waved a hand. "You're delusional."

"No, I'm not." There was another flutter in the woods;

Ali stepped closer to Spencer, boxing her in so she couldn't see. "*You* are."

Anger flashed in Spencer's eyes, and she pushed Ali hard on the shoulder. Ali staggered back, surprised by the forcefulness of it. Her feet slipped on the path, and she twisted to the right, grabbing a tree branch for balance.

She straightened up and gawked at Spencer. "Friends don't shove friends."

Spencer stood tall. "Well, maybe we aren't friends."

"Guess not," Ali said. She wanted to add, *So go back to the barn.*

But still Spencer lingered. It had gotten past the point of annoyance. Now Ali *wanted* to hurt Spencer. She suddenly realized how. She licked her lips, the twist to the secret like rich juice on her tongue. "You think kissing Ian is so special," she teased. "But you know what he told me? That you didn't even know how."

Spencer stepped back as if Ali had slapped her. "Ian told you that? When?"

"When we were on our date," she lied.

Spencer's lips parted. No words came out of her mouth.

Ali edged closer. "You're so lame, acting like you don't know we're together. But of course you do, Spence. That's why you liked him, isn't it? Because *I'm* with him? Because your sister's with him?" She shrugged. "The only reason he kissed you the other night was because I asked him to.

He didn't want to, but I begged."

Spencer's eyes boggled. *"Why?"*

"I wanted to see if he would do *anything* for me." She stuck out her lip. "Oh, Spence. Did you really believe he *liked* you?"

Spencer looked dizzy. A lightning bug landed on her arm, but she didn't flick it away. Ali waited for her to whirl around in fury, but instead, she reached out and pushed Ali so hard that her feet went out from under her and her body flew back. A series of images flashed past her: the hazy lights, the huge moon in the sky, and then whiteness. A loud *crack* sounded in her ears. Her head throbbed with pain. She landed sharply on her elbow and rolled to her side. Moisture seeped into her clothes, but for a moment, she was too stunned to move.

An owl screeched in the trees. Ali opened her eyes, then felt the dirt caked onto the side of her cheek. She wiggled her fingers, then her toes, then rolled over and attempted to sit up. Spencer was still standing there, but she looked transfixed, almost like she *had* been hypnotized. Ali stood and brushed herself off. When she ran down the path, Spencer didn't follow.

Good.

She padded toward her yard. But as she reached the hedges at the back of the property, a door banged in the barn, and a new thought struck her. What if her sister had seized the opportunity and gone inside the barn with Aria, Emily, and Hanna? She might be pretending she was

Ali—or telling them everything.

She wheeled back around, her head throbbing. That had to be it! She couldn't believe she'd fallen for it.

She doubled back toward the barn, feet slipping in the dewy grass. A door slammed, and she could just make out through the windows Spencer walking back inside. A *crack* sounded behind her, and she turned. Something was moving near the Hastingses' patio. A *person.*

Ali's hand flew to her mouth. "Courtney?" she whispered, too quietly for anyone to hear.

Only, it was two people, not one. They stuck close together, moving toward the side of the house and stopping by the Hastingses' garden hose caddy. The taller of the two pushed the smaller figure up against the side of the house. Their bodies pressed together, and their lips met in a kiss.

Ali squinted hard. At first, she thought it was Ian and Melissa—they were around here somewhere. Then a car passed on the street, its headlights shining against the figures for a brief second. Her mother's long blond hair and sharp profile shimmered into view. Ali gasped and looked at the taller figure, who was now caressing Mrs. DiLaurentis's neck. The headlights touched on his face for a brief moment, illuminating his strong jaw, long and slender nose, full head of hair. He leaned Mrs. DiLaurentis against the side of the house with authority, as though he owned the place.

And then it hit Ali: He *did* own the place. The man her

mother was kissing was Spencer's father.

She wheeled backward, feeling literally struck down by the news. There was no way this could be true. Her mother *hated* Mr. Hastings, didn't she? But then she heard her mother's words on the phone: *We just need a little more cash, honey. Just to pay the rest of her hospital bills…. she's your daughter, too.*

Her insides curdled. Mr. Hastings certainly had money to pay hospital bills—especially for a deranged daughter no one knew about. Perhaps this explained why Mr. DiLaurentis always seemed so outrageously jealous of the Hastings—perhaps he sensed that something was going on. But what *had* gone on? He'd gotten Ali's mom pregnant while they were having an affair . . . and then what? She'd passed the twins off as Mr. DiLaurentis's, clearly. Maybe she'd tried to drop it for a while . . . until things got bad between Ali and Courtney, when she needed Mr. Hastings's financial help. Perhaps he'd helped them move to Rosewood. Got them a house next door so he could keep an eye on his daughter—and his mistress. *How convenient*, Ali thought acidly. Her father, next door, and she'd never even known.

Ali felt like she was going to throw up. Instead, she turned around and ran. That it was someone she knew, her best friend's *father*, made it even worse. How could her mother never *tell* her this? How could they move next door to the Hastingses, her real father within arm's reach but off-limits? And this made her and Spencer . . . *sisters.*

Mist swirled around her head, and she suddenly lost her bearings. She came to a stop in her yard—at least she *thought* it was her yard. Everything looked unfamiliar. The house glowed far away, up a long, gradual slope of grass. A tarp flapped next to her, and the moonlight caught a glint of a discarded tool on the ground. She hadn't realized she was so close to the half-dug hole. One false move, and she could have fallen right in.

"It's pretty shocking, huh?"

Ali jerked her head up. A figure stood opposite her, shrouded in shadow. Her face was tilted toward the kissing couple in the Hastingses' yard.

"Looks like our family tree has a lot of rotten apples," the person said, in a voice that indicated she'd figured everything out, too.

Then she stepped into the light, and Ali swallowed hard. It was her sister.

33

ONE LITTLE PUSH

For a moment, Ali couldn't move. She stared at her sister opposite her. The girl's eyes glinted. Her teeth glowed. Half her body was hidden in the mist, like she was a ghost.

Ali whipped around and headed toward the house. "You're not supposed to be outside."

Her twin caught her arm and dug her nails into her skin. "You're not going anywhere, *Ali*."

"Let go of me," Ali said, trying to yank her arm away. But Courtney's grip was firm. "I'll scream," she warned, fear rising in her voice.

Courtney chuckled. "No, you won't. You won't say anything."

"Yes, I will," Ali said. "Mom and Dad will come running."

Courtney guffawed. "Um, didn't you just see what I saw? Mom's a little busy right now."

"Then I'll call Dad."

Courtney's smile stretched wider. "Dad's passed out on the couch. Someone might have slipped something in his wine at dinner."

Ali backed away, suddenly trembling. *She really* is *crazy,* she thought.

But "Courtney" just pulled her back. "And don't think Jason's going to come rescue you," she whispered in Ali's ear. "He doesn't give a shit about either of us. And as far as your friends go, they all left. Some end-of-seventh-grade sleepover, huh?"

"Let go of me!" Ali exclaimed. Her arm was starting to sting from the pressure of her sister's fingernails, and her heart was beating so fast she thought it might explode in her chest. Her nostrils caught another whiff of that cigarette. The source was close, but it didn't seem like her twin had been smoking. "What are you doing out here?"

Courtney chuckled again, the most horrible sound in the world. "Oh, I just wanted to see what your life is like. *My* life. What possessed you to pick those girls as your new friends? To torment me? To ruin my reputation?"

"There's nothing wrong with them," Ali said defensively, suddenly feeling a rush of protectiveness for her friends. "They're really sweet."

"*They're really sweet,*" Courtney mimicked. "Do you think they'll still do everything you ask when they find out what you did?"

"They'll never believe you," Ali said, but even she heard the waver in her voice.

Courtney raised her chin. "They will if I tell them the truth about you."

Ali tensed. All of a sudden, anger rushed through her, hot and potent. "The *truth*?" she asked. "And what would that be? How you manipulated me for years? How you got *me* sent to the hospital instead of you? How you stood there and *told them* I had to go away?"

"You *did* have to go away," Courtney said, her voice eerily calm. "And you're going to have to go again. You're going to tell everyone what you did. And they're never, *ever* going to forgive you."

Fear streaked through Ali's veins, but she stood her ground. "I'm not going anywhere," she said, planting her feet in the wet, chilly grass. She laughed as confidently as she could. "Do you really think it would be easy for you to step into my life and be me? I've done things you aren't capable of. I'm better at being you than you ever were."

"It's *my* life," her sister snarled, placing her hands firmly on Ali's shoulders. "You really think I'm going to have a hard time? I can even be friends with those stupid bitches, if that's what it takes. I can do this with my eyes closed."

"No, you can't," Ali said. "You don't know anything."

Courtney snorted. "Please. I read your diary—*my* diary. I know everything about them, about you. You put every secret in there, everything important."

"Not everything," Ali snapped, thinking of Nick. Thank God she'd left him out. She wished she could lord that over Courtney right now—he had, after all, been her unrequited crush. But now that they were over, her twin would just laugh at her.

"You certainly put in enough in your diary," Courtney taunted. "That's how I figured out that we've been calling the wrong guy Dad. Watch where you store your secrets, *Ali.* Anyone can open up a diary and find out all kinds of things." She took Ali's arm. "And now it's time for you to say good-bye. Let's go find Mom and our real father, shall we? We can tell them everything!"

She clamped down hard on Ali's shoulders and tried to steer her toward the Hastingses' house, but Ali folded her body in half and twisted away. Courtney grabbed her around the waist and yanked her across the grass, but Ali stumbled, pulling her sister down with her.

"Get *up*, bitch!" Courtney yelled.

"I'm not going anywhere with you!" Ali pulled hard on her twin's hair and rolled over on top of Courtney, pinning her onto the prickly grass. The old feelings rushed back—she was that little nine-year-old girl again, fighting against a force so crazy, so manipulative, she didn't know what else to do but hit her, punch her, lose her mind.

But then, suddenly, she snapped back into herself. This was crazy. She hated her sister, but she couldn't fall back into that trap. She had to be the bigger person.

She rolled off Courtney, stood, and started toward the house. But just a few steps in, a hand snaked around her ankle, and she was sprawled on the grass once more. She felt her sister's body press on top of her. The ends of her long hair tickled the back of Ali's neck.

"I guess it's plan B, then," Courtney whispered. She moved off Ali and, before Ali could go anywhere, grabbed Ali's ankles and dragged her toward the very edge of the property as though she were a rag doll. Ali howled and clawed at the ground, but her fingers couldn't get a grip. When they passed some of the discarded tools, her heart picked up pace. Was she dragging her toward the hole?

Ali tried to call out, but she couldn't draw in a full breath. The house was so far away, the Hastingses' barn now dark. Where had her friends gone? Had they left? Then she thought of Ian, waiting for her in the woods somewhere. Maybe *he* was the one who'd been smoking. She peered desperately into the black trees, praying he saw her. But the forest was silent. No branches crackled underfoot. No one emerged.

Her twin stopped dragging her when she was at the edge of the hole. Ali tried to scramble up, but Courtney pushed her down again, her eyes blazing. "I should have done this years ago," she growled. And then she shot her hands toward Ali's neck, ready to strangle her.

"No!" Ali screamed. "Please!"

But her twin just tightened her grip. "You deserve this," she said in a detached, almost automated voice. "You deserve to die for what you did."

No, I don't! Ali kicked her legs and thrashed her arms. She twisted her neck and got a gulp of air. "I'll do anything!" she cried. "Tell the truth—I don't care! Just don't *kill* me!"

"You deserve to die," Courtney repeated.

When she readjusted for a better grip, Ali took a huge breath, her lungs screaming. "Remember how it used to be? When we used to be *friends*?"

"We were *never* friends," her twin hissed.

"Yes, we were! I loved you! You loved me! I . . . I *miss* that!"

Courtney's grip let up just a little bit, and Ali twisted to the side to free herself. She coughed violently, her lungs feeling like they'd never fill again. She scrambled backward, sat up, and looked hard at her sister. Courtney was breathing hard, her eyes wide. She stared at her hands with wonderment, as if she'd never seen them before.

Then she looked up at Ali. "I can't," she said in a small voice.

"Can't what?" Ali dared to ask.

Courtney's jaw trembled. "I want to kill you. But I *can't*."

Relief flooded Ali's body. "Of course you can't," she said. "We're sisters."

Courtney glanced at her cagily. Once more, she peered at her hands. She shifted toward Ali, her eyes flashing again.

"M-maybe we can start over," Ali bargained. If she kept talking, maybe she could keep her twin's craziness at bay until someone came looking for them. "I can be me. You can be you. You can be Alison DiLaurentis again."

Courtney blinked. "Just like that, you'll switch back?"

Ali nodded, swallowing a lump in her throat. "Just like that." She reached out and touched her sister's hand, a tender gesture she hadn't made in years. "I just want a sister again," she said softly. "That's all I've ever wanted."

Courtney's head remained down for a few more beats. A strong scent of uprooted dirt swirled through the air, and for a moment, the crickets were silent. Then she breathed out a long, slow sigh. She covered Ali's hand with her other one. "I don't know if I can do that."

"You *can*," Ali urged. "Please."

"I . . ." "Courtney" trailed off. Her eyes widened on something behind her. "You're here," she whispered.

Ali tried to turn around to see who'd come. A parent? Ian? One of her friends? But before she could, her sister's gaze hardened once more, her resolve apparent. She lunged forward and shoved her hard.

Ali expected to hit grass immediately, but she felt nothing but air. She screamed out as the world turned upside down, and then her neck banged on something sharp and metallic. For a moment everything went black, then she heard a horrible *clang* in her ears. All the air seemed to leave her body as she hit the cold, flat, unforgiving earth. Something cracked close by. After a second, Ali realized it was a bone inside her body.

She was at the bottom of the hole.

She tried to scream, but her mouth wouldn't open. Only a square of light peeked out far above her head.

Stars twinkled in the distance. A sliver of moon peeked from behind a cloud.

"Help!" she cried, but it was only in her head. Her heart shuddered inside her chest like a seized engine. A strange, snapping sensation was taking place beneath her skin, nerves gone haywire. After a moment, she realized she wasn't breathing—*couldn't* breathe. She tried to claw, tried to fight, but it felt like every cell in her body was weighed down with sand. Then she realized what was going on. She was *dying*.

A figure appeared over the hole. Ali's twin looked in, a strange mix of horror and relief on her face. She stared down at her hands again with that same where-did-these-come-from expression. Then she turned and looked at something just out of view.

"I didn't know you were coming," she said. "I thought you weren't going to make it."

At first, Ali thought Courtney was talking to her, but then a voice answered. "Of course I made it. I'll always come for you."

Ali strained to listen. It was a voice she was sure she recognized, a voice she'd heard many times before. But her brain, with its dying cells and lack of oxygen, couldn't quite put the pieces together. She tried to lift her head to get a glimpse of who it was, but her neck wouldn't move.

"Are you happy?" the voice said.

Courtney's jaw wobbled. "I don't know," she said, looking back down in the hole, a hand over her mouth. "I can't believe I just . . . *did* that."

"But it was our plan all along."

Suddenly, Ali realized whose voice it was. She tried to react, tried to scream, but she could feel herself slipping away inch by inch, first her feet, then her calves, then her knees. She struggled to stay present, but it was just too much of an effort. She stared at the top of the hole until her sister's figure was nothing but a big blob of light and shadow. She thought of the second voice, that voice she knew. Only one question screamed over and over in her brain: *Why?*

But before she could answer, the dying feeling, like a candle fizzling out, had reached her neck. She inhaled the last breath she would ever take, and then shut her eyes. After a moment, amid the dirt and the rocks and the earthworms, she breathed out and finally let go.

34

MISSING: ALISON DILAURENTIS

The following morning, the real Alison DiLaurentis watched the sun come up through the maple blinds in her old bedroom. Bands of light illuminated the vanity she'd begged her mom to buy for her in fifth grade, the blue crystal knobs on her closet and bureau drawers, the faint patina of dust on the flat-screen monitor and TV. This room even *smelled* the same, like vanilla hand soap. It felt like home.

Finally.

The aroma of coffee brewing in the kitchen wafted into her nostrils. When she looked over the railing, her family was already awake. Mr. and Mrs. DiLaurentis sat at the kitchen table, staring blearily at each other. Jason paced the hall, looking worried.

Just one family member was missing, though Ali certainly wouldn't miss her.

She glanced at herself in the mirror. Her eyes had

always been bluer than her sister's, the cheekbones in her heart-shaped face more pronounced. She was the more beautiful twin, the *rightful* queen bee of Rosewood Day. Now it was time to reclaim her throne from that bitch. Just thinking of her, just picturing her face, still filled Ali with rage. How *dare* she go outside in sixth grade and pretend she was someone she wasn't. How *dare* she show up at the Preserve during those visits and pick at her perfect manicure or text with her friends while their parents tried to make conversation. That bitch *deserved* everything she got. And now Ali would never have to worry about her again.

She walked downstairs, her head held high. But when she entered the kitchen, her family looked up and paled as if they'd seen a ghost. Mrs. DiLaurentis stepped forward and touched her arm. "I think you should go back upstairs, Courtney."

Ali stopped short. "I already told you. I'm *not* Courtney. I'm Ali."

Her parents exchanged a worried glance. A thin ribbon of fear began to niggle its way into Ali's brain. She knew that look. *It is happening again.*

And now their other daughter was missing.

Last night, when she'd come home, Ali hadn't expected her father to be awake—or for her mother to be home—but she still thought she'd pulled it off okay. They'd both caught her as she was sneaking up the stairs and yelled out her name—her *real* name.

"Hey, Mom, hey, Dad," she'd said breezily, staying in

the shadows so they couldn't see her disheveled hair or the bruise on her cheek. "The sleepover was a bust. We kind of got into a fight. I'm off to bed."

She made it to her old bedroom and shut the door. Once inside, she'd scrubbed at her hands and brushed her hair. Her brain had whirled, trying to come up with what she and her friends had been fighting about. It had looked like her sister was trying to hypnotize them or something, right? But Spencer wasn't into it. And then her sister and Spencer got into that stupid fight about Ian Thomas outside the barn—Ali heard everything.

Then a knock had sounded on her door.

She'd jumped up and offered her parents, who were standing nervously in the hall, a twitchy smile. Their gazes zipped to Ali's pointer finger, which, of course, was missing its initial ring. Then they looked at her wrist. It was naked; no Jenna Thing string bracelet. *Crap.*

"Courtney?" Mrs. DiLaurentis asked tentatively. "Honey, were you outside?"

"I'm not Courtney," Ali said, frowning. "I'm Ali. See? This is why I didn't want you to bring her home. It's so confusing."

She tried to shut the door, but Mr. DiLaurentis stuck his hand on the jamb before she could. "This isn't your room, Courtney," he said with authority.

And you aren't my dad, Ali wanted to snap. "Yes, it is," she said instead, and then glowered at him. "And please don't call me Courtney. It's insulting."

Mrs. DiLaurentis looked confused. "Were you trying to hang out with your sister and her friends? Did you go into Spencer's barn?"

Ali shrugged. "Yeah, I was in Spencer's barn—*I'm Ali.* But the sleepover sucked. We had a fight, and we all went home. I already told you."

Mrs. DiLaurentis blinked hard. "So no one's in the barn anymore?"

"Yeah. They went home."

Looking like she didn't quite believe her, Mrs. DiLaurentis walked swiftly to the window in the bathroom, which offered a view of the backyards. Ali already knew the barn's windows were dark. Seconds later, her mom wheeled back into Ali's room. "Where's your sister?"

"Courtney?" Ali stared at her innocently. "I have no idea. She's not in her room?"

Mrs. DiLaurentis poked her head into the dark guest room, then shook her head.

Ali widened her eyes. "She got out? You weren't watching her? It's the only thing I asked you to do!" She made her voice rise and fall, the same way her sister had when she'd freaked out to her mother when she'd found out that Ali had met her friends.

Frazzled, Mrs. DiLaurentis ran her hands through her hair. "We'll get it sorted out." She touched her daughter's arm. "Good night . . . *Ali.*" The name sounded awkward coming out of her mouth, like she'd never used it in her life.

"Good night," Ali had said, grabbing pajamas from the top drawer. Her sister liked Pink boxers from Victoria's Secret—so lame. But she'd dutifully pulled them on, feeling a rush of triumph. Her parents might have been a little confused at first, but they had bought it in the end. She was sleeping in her old room. *Yes.*

But this morning, with her parents staring at her and calling her Courtney, doubt crept into her mind. Maybe her panic had seemed too staged. Maybe she'd grabbed a pair of pajamas that her sister would have never chosen. Maybe they were hung up on that missing *A* ring. And she had heard them downstairs until all hours of the night, pacing, murmuring into the phone, opening the front door and shutting it again. She'd heard them moving around at midnight, and then two, and then four, and then five thirty. They might not have slept at all.

"Go upstairs, okay?" Mrs. DiLaurentis's patience was wearing thin. "Spencer and the other girls are coming over soon. I'd like to ask them questions without explaining anything."

Ali made her breathing quicken like she was afraid. "So Courtney *did* take off? See? This is why I didn't want her back! She's totally mental, Mom. That's why you locked her up. Who knows what she's going to do now! What if she tries to hurt me?"

Mrs. DiLaurentis gave her husband a plaintive glance. Mr. DiLaurentis just looked at her helplessly. She turned back to Ali. "Just go upstairs until we figure all this out."

Sighing dramatically, Ali thumped up the stairs, trying to hold it together. Once in her old bedroom, though, she sank to her knees, her mind thrumming. Why wasn't this working? Why didn't they believe her? She needed an airtight alibi. If those girls were coming over, they were probably going to ask where she'd gone last night, and when. There were probably twenty minutes that were unaccounted for–her parents would ask where she was. *Talking on the phone*, she could say. *Walking around, blowing off steam.*

But they were supposed to just *believe* her. They weren't supposed to shoo her away or question those girls without her around.

The doorbell rang. The door squeaked open, and the sounds of Mrs. DiLaurentis's and the girls' voices rang through the foyer. There were footsteps, and then the scrape of the chairs being pulled back for everyone to sit. Ali crept out of her room and slipped to the bottom of the stairs. All four girls sat around the table, staring at their hands. All of them were quiet, as though they were hiding something. Emily picked at her cuticles. Spencer drummed her fingers on the table. Aria inspected a pineapple-shaped napkin holder, and Hanna chewed voraciously on a piece of gum.

"Alison hasn't come home," Mrs. DiLaurentis said.

The girls all looked up, shocked. Ali clapped a hand over her mouth by the stairs. *How was this happening?*

"Now, I don't know if you girls had a fight or what, but did she give you any hints as to where she might have gone?" Mrs. DiLaurentis continued.

Hanna twisted a piece of hair around her ear. "I think she's with her field hockey friends."

Mrs. DiLaurentis shook her head. "She's not. I've already called them." She cleared her throat. "Has Ali ever talked about someone teasing her?"

The girls glanced at one another, then looked away. "No one would do that," Emily said. "Everyone loves Ali."

"Did she ever seem sad?" Mrs. DiLaurentis pressed.

Spencer wrinkled her nose. "Like depressed? No." But then a troubled look came across her face. She stared blankly out the window.

"You wouldn't know where her diary is, would you?" Mrs. DiLaurentis asked. "I've looked everywhere for it, but I can't find it."

"I know what her diary looks like," Hanna offered. "Do you want us to go upstairs and search?"

Alison scampered halfway up the stairs, picturing the diary in her mind's eye. *She* knew where it was—somewhere very, very safe. But she wasn't telling.

"No, no, that's all right," Mrs. DiLaurentis answered.

"Really." Hanna scraped back her chair. There were footsteps in the hall. "It's no trouble."

"Hanna," Ali's mom barked, her voice suddenly razor-sharp. "I said no."

There was a pause. Ali wished she could see the looks on everyone's faces, but her view was obstructed. "Okay," Hanna said quietly. "Sorry."

After a while, the girls filed out. Mrs. DiLaurentis shut the door behind them and stood for a moment in the hall, just staring. Ali crouched behind the wall on the second floor, barely breathing. She had to think—and *fast*. She needed to convince everyone she was the real Ali.

She ran to her old bedroom window and watched her sister's friends as they stood in a circle in the yard. They looked worried, maybe even guilty—especially Spencer. Emily burst into tears. Hanna gnawed nervously on a handful of Cheez-It's. It seemed like they were arguing, but Ali couldn't really tell. Should she go outside and talk to them? Maybe she could tell the truth—that there were twins, that the other girl was a crazy Ali impersonator, that she'd gotten out last night but her parents were confused and thought the girls had switched places. She needed those stupid bitches to convince the world, just as her sister had used them a year and a half before.

She started down the stairs, but suddenly there was a deafening grumble from the backyard. It was the bulldozer. It barreled toward the hole, its huge tires ripping up the grass.

"Just what we need right now," Mrs. DiLaurentis groaned. "That thing is so loud I can hardly hear myself think."

"Do you want me to tell them to stop?" Mr. DiLaurentis asked.

The words rippled through Ali. A horrible thought gonged in her brain. Her parents could *not* go out there.

What if they saw her sister at the bottom of the hole? She'd piled a lot of dirt on her, but it had been dark out—maybe she hadn't been thorough enough.

She sprinted to the window in the bathroom and looked out. Men stood around the hole, positioning a chute that connected from the cement truck to a spot just inside. No one looked down the hole. There were no shouts of terror or backward steps of surprise. Ali thought again of the handfuls of dirt she'd thrown on the body, then about the person who'd helped her. She was glad her accomplice had shown up, just as she'd asked. For a few weeks there, she wasn't sure if it was going to happen.

The mixer started to turn. Gray cement poured down a chute into the hole, slowly filling it. The men stood around, smoking cigarettes. One of them told a joke, and a few of them laughed. Ali kept expecting them to turn toward the hole and suddenly scream out in terror, but no one did. The mixer whirled and whirled. The sludgy cement rolled down the chute. Ali assessed her feelings, but she didn't know what she felt. Relief, sort of. But also worry.

There was a knock on the bathroom door, which was ajar. Mrs. DiLaurentis stood in the hallway, fiddling with the hem of her T-shirt. "You have to tell us what you know, honey," she begged, her eyes full of tears.

Ali shrugged. "Why would you think I'd know something?"

Mrs. DiLaurentis blinked at her. Ali looked down,

trying to remain calm, and reached for her sister's cell phone, which she'd found on the grass last night. But then she heard the mixer click off. It was all over. The hole was filled. Her sister was buried. Gone. *Done.*

Her fingers started to shake uncontrollably.

She shoved her hand under her thighs. Then she caught a glimpse of her freaked-out expression in the mirror. When she looked up, Mrs. DiLaurentis's mouth hung open. All the blood had drained from her face. In an instant, Ali knew that she knew.

Mrs. DiLaurentis set her mouth in a line. "Pack. *Now.*"

Ali blinked. "Why?"

Mrs. DiLaurentis turned toward the stairs. "Kenneth?" she screeched. "Kenneth, I *need* you."

Mr. DiLaurentis bounded up the stairs fast. Mrs. DiLaurentis whipped around and pointed shakily at Ali. "Honey, she . . . Alison . . . she . . ." And then she burst into tears.

Mr. DiLaurentis lunged for Ali as though he'd been planning the move for hours. Before Ali knew what was happening, they'd shut her inside the guest room and locked the door from the outside. "What the hell?" Ali screeched. "What's going on? Why are you two acting like freaks?"

She could hear their voices in the hall, low murmurs. *She did something. I don't know what, but something horrible has happened. We have to get her out of here.*

Ali's spine stiffened. *Out* of here? They didn't mean . . .

the Preserve, did they? But they couldn't. No freaking *way*. Ali's heart began to pound just from the thought of it. She'd spent eighteen torturous months in that place. Hours inside that dark room. Days locked inside her head, so drugged-up from those indifferent nurses. And the doctors, oh, the *doctors*, they were even worse. Cruel. Careless. They forgot her name. They forgot her situation. When she said, tearfully, *I'm Ali, I'm Ali,* they stared at her like she was nothing more than a number, a case study.

Moments later, when her parents came back into the room, Mrs. DiLaurentis yanked the suitcase from the floor and began stuffing T-shirts and underwear inside. "Mom," Ali said shakily. "I don't know what you're doing, but—"

"Don't talk," Mrs. DiLaurentis interrupted. Her husband was on the phone. After a moment, a voice answered so loudly that Ali could hear her through the receiver. "Good morning, the Preserve at Addison-Stevens, how may I help you?"

Frightened tears came to Ali's eyes. She tried to grab the phone from her father's hand, but he twisted away. "You can't send me back there!" she screamed. "I didn't *do* anything!"

Mrs. DiLaurentis pushed her palms against Ali's shoulders with surprising force, shoving Ali back to the bed. "Stop lying," she warned, her eyes full of tears. "Just stop all the lying!"

Ali screamed and tried to roll off the mattress, but then Mr. DiLaurentis appeared and grabbed her around the waist. Her feet kicked as they hauled her down the stairs. She screamed so loud, she was sure the workers in the back would come running, but no one did.

"You don't understand!" she moaned to her parents. "I'm Ali!"

But they didn't listen. She caught snippets of things as they dragged her to the car: the calligraphy lettering on her sister's seventh-grade diploma on the kitchen island, her sister's field hockey stick propped up in the corner of the laundry room, the whirling mixer in the backyard. The sky was so perfectly blue, the yards so pristinely manicured.

"I'm Ali!" she howled again in the garage, a desperate plea to the Cavanaughs, the Vanderwaals, even the Hastingses. But still no one came to her rescue. Her father shoved her into the backseat, and her head hit the opposite window hard. She tried to scramble out the door again, but her parents had already climbed inside the car and child-locked the doors. Then the engine growled. Then they were going in reverse. Ali's vision was clouded by tears now. Her throat felt sore from screaming. She peered out the window at the impassive houses all along the cul-de-sac. No one cared about her. She hated everyone on this stupid street.

And with that, they were gone. "You don't understand, I'm *Ali*," she repeated a few more times, but as they pulled out of the driveway, she realized it was futile. They *didn't* believe her. Her plan had backfired. She'd never, ever be

Alison DiLaurentis again.

And worse, they'd somehow figured out what she'd done. Perhaps they thought they were being kind. They could have called the police, could have had her locked up in jail.

But it didn't seem kind to her. She would have *preferred* jail. At least she would have gotten a trial. At least she would have gotten her name back.

Mr. DiLaurentis's face was splotchy as he pivoted to the right and started down the street. Shell-shocked, Ali cranked her neck to the side and watched as the cement truck topped off the hole, leveling it with the rest of the yard. *She's buried forever.* Her sister's words spiraled through her head: *I just want a sister again. That's all I've ever wanted.* It had stopped her, at least for a moment. They passed the Hastingses' house. Spencer stood on the porch, looking worriedly into the yard—maybe she'd heard Ali's calls. "Get *down*," Mr. DiLaurentis barked, roughly shoving Ali's head into the footwell just as Spencer noticed the car.

After they passed, Ali sat up again and stared at Spencer's back. *She* was Ali's sister, too. Except all Ali felt for her was hate. When you got down to it, this was all Spencer's fault—and Aria's, Emily's, and Hanna's. *They* were the ones who'd intercepted her sister in the yard that day a year and a half ago. *They* were the ones who'd facilitated Courtney's ascent into Ali-dom. A new batch of hate flooded her body. It was no longer her sister she was angry at. It was *them*.

Mr. DiLaurentis put on his blinker at the corner. Mrs. DiLaurentis let out a tormented sniff as they turned onto the main road, leaving their quiet, happy little street behind. Ali peered out the back window, wondering if she'd ever see it again. She *would*, she decided. She would find a way to come back here, to clear her name. And once she did, she would get her revenge—for real this time. She'd make those bitches pay. She'd make them wish they were never Alison DiLaurentis's friends in the first place. She didn't know how, and she didn't know when, but at least she had one person she could count on to help her carry it out. Together, they were going to make it happen.

Even if it killed her.

ACKNOWLEDGMENTS

This was such a pleasure to write! I've wanted to get inside Ali's head for a long time now, and I had a great time doing so. I have many people to thank for making this book such a success: my wonderful editorial team, which includes Lanie Davis, Sara Shandler, Katie McGee, Josh Bank, and Les Morgenstein at Alloy, and Farrin Jacobs and Kari Sutherland at Harper. (Thanks especially to Kari for all of her PLL sleuthing, sifting through previous books to make sure all of the details matched up. It's tough to go through all those books again, so you're a lifesaver!)

Thanks also to the awesome people who work on the *Pretty Little Liars* show on ABC Family—the fantastic writers and crew, the talented actors, and Marlene King, who has stayed true to the series while also pushing it in new directions. I love watching Ali on the show, so it was fun to bring a little bit of that into this book.

Thanks also to my family and friends, especially all of

the people in Pittsburgh, including the Shepard family and the Lorence family. A huge hug to Samantha Cairl, who gives me a bit of time to write every day. And a really, really big hug for Kristian. *Pretty Little Secrets* was dedicated to you as well, but when I was writing it, you weren't even here yet. Now you're a happy, walking, playing, "wow"-saying busy boy who has utterly changed my life. So, again, "wow!" I love you, big guy.

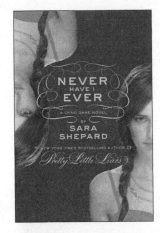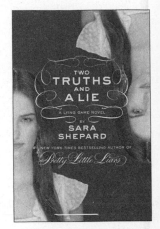
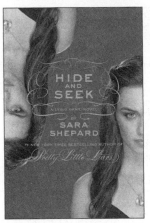

THE HIT ABC FAMILY ORIGINAL SERIES RETURNS
Pretty Little Liars
Time to bring your A game.
© ABC Family
tuesdays at 8/7c
abc family
a new kind of family

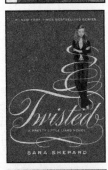